SHADOW HAWK

Patricia Hengeveld
Shadow Hawk

Published by Spines
ISBN: 979-8-89383-102-3

Shadow Hawk

Lane Kensington

Contents

ACKNOWLEDGMENTS

Without the help of these people I never would have gotten Shadowhawk this far. I want to thank my best friend Sheila for standing beside me and pushing me, my daughter Holly who said, "Mom you're going to be a great writer!" Unfortunately she is in heaven now watching down over me. To my dad who loved the story and unfortunately died before I had written the ending, and to Snake Blocker Jackson, an Apache that I met when I was in Arizona. These are just some of the people that I owe Shadowhawk to.

To all of you thank you

Chapter One

The Yuma territorial prison sat among miles of desolation and scorched earth. Nothing save rattlesnakes, scorpions, cactus and mesquite could survive here.

As the sun beat down, the hot air sucked the moisture out of every living thing. Canyons of limestone and sandstone seemed to glow in the furnace like heat.

In this hellish environment the only things that survived were the cactus and the Mesquite. The foreboding, massive Suguaro cactus stood with it's arms outstretched along side the pipe organ, the barrel and the cholla with it's twisted arms and knife like spines flourished in this land of sand and death.

Beneath the blistering sun, the mesquite grew slowly, its trunk twisted grotesquely from the never ending heat and lack of water.

It was also home to desert predators like the wolf, mountain lion and the most fearsome; the Jaguar, known by the Indians, as the desert tiger.

The Yaqui Indians called this land home and lived within this hellish landscape. They knew the location of the few waterholes here; the life giving blood of the desert. They knew the hot red canyons, the ravines and gullies where those that had tried to escape before, had failed.

Known as uncompromising and ferocious, they were recruited to go after those who would try to escape. Those who tried generally were returned dead; killed by the desert itself, or by the Indian trackers, no one ever questioned them.

Inside the small cell the heat was stifling as Clay Stanford stood impatiently at the door waiting for the guard to come and let him and the others out. He and his partner Roman Kincaid had been here now five years. Both put here by one man, Travis McCord.

Standford's fists clenched and unclenched in rage as he thought of McCord. He thought of what he had been reduced to; living like an animal in a cage. Angrily he waited for the guard to open the door.

Sweat poured down his face and darkened the prison garb he was wearing. One by one the cell doors were opened as the men were allowed outside.

Stanford strode angrily over to Kincaid, bending over he picked up a rock then threw it hard at the fence surrounding them.

"Kincaid," whispered Stanford, his dark eyes narrow and glowing with anger, "McCord did this to me, to us, then he steals my girl and gets married. So help me God he will pay for what he has done to me. This time," he snarled through gritted teeth, "he will pay with his life." Staring hard at Kincaid, Stanford then turned his angry gaze toward the endless desert surrounding the prison.

"You got a plan?" Questioned Kincaid.

"Yeah." Was Stanford's quiet reply, his face twisted with hate, he gave Kincaid a hard stare. "I got one."

In the time he had been there he had worked his way into that of a trustee. He and one of the guards a Juan Montoya, would go once a week into the town and get supplies. On one of these trips he had met a girl.

Magdelena was the sister of Montoya. For a year now she had been visiting him at the prison and had fallen in love with him. The last time they had gone for supplies, Stanford read about the wedding of McCord and the girl he loved Carrie Fitzgerald.

Knowing how she felt, Stanford knew his best chance of escape was to convince Magdelena to help him. Over the next few weeks, they hatched the escape plan. Magdalena pleaded with Montoya and finally he had agreed to help them.

The night was black dark when Stanford, Kincaid, along with Charlie and Shane Ault made their escape. They worked their way through the blackness of the night to the fence, as planned Montoya was there with his key to unlock the massive gate lock. As they shook hands, Stanford pulled a knife he had made and stabbed him instead.

"Dead men don't talk." He growled to Kincaid as they carried the body to a ravine and dropped it over the edge.

As planned Magdalena was waiting for them with horses and pack horses a short distance away.

"Where's Juan." She asked, glancing around.

"He ain't coming." Was Standford's reply. Adding, "and neither are you."

"Now Magdelena," Standford said quietly, as she started to argue with him, "that desert ain't no place for a woman like you,. Adding, as he put his arm around her, "You know I love you and I'll send for you when we get settled."

"But Clay," She sobbed, "I wish to be with you.

"No," He snarled, "It will be too hard and you will hold us up. Can't you see with the indians tracking us it just would not work."

As tears flowed, he put his arm around her and kissed her, as her body melted to his he brought up the knife and stabbed her in the heart,

"It just would not have worked my darlin'." He whispered as he laid her body down in the sand.

"Let's go." He said as he mounted a horse and motioned for the others to follow.

Knowing they had just a few hours before the Indians would start tracking them, they hurriedly left toward the White Mountains and the Big Sandy river two hundred fifty miles away.

Beneath clouds of stars, they pushed the horses hard into the night, They wanted as much distance between them and the trackers they knew would be on their trail.

Dust lay heavy in the air as they made their way toward the first waterhole on the map. As the sun began to rise, they entered a deep canyon, according to the map Montoya had drawn, there was a waterhole there.

As they approached the it, Standford swore quietly, It was dry! Crumpling the paper up he threw it hard onto the ground and glared at the others around him.

That son of a bitch," He swore, "he set us up!"

Knowing they were being tracked, they took what they could carry on horseback and left the packhorses, putting as many miles behind them as they could.

Beneath the blistering sun, they rode warily through the brush and cacti, within days they were burned and blistered from the uncompromising sun.

One by one the horses bogged down in heat and died, finally, left on foot, Standford knew their only choice to reach the Big Sandy river was to continue to move during the heat of the day. With the saddlebags hung over their shoulders, the four men stumbled forward stopping only to to drink and eat the jerky from the packs, knowing behind them the indian trackers were gaining ground.

At night they could see the torches of the Yaqui tracking them, forcing them to keep moving, pausing only long enough to cut into the cactus and eat the moist pulp. Day after day the wind blew hot and dry, like a furnace sucking the moisture out of them.

Within days, their tongues swelled, their faces caked with dust and salt from their bodies, they began to stagger, "how much more." Thought Stanford as he helped Kincaid to his feet as the Yaqui drew closer.

Just as they were about to give up, Standford saw the ragged outline of the White Mountains shimmering through the haze, which meant the river was close.

The Yaqui's knew this as well, they began to try to run down the four men as they struggled to stay on their feet. Barely able to walk, their clothes in tatters and with the trackers right behind them they fell into the cool water of the Big Sandy river. Barely alive they fought their way across and collapsed on the other side. They had beaten the odds and knew the Indian trackers would not cross the river.

They needed food desperately, from the top of a ridge, Stanford spotted a ranch not more than three miles away. As the moon began to rise they quietly entered the yard. Keeping to the shadows the Ault Brothers carefully made their way toward the corral, while Standford and Kincaid crept toward the door.

The smell of food cooking filled the air as Kincaid kicked the door in and surprised the man and woman.

"Mister," Started the man fearfully, "we'll give you anything you want just don't hurt my wife."

"We need food, water and horses." Stated Stanford, adding, "anyone else here?" As the man shook his head no, Stanford shot him.

"Take her to the bedroom and lock the door." Said Standford as he walked into the kitchen.

Beans were bubbling on the stove, tortillas were on the table alongside a slab of beef, Sitting down he piled a plate full of beans and the meat and began to eat. Moments later all four sat quietly and ate the first meal they had had in eight weeks. When they had finished, they filled the canteens with water and loaded the saddlebags with hardtack and jerky.

"What about the woman." Asked Kincaid, giving Stanford a hard stare.

"Leave her be," he said quietly, adding, "she ain't goin' anywhere without horses."

The four mounted up and headed toward the jagged peaks of the White Mountains and McCords ranch.

Carrie McCord was in the kitchen and heard the sound of approaching hoofs. She had been anxiously awaiting the return of her husband. She smiled happily as she dried her hands on her apron and ran to the front door. Happiness turned quickly to fear as she opened the door and instead of her husband it was the face of Clay Stanford!

He shoved the door open and came inside. His dark eyes glinted angrily as he glanced around the room.

"Where is he Carrie." He demanded.

"He's not here Clay." Was her quiet reply.

"Then we wait for him." He stated as he motioned for the others to come inside. Within seconds the others came inside. First was Kincaid, then the two Ault brothers.

"Why Clay," Stated Shane Ault with a smile as he grabbed Carrie and turned her toward him, "you didn't tell us she was such a looker."

"Leave her the hell alone!" Snarled Stanford as he pulled his gun and aimed it at the man.

"Hell Clay," stuttered Shane fearfully as he let Carrie go, "didn't mean nothin'."

"We're here for him," Snarled Stanford, "not her!"

"Make yourself useful," ordered Stanford as he lit the end of a cigar, "an get up in those cliffs and watch for him." Adding, "an you Carrie get in the kitchen and make us something to eat."

Carrie walked hesitantly into the kitchen followed closely by Stanford. Walking to the pantry she pulled venison jerky she and Travis had made, as well as beans. Glancing furtively her hand reached into her pocket and pulled out a small knife.

They had only been married a few months yet she and Travis had known each other for four years and she had learned some of the ways of the Apache; one thing was the Apache was never without at least two knives.

"Carrie," said Claybourne quietly as he gently turned her to him, "its been a long time."

"Clay," she pleaded, her eyes wide with fear, tears glistened in her eyes, "you don't have to do this. Her hand tightened it's grip on the handle as she added, "I'll go with you just leave Travis alone."

"As long as he's alive," Spat Claybourne hatefully, "he'll come after you and you know that! No! He will die here then you will come with me as it should have been in the first place!"

He pulled her toward him, as he tried to kiss her, her hand came up with the knife and jabbed it deep into his side!

"You Bitch!" He screamed as he stepped backward, raising his hand, slapping her hard and knocking her to the floor!

"If I had gone with you," she snarled hatefully, her green eyes flaming, "you would have to sleep with one eye open as I would have tried to kill you."

"Tie her up!" He ordered as he made his way gingerly to a chair.

"The bitch stabbed me." He snarled seeing the questioning look on their faces.

"Hurt bad?" Questioned Kincaid seeing the blood flow from Claybourne's shirt.

"No," he said glaring at Carrie, "it ain't that bad."

Carefully he stood up, giving Carrie a hateful glance, he walked with the others into the main room.

Carrie's mind was racing. They had taken her Winchester from above the fireplace, however, she knew where Travis kept his buffalo rifle and she knew how to use it. He had spent hours teaching her how to load, fire and shoot the rifle as well as hand guns.

For two days she sat tied up only being released to cook. From outside, she heard a man yell, "he's comin'!" She worked to get her hands loose, just loose enough not to cause concern but now she could reach into the pocket of her apron and pulled out a small knife. She twisted the knife around and began to saw the ropes holding her.

Finally, with one hard pull, she broke free and quickly ran toward the bedroom. Knowing they would not be watching her, she reached behind the dresser and pulled out the rifle Travis had placed there after last season's hunt with the Apache. She fumbled in a drawer and pulled out the shells. Then loaded two into the breech and put the rest into the pocket of her apron. The rifle was heavy as she carried it into the main room of the house.

The sky was blood red as McCord rode quickly toward the red ridge above his home. For the last month, he, Logan Teel and Chad McKinley had been tracking rustlers in the Muggieowns. They had found them hiding under Pinto Mesa and had surrounded them in a box canyon. Logan had offered them a deal, come with them or fight. They chose to fight.

When the smoke cleared all four lay dead. On the ride back, Logan had told him to go to his ranch and would see him in the morning.

Pulling the stallion to a stop, he gazed down at the ranch, in the fading light of day, the house and yard seemed unnaturally quiet. The stallion tossed his head and pawed the ground, seeming to sense something wrong. Murmuring softly, he kneed the horse to an outcrop of red limestone; the rocks still radiating heat from the broiling heat of the day.

This was his home, a place he had built for his wife Carrie and him. Sweat trickled down his face, leaving streaks in the fine dust that covered his face. The short hairs on the back of his neck bristled as he sat and studied the empty yard. Something was wrong, no smoke from the fireplace, no sound coming from his barn.

Carrie, his wife, would have been feeding the horses about now. He had courted her for four years and they had just been married a few months, he had thought she would be sitting on the veranda waiting for him. Yet she was nowhere to be seen.

Carefully he removed his rifle from the scabbard, cocking it, he laid it across the saddle. Sweat beaded on his forehead and trickled down his face, fear for his wife knotted his stomach as he kneed the stallion down the slope toward his house.

As he passed the last stand of Joshua trees a bullet spat dirt in front of the horse. The stallion half-reared and backed up tossing it's head.

"Welcome home marshal." He heard a familiar voice say, Now get down off of that horse!" It was the voice of Clay Stanford a man he thought was still in prison at Yuma!

"Clay," snarled McCord, "where's Carrie."

"She's safe," replied Stanford as he stepped out of the shadows. Adding, "we just want you not her."

As he stepped off the horse he pulled his rifle, turned and fired where Stanford had been. As he rolled to the cover of a water trough as bullets flew like hornets around him. Firing at the muzzle flashes, he heard a yelp of pain from the encroaching darkness as something burned deep into his right shoulder!

"Clay! I got him!" As he heard another familiar voice yell, it was the voice of Roman Kincaid; he and Logan had arrested both of them and sent them to prison.

His head roaring in pain, his vision blurred he saw Stanford and Kincaid approach him with guns drawn. To their left and right were Charlie and Shane Ault; two more he had put into prison. Without warning, the door to his house opened and Carrie stepped out, tears streamed down her face as she saw Travis lying in the dirt.

"Throw your guns down Clay or so help me God I will Kill you!" She screamed as she aimed the rifle at Standford's chest.

"Get back in the house Carrie!" Screamed McCord struggling to his feet.

He staggered toward her as another bullet tore into him. It's force threw him forward, weakly he tried to reach her. Through a fog of pain he heard the deep throated roar of the rifle.

Slowly the barrel of the rifle that Carrie was holding and tipped down, there was a look of surprise on her face as her legs slowly folded. Tears fell as she reached out toward him, her eyes wide with fear, with her last breath she gasped in a whisper. "Travis."

"No!" He screamed, through a red haze, he saw her fall. He fought his way to his feet, "You son of a bitch! You killed her!" He screamed.

Seconds later he was slammed to the ground as another bullet tore though his chest. Knocked to the ground, seemingly from far away, he heard Standford scream to someone, "You stupid son of a bitch, you killed her!" Then the sounds of retreating hoof beats filled the air around him as blackness enveloped him.

How long he'd been out he did not know, blood flowed from three gunshots, he tried to stand but could not, through blurred eyes he saw Carrie's body lying on the veranda. Tears streamed down his face, his vision blurred as he crawled to her. Painfully, his head pounding, his breath coming in labored gasps, he made his way toward her crumpled shape.

"OH...... MY........GOD...... NO!" he whispered, gasping as pain knifed through him as he gently pulled her body to him. Tears fell as he held her still body next to his.

"No!" He sobbed over and over. Hesitantly, he touched her face, then gently kissed her still lips. His face streaked with blood, dirt and tears, he held her body next to him as he leaned back against the wall of the house.

With his last ounce of strength, he screamed into the blackness of the night, "There..... ain't....no.....where... you...... can... go ....where.... I.... won't..... find..... you!" the last said in a whisper as his eyes closed and he fell into the black void of unconsciousness.

Through the heat waved horizon, the town of Tucson seemed to appear, as Logan and Chad made their way slowly to the small building they used as a jail and office. As they dismounted a man came running up to them.

"Marshal," He said breathlessly, as he handed Logan a message, "this wire came for you a few days ago"

The message was from the warden at the Yuma Prison. As Logan glanced at it then threw it to the ground, his face turned hard, his gray eye's turned to steel.

"Chad get some fresh horses," He ordered, then added, "and round up some of the the others for a posse we have to get to McCord's ranch now!"

"Stanford, Kincaid and the Ault brothers broke out of Yuma a month ago." snarled Logan hotly, adding his voice nearly a whisper, "The warden says they lost the trail at the Big Sandy close to McCords ranch."

McCord's body screamed in pain. He was aware of hands rolling him over. Through the fog he heard Logan's voice scream, "He's still alive!" As he faded into the painless black void.

The soft glow of an oil lamp was the first thing McCord was aware of as his eye's blinked open. His head roaring in pain, he gasped as he weakly tried to raise himself up but could not then he saw Logan's worried face above him.

"She's dead," he whispered hoarsely as Logan gently held him down. "those..bastards... killed... her." He breathed as his eye's closed and he fell back onto the pillow into unconsciousness.

"Yeah I know Travis." Logan stated quietly. "You rest easy." Adding, "Somebody get the doc now!"

Minutes later Doc Stevens ran quickly into the room. He checked the unconscious man then stood up shaking his head.

"Didn't think he had a lick of a chance." He muttered quietly to Logan. Adding "Never seen the like. Most men would have died." Turning around he walked out of the room turning as he walked out the door, "never seen the like." He restated.

Within a month McCord was finally able to get up and with Logan's help he was able to walk. Logan noticed the change in his friend immediately, his friend was quiet, angry and withdrawn.

It had been two months since the attack on his ranch. Not yet fully healed, he watched as McCord limped to the door. As he tried to stop him, Travis just gave him a look that sent a cold chill down his back as McCord shook off his hand and continued walking toward the livery. He was saddling a horse when Logan surprised him in the barn.

"You heading out after them?" He asked?

"Yeah." Was his reply as he jerked the cinch tight.

"Travis you ain't ready," Argued Logan, "you heard what the Doc said, nothing for at least another month!"

"Don't give a damn what he said." Growled Travis angrily, as he jerked the cinch tight.

"Then," Said Logan matter of factly, "I'm going with you.

"NO!" Snapped McCord as he turned to face Logan, "Not this time this is something I have to do alone!" Adding, his voice soft and low, "Logan, I.....I... I promised her...

"But Travis," interrupted Logan, his voice low and quiet, he placed his hand on his friends shoulder, "She was my friend too an............an................I.........I loved her as well. You know that............."

As McCord shrugged him off, he angrily turned back to his horse, then, without warning, spun around and hit Logan hard with his fist! The blow knocked him to the ground, as he struggled to rise, McCord put his arm around Logan's neck in a headlock, then whispered vehemently, "You know I could break your neck right now!"

Throwing him down, he stepped back, breathing heavily, feeling pain, he pulled his gun and motioned for Logan to stand. As Logan rubbed his neck he stood up. McCords eye's were ice cold, and emotionless. Motioning for him to sit down in a chair, McCord took his lariat and tied his friend.

"Logan, you and I are friends," stated McCord, his voice soft and low, adding, " we've been though a lot together an I know you loved Carrie. But this time," he said taking a deep breath, "they came after me! No one, but no one will stop me from going after them...............if you try," he added in a dead quiet voice, "I will kill you!" With that he swung up on the horse and started to leave.

"It's been a long time Travis, you don't even know where they went." Stated Logan.

"I know where they are." He sneered angrily, his face twisted in hate as he pulled the horse up and looked down at his friend. Turning to leave, he reached into his pocket and pulled out his badge, he fingered it for a moment then threw it into the dust of the street. Glaring at Logan he paused for a moment then left.

Following the trail to his home, he guided the horse along a scant trail beneath layered cliffs of red sandstone, cresting a ridge he pulled up.

Even from this distance he could see the ranch house was riddled with bullets. The flowers and garden Carrie had planted had been trampled by horses. Tentatively he went forward. The horse walked slowly toward the new grave that had been dug.

Pulling it up, he dismounted and walked to the grave. Tears clouded his vision as he looked down and remembered that night. He took off his hat and stood nervously turning the hat in his hand, his blue eye's were like ice.

"Carrie...I vow... I will find them and they will pay for what they did to you!" He growled through clenched teeth, his voice low and soft. He bent down and placed his hand on her grave, then turned abruptly and walked toward the house.

He raised his hands to his lips and whistled, a few moments later, his stallion came racing down from the cliffs. As it nuzzled him, McCord patted the animal affectionately, then transferred the saddle and bridle from the stable horse to Raven.

His father Black Feather had presented him with Raven as a yearling. He remembered his father telling him, "The white man breaks the spirit of the horse, the Apache teaches without breaking it's spirit, if you do this, this horse will be as the warrior by your side."

Just before dawn, McCord mounted the stallion and started the long trail toward the Utah territory. The trail was cold but he knew the men he was after. He knew the Ault brothers would lay low and he knew they would go to their friend Jake Coulter for help.

Coulter was the leader of the infamous "Hole in the Wall" gang. For months he and Logan had been on his trail in these rugged canyons.

He criss crossed the deep red canyons of the Utah Territory. Only stopping to hunt. For days he would sit using his field glasses looking for any sign of the "Hole in the Wall" as it was known throughout the southwest.

His days with the Apache had taught him patience, his days as a renegade had taught him stealth. His camps at night were hidden deep in caves, safe from prying eyes. His father Black Feather had taught him to watch the birds, the animals as they would guide him to the few waterholes in this desert.

He built a bow and a set of arrows for bigger game. He also set snares for rabbits, gophers and game birds. He skinned the animals for their pelts. By following bees and wasps, he located water.

Using the medicine Black Thunder had given him, slowly his wounds healed.

Weeks passed without any sign. It had been nearly six months since he left Logan tied up in the barn. Patiently, he waited, continually scanning the trail with his field glasses.

Finally he saw what he was looking for, three men coming down the trail below him. As they past underneath, he recognized the three as outlaws, Nate McCormick, wanted for robbing trains and Jesse Dolan and

Chris Underwood, wanted for cattle rustling. Mounting his horse, he paralleled their trail from above and followed them.

Their trail led toward a red bluff then they disappeared into a deep cut. He followed them past layered cliffs of red sandstone. Smiling softly, he remembered coming up this trail many times with Logan and going right by the entrance.

It was disguised by an outcrop of fallen rock, then right behind was a notch, just wide enough for a horse and rider, he followed it to an opening and saw the valley and a town inside.

Chapter Two

The midday sun was hot, dust kicked up from his horse's hooves hung like clouds in the still air, as his horse plodded slowly down the street. Seeing the saloon he pulled up and dismounting he wrapped the reins around a pole then paused a moment and took the rifle out of the scabbard.

He carried the rifle in his left hand. Taking his hat off , he slapped it against his jeans, then stepped up onto the wood walkway, the only sound, the clinking of his spurs.

Pausing at the doors for a moment, he allowed his eyes to become accustomed to the darkened interior, then strode inside toward the bar.

He noticed four men at a table giving him a hard look. Coulter was sitting with the three he had followed. Ignoring them, he walked to the bar. his gun hand close to his holster.

"Whiskey," He drawled to the bartender.

A moment later a bottle and glass were infront of him. Taking the bottle and glass he walked to a table facing the door and sat down, leaning the rifle against the table.

Coulter had known that a stranger had entered the canyon as he had guards in the rocks. As he watched him, his hand slid toward his gun he was stopped by one of the men at the table.

"You'd be dead before your gun cleared your holster," He said, adding, "Thats the one they call el Cetan Nigren, The Shadow Hawk."

For years he had heard the stories, then he suddenly vanished, and no one had heard or seen him since. Now Coulter wondered why he was here, shaking his head he went back to playing cards as the stranger gave him a penetrating stare.

McCord had been there less than a day when he heard voices coming. He was holding a drink when three men walked in. Charlie and Shane Ault and a third man. Stepping up to the bar Charlie turned and saw McCord! Before they had time to react, with one hand McCord had drawn his gun and aimed it at Coulter and with the other he aimed his rifle at the Ault brothers. .

In a loud voice he told Coulter, "this is between them and me Coulter." then added, his voice low and threatening, "Coulter, all I want are these two. Lessen' you want to die, you will stay the hell out of this!"

"Shane, Charlie! I'm calling you out!" Snarled McCord through gritted teeth.

"He's a damned Marshal." Snarled Shane as he looked around for help.

"There's only one of him." Added Charlie loudly.

"Then Charlie," Coulter remarked, "you take him out, 'cause me an the boys here are stayin' out of this."

They walked out into the dust of the street. McCord stood alone, sweat beaded on his forehead and coursed down his face as he waited for the Ault brothers. Coulter and the others lined the walkway.

Reluctantly, Charlie and Shane walked out of the bar and into the street. They both new McCords reputation as a fast gun. Nervously they glanced at each other, in a split second, gunfire erupted.

McCords first shot hit Charlie in the chest. Charlie's gun still had not cleared his holster. His second shot took Shane down as Shane's shot went wild.

McCord walked up to him as he holstered his colt. Pulling out a knife, he grabbed Shane's shirt and pulled him up.

"You know Shane," he snarled as he laid the blade of the knife across his throat, "I rode with Geronimo," adding, his voice low and threatening, " theres a thousand ways to kill an I learned them all. Now I want to know where the hell are Stanford and Kincaid!"

"Jake......" asked Shane weakly, his eyes wide with fear as he looked to Coulter for help.

"Tell him." Ordered Coulter, as he walked up.

"Colorado......the mountains, I think." Shane panted, licking his lips nervously and giving McCord a terrified look.

McCord let go of him then turned to leave as Coulter grabbed him by the shoulder and turned him around.

"They killed my wife." Sneered McCord through clenched teeth, his blue eye's glaring as he looked Coulter in the eyes. He then watched as Coulter walked toward Shane, he took out his pistol and shot Shane in the head.

"We don't tolerate anyone killing a woman!" He remarked quietly, giving McCord a hard stare. Adding, "Because of who you are, I'm giving you five minutes to get outta' here 'fore we come after you!"

" You come after me," Remarked McCord giving Coulter a cold stare, "you will regret it and you will lose good men."

"We goin' after him?" Questioned one of his men as he came up behind him. For a moment Coulter said nothing as they both watched McCord ride out.

"No." Was Coulter's quiet reply, adding matter of factly, "it wouldn't be worth the cost."

From Utah, McCord traveled further into the mountains. He had avoided most towns along the way but rode into the small town of Meeker for supplies. He traded pelts he had been collecting for the supplies he needed.

As he waited in the bar the only conversation he heard was of gold being discovered somewhere in a place called the valley of the Eagle, and of a range war ready to erupt in the valley between two ranches the Double Diamond, owned by a Sam Claybourne and the J-Bar owned by a Morgan Jenric, knowing the two men he was after, he knew his best chance to find them was there.

The late afternoon sun shone golden in the clear blue sky as McCord rode into Defiance. In the distance dark cliffs of a canyon loomed high and foreboding as he walked his horse to the livery.

It had been several weeks since he stopped in Meeker, taking the saddle off, he began to brush his horse as a voice stated from behind him, "mighty fine lookin' animal yeh' got there mister."

"Heard Doc Holliday is in these parts." Remarked McCord, ignoring the mans statement. As he continued to brush the animal, Adding, "where I can find him?"

"At the hotel," was the mans reply, adding, "that'll be two bits, fer the horse mister." McCord paid the man then finished brushing the stallion and then fed and watered it. When done, he stretched his tired muscles and headed up the road to the Hotel Colorado.

The hotel had been built beneath a large red cliff, the building had large rock pillars lining the veranda. The outside was painted white, two large oak doors with brass handles announced the entrance.

Opening the doors he stood for a moment allowing his eyes to adjust to the darkened interior. He took off his hat, dusting it against his legs and ran his fingers through his hair. In front of him the great room opened with spiral staircases leading up to the second floor.

The room was carpeted with a dark red patterned carpet. Three large chandeliers hung glimmering from the ceiling, next to the far wall stood a large mahogany desk with a man behind it.

"Looking for Holliday." He drawled as he walked up to the desk.

"Can I tell him who's asking." Replied the man suspiciously, giving McCord a hard stare..

"Yeah, tell him McCords lookin' for him." he replied then turned on his heel and walked into the near empty bar.

"Whiskey." He drawled to the bartender.

A moment later a glass and bottle were placed infront of him. He poured himself a shot and downed it then poured another he sipped this one and waited.

"Heard you are looking for me." Boomed a voice from behind him.

McCord slowly put the glass on the bar and turned around. In front of him stood a tall, thin man dressed in black. He had a long handlebar mustache and was flanked by two others.

"Holliday". Remarked McCord, "been awhile."

Holliday's right hand moved slightly, a moment later a grin followed by a loud laugh as he found himself staring into the bore of McCords navy colt.

"Damn Travis,' Stated Holliday with a laugh as he grasped his friends hand. "you ain't slowed down at all." Adding, "Never could outdraw ya'. Charlie bring us a bottle." He added as he motioned for McCord to sit down at a table. A moment later a bottle with two glasses were set at the table as the two men sat down.

"Been what Travis," said Holliday, "five years ain't it." Then he added quietly, "Sorry I couldn't be there for your wedding." Then added, his voice soft and low, "heard what happened." Seeing McCord's questioning look, he explained "Logan wired me." Adding, "Damn I'm sorry."

"Yeah," Was all Travis could muster.

"So you think they are here?" asked Holliday as he took a sip from the glass.

"Don't know Doc." Was McCords comment as he sipped his drink, "not really sure right now, heard Kincaid and Stanford were headed into the mountains."

"Kincaid huh," mused Holliday, "heard a gent by that name is in what they call the Eagle river valley just on the other side of the canyon, and a gent by the name of Claybourne owns a ranch over there, the Double Diamond. Heard the're tearin' that valley apart an Claybourne's been importing gunmen, could be the're the one's your looking for."

"If they are there," McCord drawled, giving Holliday a hard stare, "I will find them."

At the mention of Kincaid, Holliday saw a look come over his friends face, Sitting back in the chair he looked at this man he had called friend for many years. The man sitting in front of him was not the man he knew.

It was his eyes that drew his attention. His blue eyes were emotionless and cold and sent shiver up his spine, he remembered having the same feeling the first time they had met, in Tucson. He knew he was looking at a man who had nothing to lose, a chill went up his spine as he looked into the McCords ice blue eyes and for the first time felt the fear others had felt as his cold stare seemed to go right through him.

He also remembered what Logan had told him, "Doc, if you ever have to go after McCord, you best make sure you get the drop on him and make sure he is dead." Here he had paused, then added, "because if you don't, he will track you down and he will destroy you and in the end you will wish he had just killed you". Now Holliday understood what Teel had meant by his statement.

That night, as he laid in the bed, McCord mulled over what Holliday had said. Closing his eye's he fell into a fitful sleep filled with images of Carrie, and Logan.

Holliday had told him the best and quickest way to the valley of the Eagle was through a dark canyon, known as "The Canon of the Grand".

It was a land of wild and rugged beauty. Steep walls of scarred limestone and granite, carved though the centuries by wind, sand, and rain, stood as solitary reminders of a time now long forgotten.

A turbulent river wound its way beneath these looming walls of rock and beneath red rimmed cliffs. It churned and boiled angrily among huge boulders and rock slides littering the bank; the only reminders of distant catastrophes. It's sound was deafening. This was the Canon of the Grand.

Thick stands of pinion and cedar grew beneath these massive walls. Painted with desert varnish, the canyon walls seemed to glow golden red in the hot early morning sun.

It was a land of hidden dangers and where the law was not of man, but of nature; Survival-of- the fittest.

McCord rode with a constant vigilance, a trait that has saved his life many times. Taking note of his surroundings; of the birds, of the deer and elk and their behavior.

He pulled up the horse as a flock of birds suddenly took to the air seeming confused and panicked. A moment later an Eagle flew low, skimming the walls of the canyon, then soared high into the crystal blue Colorado sky and out of view.

Carefully, man and horse moved slowly along the scant trail that hugged the massive walls of rock. At times he had to dismount and lead his horse over fallen tree limbs, past thorn laced bushes, and around large boulders.

For two days, man and horse made their way though the canyon. It was mid-day as they made their way slowly toward it's mouth. Sweat beaded on his forehead and streaked his shirt.

Within the shadow of a granite boulder lay a small clear pool of water. McCord pulled his horse up and dismounted. Kneeling down beside it, he took off his neckerchief and dipped it into the water then wet his face and neck, the coolness of the water surprised him as it dripped down his shirt.

It revived him, taking off his hat, he ran his fingers through his hair and leaned tiredly against the boulder as his horse drank thirstily.

Reaching into his pocket he pulled out his small bag of tobacco and rolled a cigarette. As he lit the end and exhaled he looked at the vortex of the canyon walls and caught just a glimpse of the valley of the Eagle. From what Holliday had said this would be his best chance.

"If your here," he thought, "I'll find you." His blue eye's glinted like steel as he thought of the two men Kincaid and Standford.

Deep in thought, he remounted his horse and continued on the trail toward the vista of the canyon and the valley of the Eagle. As they rounded the last curve he pulled the horse to a stop and gazed out at the valley before him.

Surrounded by mountains their jagged peaks still glistening with the snow of the last winter, they were in stark contrast to the valley below.

The valley lay like a jewel, thick green grass, horse belly high, rolled like waves in the slight wind that blew and were covered with red and yellow wildflowers intermixed with purple thistle and sage.

The stillness of the moment was shattered by the sound of gunfire. Within seconds he was on the ground, crouching, his rifle in hand. Leaving the horse groundtied, he carefully worked his way up a granite outcrop.

From his vantage point he saw a clearing surrounded on three sides by thick stands of cedar, pine, and scrub oak and a road winding its way through the brush and trees.

A wagon lay on its side, its contents having spilled out, its wheels still turning. Two people lay trapped behind it. One an older man with white hair the other what appeared to be a boy.

Gunfire exploded from above him, bullets slammed into the dirt surrounding the wagon, and into the wagon itself. From his vantage point he saw they were surrounded, from the muzzle flashes he counted five.

Five against two, think I'll even the odds a bit." He thought, as he raised the rifle to his shoulder. With careful aim at a puff of white smoke, he gently squeezed the trigger and saw a man fall.

A moment later, bullets bounced off the rock all around him like angry hornets. Squeezing off another round, he saw another man clutch his chest then fall.

Twice more he fired, then as quickly as it had started, it ended with the sound of hoof beats fading fast in the distance.

Carefully he stood up not knowing what kind of reception he would have. He approached the wagon with his rifle by his side. A moment later, a bullet spat dust in front of him as a raspy voice said angrily, "Mister drop that rifle and raise your hands over your head!"

Doing as he was told, a grizzled old man stepped out from behind the wagon. His hair white, his face weathered brown with deep-set wrinkles; he walked bandy-legged toward the stranger with a limp.

"You got any more of your friends out there." He demanded, glaring at him suspiciously.

"It wasn't me". He drawled.

"Hey Charlie," said a voice, a definite female voice, from behind the wagon". "that's the gent that saved our bacon."

A moment later a young woman emerged from behind the wagon, wiping dust and dirt from her clothes. Tall, dressed in mens riding pants, her hair was the color of wheat and tied back, her eyes a violet-blue.

"Thank you mister, don't know what might have happened if you hadn't shown up." She said smiling as she held out her hand. "If it hadn't been for you, we both would be crow bait, the names Morgan, Morgan Jenric and this here grouch" she added, " is Charlie Dumont."

"Glad I could help ma'am," he drawled with a smile, "the names McCord, Travis McCord"." grasping her outstretched hand in his.

He walked around the wagon checking the rigging then said, "It don't look like it's been damaged all that bad; let's right this thing."

With both men's muscles heaving, the heavy wagon swayed once, as they pushed again, it swayed again then righted itself.

"Damned horses took off at the first shot." Remarked Charlie breathlessly as he leaned against the side of the wagon.

Nodding his head, McCord raised his fingers to his mouth and whistled. A moment later, a large black horse appeared and he swung on to it's back.

"If they're still around, I'll get em' for you." He said as he kneed the horse back up the road.

"Think he's one of them guns that Claybournes been hirin'?" Asked Charlie suspiciously as he watched McCord ride away.

"Don't know Charlie," Stated Morgan quietly as her eyes followed McCord, Pausing, she added whispering, "I really hope he's not."

They walked to the wagon and began to reload it.Picking up the last sack Charlie threw it in the wagon as McCord rounded a turn leading two horses.

"Found them up the road a ways." He said as he dismounted.

"From the looks of the hub, your gonna need a new one," said McCord as he pointed to a crack in the metal hub. Adding, "If your careful it ought to get you back to town."

"We're not that far from my ranch; we can fix it there". She stated, shaking her head no.

As he turned to leave he tipped his hat to them as again Morgan said thank you.

"I know I seen that gent before." Thought Charlie, his eye's narrowed as he watched McCord disappear out of sight. Helping Morgan up into the seat, he turned and climbed into the boot, deep in thought, he wondered "where have I seen him before."

Slapping the reins, the wagon lurched forward, heading into the high mountain known as Storm King, toward the J-Bar.

Chapter Three

Several hours later, McCord pulled his horse up as the town of Castle emerged out the heat waved horizon.

Like others he had seen, the town had been built not far from the Eagle river. The air was heavy with dust. The heat was like a that of a furnace, in this the high plains desert of Colorado. Sweat beaded on his forehead leaving streaks through the thick dust on his face and arms.

As he passed McDonald's Mercantile, Garret Shannon paused from putting bags of feed into a buckboard. Sweat trickled down his face, wiping it, he glared at the stranger as he rode by.

"Probably another of Claybourne's hired guns." Shannon thought, his eyes narrow and his teeth clenched in anger as he watched him ride past.

"Best tell Miss Morgan about this gent." He thought as he watched the man ride slowly past him.

He finished loading the wagon then climbed into the boot, clicking at the horses, he slapped the reins and left out of the town toward the mountains.

In the thick heat of the afternoon sun, McCord's horse plodded slowly down the deserted street toward the livery. Seconds later, the animal half-reared as a dog charged out from the shadows barking at the legs of the horse.

A gun seemed to materialize in his hand; he aimed it at the dog and was about to pull the trigger when a boy ran out and grabbed the dog.

"Don't shoot him mister. Please!" Pleaded a boy of about nine, his eyes wide with fear, as he sat in the street holding the squirming animal.

"Son, you best keep that dog away from horses," McCord drawled with a gentle smile, adding, " 'cause next time, you might not be so lucky." As his horse moved nervously beneath him, he lowered his gun and put it back in the holster. Tipping his hat to the boy he turned the animal back toward the livery at the west side of town.

People stopped and stared as he rode down the street. He was a man who commanded attention, well over six feet, tanned and muscular, his eye's a steel blue, his dark hair hung just below his ears. His hat was black with a silver headband, and wore a light blue denim shirt with the sleeves rolled up to his elbows.

But it was his gun, that drew people's attention, a black navy colt with a well worn handle and engraved in silver, was the head of a hawk.

As he passed the saloon, a man inside, nervously looked at him, pointing his finger, "Mister Claybourne," he whispered, "that's the gent! That's the one that showed up an helped that Jenric gal!"

The man he was speaking to raised his gun and using the barrel opened the curtain just enough to see the man as he passed the saloon. His face turned white.

"Ride to the ranch tell Kincaid to come here, tell him we got a problem!" He snarled angrily at the man. His dark eyes hard and narrow.

Closing the curtain, he turned to the bar, grabbing a bottle of whiskey and a glass he strode angrily to the back office.

"When Kincaid gets here, tell him I need him now!" He snarled as he turned around to the bartender his dark eyes flaming, opening the door to the office, he stepped inside and slammed the door behind him.

As McCord pulled up to the livery, he dismounted then led his horse inside, he had learned many years ago that taking care of his horse was a matter of life or death, and not something to be trusted to strangers.

"That'll be two bits mister." Said a voice from behind him, turning around, he saw an older man leaning against a stall chewing a piece of hay.

"Think that'll cover it for the time being." He drawled smiling, as he tossed him a silver dollar.

"Oats are in that bucket over yonder, help yourself mister." Said the man with a smile, as he bit the end of the coin.

"Know where a stranger can sit and lite for a spell." He drawled, as he brushed down the horse.

"Bernice's Place, north end of town, best grub in the valley; an she rents rooms." Said the man

Nodding his head, McCord , brushed the stallion down then ran his hand down each of the horses legs, grabbing a bucket, he walked out to the trough and filled it, then gave it to his horse along with fresh straw and a bucket of feed with oats mixed in.

Walking out into the blinding sun of the late afternoon, he paused for a moment to allow his eyes to become accustomed to the intense light. In the distance he saw Bernice's Place. A few minutes later, he stepped up on to the planked side walk, his spurs jangling in the silence, his boots echoed against the wood walkway as he stepped inside the swinging doors.

Taking off his hat, he stood for a moment allowing his eyes to adjust, he was aware others were looking at him. Hot and tired, he ignored the looks and walked to a table and sat down in a chair facing the doors. As he eased his himself down, an older lady wearing an apron walked up to him.

"Mister, if anyone needed a cup of my coffee, I'd say it's you. The names Mattie." she said with a broad smile.

"An some beans if you got em." He said smiling back at her.

"Be right back," she said. A moment later, she returned with beans, cornbread, and a tortilla along with the coffee.

"Need anything else, just holler." she said, wiping her hands on the apron and walked back into the kitchen.

The coffee was hot and black. Leaning back in the chair, he sipped the coffee as he looked out the window. Outside, he could see the peaks of the mountains, he understood now what would attract men, like the two he was looking for; to here, the high mountains of Colorado.

It's remoteness was the key. If someone wanted to hide from the law they would come into the mountains. There was no law here, there were no roads and for less than three months out a year, these mountains were almost impossible to travel through.

Huge deposits of placer gold, small flakes, almost like salt, had been discovered here; all along the rivers and streams makeshift towns like Dotsero and Dowds Junction sprang up almost overnight.

Located on the bank of the Rio Aquila(Eagle River) these towns were the jumping off places to the gold fields. He watched as wagons pulled by teams of horses and mules rumbled their way up the street loaded with supplies destined for the mining camps.

"This," he thought, "would be the perfect place for them to hideout."

As he wiped the plate clean with the cornbread, he leaned back, rolled a cigarette, and allowed himself to relax for the first time in days.

His eyes, rimmed red by the intense sun, burned and suddenly he realized how tired he was. His body ached from the long hours in the saddle.

"Any rooms available?" He asked Mattie, with a tired smile.

"Three dollars a day mister ah McCord is it, as she glanced at the register, then added, Breakfasts at six if your amind too," she replied smiling as he paid her she handed him a key. "your room is the second door on the left."

Nodding his head, he walked up the stairs to his room. As he entered it he walked to the pitcher of water on the stand. With his neckerchief he wiped his face with the tepid water then sat down on the bed.

"It's been awhile." he thought, as he took off his boots and eased his tired body back into the crisp sheets and rested his head on a pillow. Clotsing his eyes, he drifted into a restless sleep, again he saw the flashes from the guns, and again he felt the bullets tear into him as he saw Carrie fall.

The late afternoon sun burned hot as a man rode his horse at a full gallop into the town, racing toward the saloon. As the horse half-reared, the rider jumped off and ran into the saloon.

"Mr Claybourne's been waiting for you." stated the Bartender, then added, "An he ain't happy, been out here every few minutes lookin' for you."

Nodding his head, the man known as Kincaid strode quickly into the back office where he saw Claybourne looking out the window.

"Took your good old time getting' here." Claybourne snarled without turning around. Finally, he turned the chair so he could see his partner.

"He's here." He said quietly as he picked up a shot glass, fingering the sides then poured himself a glass of whiskey, downing it in one gulp, he looked at Kincaid.

"Mind tellin' me who we're talkin' about." questioned Kincaid, as he poured himself a drink.

"McCord!" Claybourne hissed angrily, "The man you said was dead!"

"You sure it was him," Breathed Kincaid. Sinking heavily into a chair in front of the desk.

"Yeah I'm damned sure it was him." Retorted Claybourne angrily.

"Did he see you?" asked Kincaid as he reached for the bottle of whiskey and a glass and stared fearfully at Claybourne. His hand shook as he filled the glass then drank it and poured another.

"I'm still here ain't I." Snarled Claybourne taking another drink and giving Kincaid a hard stare.

"Been hearing rumors," said Kincaid, "they say he killed the Ault bothers up in Utah."

"You heard rumors 'bout him an you didn't tell me!" Snarled Claybourne angrily, leaning forward his eye's narrow, he stared hard at Kincaid. "Why." he demanded angrily.

"Thought they was wrong Sam," stated Kincaid quietly, adding, "hell you saw him when we left, thought for sure we killed him."

"Thinking a moment, he added, his voice soft and quiet, "You know," he paused, turning the glass in his hand, "it may not be be as bad as you think."

"What the hell do you mean by that." Claybourne demanded as he leaned forward, staring hard at his partner.

"We know he's here, but he don't know we are." Kincaid said thoughtfully, taking another sip, he fingered the glass, slowly turning it in his hand. Putting the now empty glass on the desk, he gave the man Claybourne a cold stare.

"Sam," he said, his voice soft and low, "you know, there's a lot of ways to die up here, an a thousand different trails to hide a body. Why it just might be he could get hisself lost or fall off his horse, you know, just like Morgan's pappy did." He added with a sly smile, leaning forward, his eye's narrow, his face dark with anger as he poured himself another drink, then threw he head back and downed it.

"Tonight. The sooner the better, you know his rep." Said Claybourne as he turned back to the window.

"Yeah," whispered Kincaid, "I know his rep." As he fingered his now empty glass.

"This time we make damned sure he's dead!" Snarled Claybourne, turning back to the window.

Kincaid left walked out the door and into the bar. Once outside he paused for a moment and stared into the almost empty saloon.

"So Marshal, you done found us." He thought as a slight smile crossed his face and his hand fingered his pistol. Looking at his bartender he ordered a drink.

"You an me," He thought as he downed his drink, "We got us a score to settle." Standing at the bar, his fists clenched and unclenched as he thought of McCord, his dark eyes narrow with anger, his jaw set as he lifted the glass to his lips again.

It was early evening when Travis awakened with a start. He leaned back as he realized where he was. Drenched in sweat he sat up and pulled on his boots and walked to the water pitcher.

He poured water into the bowl then splashed his face, neck and arms. Grabbing the towel he looked into the mirror and was surprised at what he saw. His hair was dark brown with a touch of gray along the sides, curled just under his ears.

His face was gaunt and tanned deep by the sun and was covered with a weeks worth of whiskers. His well muscled chest was scarred, three healed bullet wounds showing bright red against the white of his skin.

He wore a piece of leather around his neck with a brown and white piece of agate dangling from the end.

Reaching into his saddlebag he pulled out a clean shirt. He buttoned all except the top button and then rolled the sleeves half way up each arm. Tucking his shirt, he buckled his holster and tied it down, then walked out into the hallway and down the stairs.

"Mister ah McCord is it." Remarked Mattie approvingly as she gave him a smile., "Your looking a sight better than you did when you came in earlier."

"Feel better thanks; that stew smells mighty good." he replied with a grin.

"Set down," she said, adding, "be back in two shakes."

A few minutes later, she came back with a large plate of stew, biscuits and coffee. Thanking her he wolfed down the stew, the coffee was hot. as he sipped it he heard in the distance the pinging of the piano down the street at the saloon.

He knew the best place for information would be there. Wiping his plate clean with a biscuit he finished, stood up and walked into the early evening toward the sound of the piano.

He stopped as wagons loaded with supplies and men rolled past him, headed for the mining camps just a few miles away.

The sound of gunfire exploded in the night as riders raced their horses down the street, shooting into the air, Several men staggered drunkenly down the walkway, carrying their bottles and drinking as they walked. McCord went to pull his gun then thinking better of it as he continued toward the saloon.

Pushing open the swinging doors he was hit with the thick smell of cigars and cigarettes. The place was crowded with ranchers, gamblers, miners and cowboys. As two men stood up from a table to leave, McCord took their place.

The table was in the back of the saloon next to a large fireplace, he sat down facing the door. A moment later he had a bottle of whiskey and a glass in front of him.

He poured himself a drink then leaned back in the chair sipping the warm amber fluid. He heard conversations ranging from the weather, the lack of gold at the river, to cattle. As a tall man with gray hair pushed through the doors men turned to greet him.

"If it ain't George Morrison, your a sight for sore eye's." Said one of them as he slapped him on the back.

"Don Stark," remarked George smiling, "what brings you down from the hills."

"Needed to clean these old rusty pipes." smiled Don as he took a drink.

"Ain't seen you since Morgan's pappy Carl was laid to rest." Said George nodding his head to the bartender as the bartender poured him a drink.

Seeing another man George asked, "Pearly you been visited lately?"

"Yeah George, offered me beans for my place they did." Looking at his drink, Pearly stared hard at George then said, "can't do it George. Too many memories. Hell that's Enis's grave up there. Lost her to the cholera. Then Cassy died. I....I just can't leave it. You know George."

"Yeah Pearly I know." He said gently, as he patted the man on his shoulder.

"George, did you ever hear back from that letter you sent to the Governor?" Asked Don.

"No." Said George shaking his head. "I was hoping that by now the army would be here, but with the problems their having with the Sioux on the plains, I don't see that happening for a while." Taking a deep breath he added, his voice soft and low, he stared at the glass as he turned it in his fingers then gave the other two men a hard look, "So I guess it's up to us."

"You talking vigilante George?" Breathed Pearly. As George nodded his head, he stared hard at Pearly and Don.

"I don't think we have a choice, all I know is if he tries to take my land or cattle," he said softly, he's gonna wish he hadn't."

"George, you know we're with you." Said Don quietly. "And you know Morgan will be there as well." He added giving George a hard stare.

Having heard enough McCord paid for his drink and walked out into the star-studded night, in the east lightning danced along the peaks.

Deep in thought he walked back toward Bernice's. He stopped for a moment, leaning against a building, he rolled a cigarette then lit it. As he exhaled the blue smoke drifted away in the gentle breeze that was blowing.

He watched bolts of lightning flash and dance along the peaks and heard the distant crash of thunder, the almost sickening sweet smell of jasmine from the sage hung thick in the air.

"If this man Claybourne is riding with Kincaid, then he's changed his name and he must be Stanford!" he thought, his eye's narrow, his lips tight as his left hand took out his gun. He held it in the light of the lamppost, with his thumb he spun the cylinder, his eyes narrow, his face set hard, he walked into Bernice's toward his room.

Oil lamps cast a dim light as he walked up the stairs. Pausing outside his room, he felt something was wrong. The small hairs on the back of his neck stood up. A sixth sense that had saved his life many times in the past.

He pulled his gun as he put the key into the lock and the door opened slightly. Using the barrel he pushed the door open further. Glancing into the darkness of the room, he saw nothing, but he could not shake the feeling.

He quickly stepped inside the room. From out of nowhere it seemed, he caught the flash of the barrel of a gun. Instinctively he raised his left arm to block, instantly, pain shot through his arm as the barrel hit it hard!

His gun was knocked out of his hand and fell to the floor. He turned on the balls of his feet throwing a right jab at his attacker!

As his fist sank deep, his head exploded in a bright flash, as a barrel of a gun knocked him to his knees! Strong arms pulled him up as a meaty fist slammed him in the jaw.

The pain was blinding! Stumbling forward, he was slammed to the floor! Half conscious he rolled to his left avoiding the fist that slammed down next to his head.

As he pushed himself to all fours, head hanging, he struggled to rise when again the barrel flashed, his head exploded in lights as he fell to the floor unconscious!

"Make sure it's clear. Then get him down to the horses." Said Stanford, breathing heavily, as he glared hatefully at the unconscious body of McCord.

Kincaid opened the door, the hallway was clear, apparently no one had heard the commotion. Picking up McCord's limp body, he carried him down the stairs then out the back door to three waiting horses. Kincaid draped McCords body over one of the horses. Then tied his hands and feet.

"Welcome to Colorado Marshal!"Stanford whispered evilly as he grabbed McCord by his hair and slammed his fist hard against McCords cheek bone, his cheek split open.

Turning on his heel he mounted his horse and motioned for Kincaid to follow. They rode through the alley and out into the deserted street. Crossing the bridge, they headed up into the mountains.

They rode for more than an hour, with the wind beginning to blow and lightning flashing overhead, the sound of thunder echoing in the distance, they pulled into a clearing.

McCord was still out, dried blood caked his cheek where Stanford had hit him. They cut the ropes holding him on the horse and watched as his limp body slid out of the saddle and hit the ground. Taking water from his canteen, Kincaid poured it on to the unconscious mans head.

Slowly McCord came around. He felt strong arms pull him to his feet, struggling to stand, his vision blurred then cleared and he saw Stanford!

As he moved to go after him he was restrained by strong powerful arms. Stanford grinned as he took his fist and slammed it hard into McCords midsection, knocking the breath out of him.

"You know Marshal," he said conversationally, as he took off his jacket, "you cost Kincaid and me five years of our lives in that rat hole prison you sent us too." Pausing he added viciously, "And the only woman I ever loved."

"Carrie was never yours to have." McCord spat defiantly, as he stared hard at Stanford. Then added, "See your still runnin' with your dawg." He sneered at Stanford.

"I ain't his dawg, McCord!" Growled Kincaid as he gripped him harder.

"You son of a bitch." Screamed Stanford as he slammed McCord hard in the mouth," then added, "I'm gonna enjoy this before we kill you!" With that he jabbed his right fist hard into McCords midsection and a left cross into his jaw!

Tasting blood, his head roaring, McCords legs folded, he felt pulled up again, gasping for breath as again Stanford hit him hard in his stomach! Barely conscious he knew his only hope to survive was somehow to get away into the black dark of the night.

He let himself fall. As Kincaid struggled with the limp body, he felt Kincaid's grip loosen and let go of him for a second.

In that second, he forced himself to roll away from his attackers, blindly he reached out and his hand felt a large rock.

Rolling on his back, his body screaming in pain, he threw the rock at the direction of the voices and heard a scream as the rock found it's mark! Knowing they could not see him, he crawled to the shelter of a boulder.

"Get him!" Screamed Stanford furiously, as they ran after him with guns ready.

"There he is...shoot!" Stanford screamed, as lightning flashed and for a moment he was illuminated!

Thunder crashed! Seemingly from far away he heard a shot! The ping of the bullet bouncing off the granite just inches from him showered him with small shards .

Panicked, on shaky legs he ran! His legs gave out as he tripped and fell over a boulder. Landing on his left arm, he gasped, his face twisted in agony, as pain knifed down his arm.

Vaguely he was aware of footsteps getting closer. Somehow he fought his way to his feet and stumbled forward into a thick stand of brush and crawled behind a large deadfall. Half concious he knew his only hope was to lay there.

As the footsteps came closer, the rain began. Slowly at first, then the wind picked up and the rain fell harder.

"He's got to be in there!" Said Kincaid pointing to the brush, seconds later, Kincaids gun spat as he emptied the gun into the stand of brush.

As the wind began to howl and rain began to fall in earnest, both Kincaid and Stanford mounted their horses, Stanford pulled his horse up and looked back as a flash of lightning lit the clearing and the stand of brush, he saw nothing then turned down the trail they had come.

McCord lay still as the rain pounded him. Barely conscious, he knew he was hurt, but how bad. His left arm felt useless. Every breath he took was pain filled. The rain driven by a now hard blowing wind, like icy needles, chilled him to the bone.

His teeth chattering and shivering from the cold, his breathing labored, he knew he had to move or he would die. He fought his way to his feet. His legs were unsteady, using a boulder for support he took first one unsteady step then another fighting his way into the sheltering darkness.

The anger inside him drove him forward and would not let him quit, visions of Carrie haunted his every step; the rain helped keep him conscious and on his feet.

Leaning on a boulder, breathing heavily, each breath torture, he kept whispering, "I .....won't.... let.... them....win!" He knew his only hope was to find some kind of shelter from the icy rain and the stiff wind.

His vision blurred as lightning lit the slope ahead, stumbling forward, his ankle turned and sent him headlong into a ravine! Blackness enveloped him as rolled down into the thick brush and into a boulder.

It was the cold that brought him around, his body shivering, he teeth chattering, he knew if he stayed there he would die.

"They......won't......win!" He mumbled as the hate drove him forward, visions of Carrie floated in front of him, he reached for her but she was not there. Then the hated faces of Stanford and Kincaid appeared, his face twisted in hate, he swung at empty air and fell.

The rain came hard. The drops, like needles kept him conscious, again he forced himself to his feet. His body numb from the cold. Thorns dug deep into his flesh, each step sent waves of pain through his body. Finally unable to go any further, he slowly sank to his knees into the red mud.

His face streaked with blood and dirt, tears fell and coursed down his face, raising his head toward the heavens as the rain pounded him.

"Carrie , I'm sorry.... my... darling." He mumbled through thick lips as the rain battered his face Taking a deep breath he fell unconscious into the mud.

Chapter Four

The sky was overcast, a gray mist covered the slopes of the mountain known as Storm King, a chill wind blew as two riders made their way slowly up a deep ravine.

"Charlie, that storm last night was one of the worst I have ever seen." stated Morgan worriedly.

"Sure was Miss Morgan," he said, then added, "them cattle are scattered all over by now."

"Say Charlie, what do you make of that?"said Morgan as she stood in her stirrups, and pointed to a flock of black birds circling just ahead of them.

"Probably one of my cows dead or injured." She snarled angrily, not waiting for his answer.

"What the hells wrong with this lop-ear son of a bitch." She growled as her horse half-reared and snorted, as it sidestepped, she nearly fell off.

As Charlie sat and laughed at her, she looked down and saw the muddied body of a man in the rocks just off the trail.

"Oh my God," She breathed as she jumped off her horse then cautiously approached the body.

"Charlie," she breathed, "it's...it's a man!"

"Is.....is he dead?" Questioned Charlie. As he ran to her. Gently they turned the man over, his head lolled limply to one side.

"No... not yet anyway." whispered Morgan, realization struck as she said, her eyes wide with fear, "ain't this the man that helped us?" Pausing, she added, glancing up at Charlie, "Somehow I don't think he's working for Claybourne."

"Get to the ranch and bring back the buckboard," She said quietly.

"He's in bad shape Morgan." Breathed Charlie hesitantly as he mounted his horse.

"Get moving now! Maybe, just maybe we can save him." She said lowly, as she gave him a hard stare.

"Yes Ma'am." He said, nodding his head as he sent the horse down the trail. Morgan grabbed her canteen and and pulled off her bedroll. The man was barely alive, he seemed cold to the touch, his color was ashen, his lips blue.

Knowing she had to somehow warm him, she started a fire, as it caught, she placed several rocks in the flames and heated them. Then wrapped them in an extra blanket and placed them next to the mans body and covered him with the bedroll. She wet her neckerchief and gently cleaned the man's face and was appalled at what she saw.

His right eye was swollen shut and his face was bruised. Across his cheekbone was gash, his left arm seemed broken. It was obvious he had been beaten. Knowing she had done all she could for the moment, she kept the fire going and waited for Charlie to come back.

For what seemed hours she waited then finally, in the distance she heard the jangle of traces of the horses pulling the wagon.

Moments later the buckboard came into view with Charlie and her top hand Garret Shannon. The two men ran up to her and with their help put the injured man in the back of the buckboard.

Though the blackness, McCord fought his way back. Waves of pain enveloped him as he was jostled by the wagon. His one eye opened, above him was the blurred face of a woman above him.

"Carrie!" He whispered hoarsely. As the buckboard hit a rock, he gasped in pain, then passed out again.

It was voices that brought him back, hearing the voice of a woman say, "Ride to town and bring back Doc Clemins."

"No....no... Doc." he gasped, as panic gripped him, he tried to get up but was enveloped with pain, falling back he whispered hoarsely, "they got to think I'm dead."

"Mister...just rest easy no Doc."She said giving Charlie a look,

McCord fell back, gasping as wave after wave of pain wracked his body.

"You heard him Charlie," Said Morgan quietly. Then added, "Bring me hot water so we can at least clean him up and see what we're dealing with."

For over an hour they worked on him. His right eye was completely swollen shut, his lips were swollen, there was a deep gash across his cheekbone, "probable done by a ring" she thought angrily.

His ribs were a mottled blue and gray, at least three ribs were either broken or cracked. There was knot the size of a rock on his left arm, it was badly bruised but not broken. They did what they could.

Finally finished, Morgan joined Charlie in the kitchen. Pouring a cup of coffee she sat down across from him.

"So." she asked sipping the coffee as her eyes searched his face.

"Morgan," he started quietly, "there's only two kinds of men that have as many scars as he does" he paused, sipping the coffee, his eyes narrow and worried, he continued, "they're outlaws or hired guns. That rock thats hangin' round his neck is his good luck piece, and them marks on his shoulder, Morgan thems Apache.

Saw a lot of them whilst in Arizona." Then staring hard at her, he questioned quietly, "what happens if he dies."

"Charlie we've done what we can." She said taking a sip of the coffee, Pausing, she added, "an hope to God he don't die."

In the black void of unconsciousness McCord relived that night over and over, again he saw the flashes of guns, again he felt the bullets dig deep into him, and again he saw Carrie die.

For over a week McCord lay in the grips of a fever, screaming unintelligible words sometimes it seemed he was speaking in a different language. He was tossing and turning so bad, they had to tie him down.

Morgan sat next to him putting moist cool compresses on his forehead. In his delirium he called out the name Carrie many times. Straightening a piece of his hair, she looked down at him and wondered who this Carrie was.

His eyes blinked opened, fear gripped him as he tried to move but could not. As he moved his head, he saw a man standing over him. His vision blurred then focused on the man.

"Easy mister," adding softly, "your among friends; just take it easy." Panic stricken he struggled against the ropes holding him as the man gently forced him to lie back.

"Morgan," yelled Charlie, "he's comin' around!"

As he closed his eye's against the pain, he was vaguely aware of someone else. Blinking his eye's he saw a woman above him. Her voice helped to calm him down as he closed his eyes and for the first time slept.

It was the smell of coffee that woke him next. The pain seemed less this time. For the first time he was aware of others in the room.

"Water." he whispered hoarsely, as he cleared his throat and licked his lips.

Seconds later, the woman whose face he vaguely remembered, was by his side and helped him sit up in the makeshift bed he was on. She held a glass of water to his lips. Coughing, he laid back down.

"Glad to see you finally awake." She remarked quietly.

"How..................how ...how long has it been?" He whispered hoarsely, as he closed his eyes to the pain.

" Been quite a while, about three weeks." Was her quiet reply,

"Been...... here...... too...... long." He whispered, then tried get up, but she pushed him back

"You are in no shape to be going anywhere." She stated matter of factly.

"Best listen to her son," stated a man with white hair, smiling as he walked up behind Morgan, "The names Charlie, and this here lady is Morgan; we met on the trail a few weeks back."

"Yeah, I remember that." Breathed McCord weakly. Closing his eyes he leaned back in the bed.

By the fourth day he finally felt good enough to try to sit up on his own. As he did so, Charlie walked into the room with two cups of coffee.

"Thought you might like this." He said as he handed on of them to McCord.

Nodding his head, McCord gratefully took the cup. Taking a sip, he leaned his head back on to the pillow.

"Don't know what to say Charlie, if you an Morgan hadn't found me, I....I would not be here today." he said quietly,

"Been wanting to talk to you 'bout that. Who done this to you," questioned Charlie as he leaned forward in his chair staring hard at the man in the bed.

"Can't... the less you know the safer you are." replied McCord softly, Pausing, he looked at the ceiling then said, "it's my fight and mine alone."

"McCord ain't it?" questioned Charlie, his eyes hard and narrow, he added with a whisper, "I know who you are."

As McCord looked at Charlie questioningly, he continued, "See when I first saw you, I knowed I'd seen you before. Took a while for me to remember but I did.

Back ten years ago I was in Winslow Arizona with a herd that John Chisholm an me were bringing up from Mexico. Heard of a gent then that they said was the fastest gun this side of the border. Called him El Cetan Nagin, the Shadow Hawk. They said this man was more 'pache than white.

See we had stopped in Winslow, to let the cattle rest, we'd been runnin' 'em hard for a week fightin' rustlers an such. We needed to let them graze and put weight on before taking them to Phoenix where the buyer was waitin'.

We was in the saloon. Saw this gent standin' at the bar. There was just somethin' 'bout him that kinda made you feel, …...well,........ uh, …......nervous. You know, like not to tangle with him... he just had that look.

These three gents come in an looked around. When they saw him, one nudged one of the others an pointed to him. Two flanked this gent an' the other walked up an started talkin' to him. When he wouldn't talk, the man took his hand and grabbed his shoulder.

When that other man put his hand on him, that gent spun on his heel, put the man's head in a headlock and twisted his arm up behind him and shoved him toward the other two!

They fell back into a table! As the gent turned to leave, they pulled their guns. He turns around , fanning his colt, he took out all three. He looked at them, shook his head and walked out. I tell you, I never saw the like!

One of the other men sitting at a table said kinda quiet like, "you know who that was?" When the other man shook his head no his friend said, "that was the one they call *El Cetan Nagin, the Shadow Hawk*," Giving McCord a hard stare he said. "That man is you ain't it!"

"That was a long time ago."stated McCord quietly as he closed his eyes.

"So you are him!" Stated Charlie triumphantly. Adding with a smile, "I knew it was you!"

"Now," said Charlie, his voice low and quiet, "what I want to know is what's a man like you doing here!"

"I told you Charlie," stated McCord, his voice low and even, "it's none of your concern!"

"McCord, if anything happens to Miss Morgan because of what she done for you, it will be my concern and I will hunt you down, an' I don't give a damn what your rep is! I will kill you!" Stated Charlie as he stood up. Looking down at McCord he gave him a cold stare then turned on his heel and strode angrily out of the room.

In the days that passed, McCord continued to improve. He and Morgan began taking long rides into the foothills of Storm King mountain the home of the J-Bar. They passed herds of elk and deer, watched moose then would ride to check the herd of cattle at Windy Gap.

"My pa and the rest of the ranchers have an agreement with an army buyer for a thousand head of cattle." She told him, then added, "A man named Claybourne knows about the contract. Showed up here about a year ago with his fancy gunman Kincaid. He's trying like hell to get all our ranches. And," she snarled angrily, her voice soft and low, staring hard into McCords eyes, "I can't prove it but I know he killed my Pa!"

Turning to him, her eye's flashing in anger, slow and deliberate, she said, "There ain't no way in Hell he will get his hands on J-Bar land.

George Morrison of the Running M and me, we both sent a letter to Governor Grant down in Denver. Ain't heard nothing back yet and George says he's about to turn vigilante if Claybourne tries to take his ranch." Pausing, she added, her voice soft and deliberate, " McCord I'll be right there by his side! My men know what's at stake here and they're doing everything they can to help me. If we default on this, my ranch is gone as is all the other ranches up here. We have a lot to lose."

McCord thought about what she said, the fact the man's name was Claybourne and not Stanford, he knew now they were one and the same.

Charlie and Travis had become friends, even though Charlie still did not trust him. Several weeks passed then early one morning, near dawn, Charlie heard the front door close. Looking out the window he saw McCord quietly saddle a horse and leave. Getting up, Charlie followed him to a secluded valley. Then watched from behind an outcrop as McCord drew his gun over and over.

His movement was easy and fluid. Several times he watched as McCord ran and threw himself down rolling then coming to one knee, pointing the pistol then shooting at a can. Each time, he hit his mark.

"Charlie." yelled McCord with a smile as he reloaded his gun, "no need to hide up there."

"I should have known you'd spot me." Smiled Charlie as he walked down to him. Adding, "What with your rep an all." Grasping McCord's outstretched hand.

"So," he added, with a questioning look he then asked "why." as he mimicked McCords shooting.

"My arm is still a little stiff.," replied McCord with a smile at Charlie's actions, as he rubbed his left arm.

"Your leaving ain't cha'." said Charlie quietly,

"Been here too long." replied McCord matter of factly as he thumbed cartridges into his colt, His eyes like ice, he looked at Charlie, then added, "the longer I stay here, the harder it will be for Morgan."

"The men I am after," he said, "will come after you and Morgan if they find out that you helped me. I told you once," he stated, his voice deadly quiet, "every minute I'm here, puts you and Morgan in danger." then his face broke with a smile, "besides Charlie I wouldn't want to tangle with a gent like you."

The last rays of the sun glowed orange as it began to set. The two men mounted their horses and rode back to the ranch. Most of the way they rode in silence, deep in thought. Pulling up at the gate, Charlie offered McCord a cigarette then lit one himself.

Looking at the man next to him he just shook his head. Kneeing his horse through the gate, he waited for McCord.

"When." He asked quietly.

"Tonight." was McCords reply.

Putting the horses away they both walked into the ranch house. The smell of stew and biscuits filled the air.

"Where were you two all day."" she asked with a smile as she set plates down for them.

"Checking the cattle up to the Gap." Replied Charlie as he gave McCord a knowing glance.

"Enough feed up there?" Asked Morgan as she dished out the plates and put it in font of the two men. Adding, " Garret said the fences needed mending, I sent him to town for the supplies."

"Yeah noticed that myself." Replied McCord, looking back at Charlie. The rest of the dinner was eaten in silence each man sat deep in thought. Morgan looked questioningly at both but said nothing.

That night, McCord waited until all were asleep. Quietly, he pulled on his boots and walked through the hall. He paused at the door to Morgan's room, for a brief moment he stood there, then thinking better of it he shook his head and continued past her door and out through the main door.

He entered the barn and lit a lantern. He began to saddle the bay he had been riding, as he put the saddle on something caught his eye. In one fluid movement, he turned on the balls of his feet pulling his gun. Charlie stepped out of the shadows with his hands raised.

"Just thought I'd say goodbye." He said quietly. Then handed McCord a sack. "thought you might need some grub an things. There's a pot an coffee, some extra shells, blankets and some other things I thought you might need."

"Found this in McDougal's, Charlie added quietly. "they was tryin' to sell it," as he handed him a gun and holster. It was his gun and holster. "I figured it was yours what with the silver an such."

"Charlie," stated McCord quietly as he took the gun and buckled the holster, then as he mounted the horse he grasped Charlie's hand warmly.

"Don't know what to say Charlie except thanks for all you and Morgan have done for me."

"Just tell her I will see her again." He added quietly, he mounted the roan, his eye's like steel he kneed the horse out of the barn and galloped out of the yard.

Chapter Five

The night was black dark as McCord headed the animal south toward the town of Castle. As they came to the bridge he dismounted and left the horse groundtied in a deep ravine. Climbing up to the road, he kept to the shadows as he crept silently past the darkened buildings of the town, making his way toward the livery.

The night was lit with the soft glow of oil lamps. The sound of the piano and loud voices from the saloon filled the air. Staying in the shadows he avoided the wagons and men as he stayed behind the buildings. The barn was not far away. Glancing over his shoulder he opened the door to the livery.

Once inside, he heard the nicker of his horse. He opened the door quietly and quickly stepped inside.

He petted the stallion as he whispered in Apache *"le mita cola ciye "* greetings my brother.

Hearing voices outside he opened the door and the stallion followed him out into the barn then he swung up on to its bareback and waited in the dark as the stallion moved restlessly beneath him.

"Come on John." Stated one of the men laughing, "you said you could ride that devil of a horse now prove it!

"Heard that black devil stoved up Chris and Miguel pretty bad an' the're pretty good riders" Said another with a smirk.

"Hell," answered John laughing loudly, " There ain't a horse that can't be rode or a man who can't be thowed..... till now."

As they opened the door to of the livery, the stallion lunged forward it's left shoulder knocked the man named John into the street. The others fell back as the stallion, it's ears pinned back, its teeth bared, charged at them!

Hanging low on the stallions side, McCord seemed invisible as the stallion raced up the street towards the ravine where the other horse waited. It's ears up, it nervously watched the approach.

The stallion ran at full speed as McCord leaned low over it's neck and grabbed the reins of the waiting horse. Then the two horses disappeared into the cover of darkness.

"What the hell....." stammered the man named John as all three stood up and dusted themselves off. Trying to figure out what had just happened.

"Jake," said one of the men, "best get to the ranch and tell Mister Claybourne that black devil of a horse just got loose." Adding, "let him know we'll head out after it as soon as the sun comes up."

"Somebody owes me for keeping that hay burner." Yelled the livery man as he ran out from behind the barn as the three men ran toward their waiting horses.

At sunrise McCord was on J-Bar land, just a few hundred feet from the gate. He took the saddle off the bay and saddled the stallion. Both animals had been run hard and were wet with sweat. He unsaddled the bay and saddled the stallion then headed north into the foothills of Storm King Mountain.

As the sun began to paint the sky pink, Garret Shannon rode toward the yard of the J-Bar, in the distance he saw two men studying a horse in the meadow. Pulling up, he used his field glasses and recognized them as riders of the Double Diamond.

The two men had been tracking the stallion, at the ravine just outside of town, they then picked up the trail of two horses heading north towards the J-Bar ranch.

Once on J-Bar land the trail split, the stallion was heading into the foothills of Storm King and the other horse they saw grazing peacefully in the early morning light.

Its coat still dark with sweat and looked like it had been run hard. The men looked at each other and turned their horses south toward the Double Diamond ranch.

"What do you make o' that'" Questioned one of the men as they turned their horses toward the Double Diamond.

"Don't know." Remarked the other, then added, "Best tell Mr Claybourne 'bout this."

Shannon waited until they were out of sight, then rode down the hill toward the bay in the meadow. Dismounting he approached the animal cautiously. He noticed it's sweat darkened coat, murmuring softly he put a rope around it's neck then led it to his waiting horse.

As he rode into the yard, he saw Morgan and Charlie looking at him questioningly as they noticed the horse he was bringing in.

"Saw some riders from the Double Diamond looking at this horse." He said as he dismounted.

"Charlie, ain't this the horse McCord's been riding?" Asked Morgan as she took the lead from Garret. "You seen McCord?" She added quietly giving Charlie a hard stare.

Looking at the ground, Charlie scuffed the dirt with his boot then looked up at her, giving her a sheepish look.

"Morgan, he's gone. Left last night." He said, his voice almost a whisper.

Not knowing what to say, she turned on her heel and walked into the house. Going to the big window in the main room, she saw a hawk gliding high above the valley.

The mountain known as Storm King was dark as storm clouds hung low along it's slopes, snow from last winter still lay within it's crevices as the peak seemed to cut into the dark sky. Lightning flashed along it's summit; the mountain seeming to echo how she felt, angry and alone.

Tears coursed down her cheek. Feeling an arm come around her, she looked up at Charlie.

"He didn't know how to tell you." He whispered gently as he held her close.

Turning back to the window, she watched as the hawk circled the cliffs then dove low over

the trees, then back up into the dark clouds.

"He didn't need to leave." she said in a whisper, her face stained with tears.

"You could have said good bye." she whispered. Gazing out the window she watched the rain begin to fall as she angrily brushed away the tears.

CHAPTER SIX

Jake rode into the Double Diamond just after dawn, pulling his horse to a sliding stop, he jumped off, ran on to the veranda and loudly knocked at the door. A sleepy eyed Kincaid opened the door.

"Mr Kincaid," he started anxiously, "that devil of a black horse got loose last night! Almost killed John, Victor an me!

"What!" Exclaimed Kincaid, adding, "How!"

"John said he could ride that devil, so we went to......."

"So you let that horse go!" Interrupted Kincaid angrily.

"No!" Stated John excitedly, "all we did Mr Kincaid was open the barn door and that horse come a running out! I swear!" he added. "Sides' Jake an Victor, they're headed out now to track it." He added anxiously.

Nodding his head, Kincaid closed the door. As he turned around he saw Claybourne standing there.

"You heard?" Questioned Kincaid giving him a hard look.

"You find his body yet?" Asked Claybourne anxiously.

"No." said Kincaid, "but Sam there ain't no sign up there, the boys an me, we been up there scouting. You saw him," he added as he poured himself a cup of coffee. "ain't no way he could have lived.....least ways not without help."

"That's what you said when we left Arizona!" Remarked Claybourne worriedly, "Then he shows up here. Dammit Roman we shoulda' made sure." His eyes showing a hint of fear. "Now what." He added, worriedly, "What now."

"We wait." Stated Kincaid quietly as he gave Stanford a hard glare.

Dark clouds lay heavy on the horizon as the two men rode into the yard. Seeing Claybourne standing on the porch. They looked at each other then walked the horses to the house.

"Mr. Claybourne," started John. "that black stud of yours, he ain't know where to be found, but, found the trail an it led to the J-Bar and there was this horse out in the pasture all sweaty, looked to us like it had been run hard then I picked up a trail leading into that mountain they call Storm King.

"Go to the bunkhouse an get some breakfast." Said Claybourne quietly, as Kincaid stepped out of the shadows.

"Should have known that girl might have something' to do with this." Kincaid snarled angrily.

"Damn it anyway." added Kincaid, "now what."

"Like you said Roman." Answered Claybourne quietly, looking out at the foreboding dark form of the mountain he added quietly, "We wait."

The rain began as a gentle mist as McCord aimed the stallion toward the white gypsum mountains. Riding through scant forests of pitch pine and aspen he watched herds of deer and elk as he looked for a place unseen from the valley.

He still had twinges of pain and knew that he was not ready yet for a confrontation with the two men he now knew were here.

He had been surprised in the room and it angered him that he had been surprised. Knowing what he had to do, he looked for a safe unseen place.

Forty two hundred years ago, a volcano exploded here, it's lava flow went right into the river and changed its course.. Even now it was difficult to go through. Surrounded by mountains of white gypsum a fine powdery dirt, and scrub oak, the malapaise, as it was called, named by the Spanish explorers, was fragile and broken. Huge blocks of basalt lay in disarray all over the plain.

Within the shadow of the volcano known as Blowout Mountain, lay walls of granite, during the eruption the earthquake shook walls of granite and sandstone loose from the cliffs above, as they fell, they created small unseen valleys.

He sought shelter from the rain inside the cover of a large granite wall, a remnet of the long ago explosion. As he sat waiting for the rain to let up his horse moved slightly and he saw the notch. Looking further he found it wide enough for him to go through. He guided the horse through the slight opening and found what he was looking for; a small valley.

The valley was lush with grass, a small stream, fed by a waterfall from the high cliffs, flowed gently through the valley. A forest of pitch pine and Aspen grew towards the back. Above lay the red rim of a canyon. An animal trail led up the side into the rim. As the rain let up, he immediately began to work to building a shelter for protection from the weather.

Several times, he rode the stallion and followed riders into the Double Diamond. On one of these, he was on a ridge when he saw Stanford riding with Kincaid. He pulled the rifle then put it back into the scabbard.

"Soon," he whispered vehemently, "You bastards you shoulda' made sure!" Turning the horse's head back to his valley. He pulled the stallion to a stop and looked back, "You sons of bitchs," he snarled through gritted teeth, "you shoulda' made sure."

Over the course of several weeks there were times Stanford known as Claybourne felt he was being watched. He would look and not see anything.

The fact that a horse that had been ridden hard was seen on J-Bar land reinforced his anger at Morgan.

It had been three weeks since the stallion had escaped. Claybourne seethed with anger each time he thought about her. The sun had been up for several hours when Claybourne walked into the ranch house and confronted Kincaid.

"You know Kincaid, we haven't paid our respects yet on Morgans pappy dieing." started Claybourne his voice low and deadly, "I think it's time we do so now. Get the boys!" He ordered as he strode angrily into the house and slammed the door behind him.

As the heat of the noonday sun beat down on him, Garret Shannon dug into his pocket and pulled out his tobacco and built a cigarette. As he exhaled, the blue smoke floated away from him in the gentle wind. He saw a cloud of dust over the horizon.

Using a spyglass, he saw a group of riders heading fast toward the ranch house led by Claybourne.

Running to his horse, he leaped on to it's back and spurred it. Racing into the yard, he jumped off the back of the still running horse.

"They're coming!" He yelled as he ran to the barn. Morgan grabbed the Winchester from above the fireplace , while Charlie grabbed his gun and ran toward the bunkhouse. For weeks they had waited for this so her plan was simple.

She had sent most of her riders to Windy Gap to protect the cattle. She figured Claybourne, being new here would not know about the gap. This was done as a precaution. But with only three to protect the ranch she had to figure out, how to beat the odds.

The bunkhouse was on the right side of the main house directly across from the barn. Garret would be in the hay window, Charlie in the bunkhouse and she would stay in the main house. They would catch them in a crossfire.

The riders lead by Claybourne rode at a walk toward the house. Morgan raised her rifle then yelled. "Sam you'd best stop there." adding, "what do you want."

"Morgan," He said, tipping his hat, as he rode the chestnut forward, "is this how you greet a friend?"

"You are not and never will be a friend!" She snarled angrily. "Now say your piece and get the hell off my land!"

"Why Morgan,,,,,,,," he said in a cajoling tone kneeing his horse closer.

"Any further," she warned, her voice quiet, soft and threatening, "Sam you know how I value horses but if you come any closer I will shoot that skittish chestnut stud your riding." With that she shot a round into the dirt in front the horses hooves.

The horse immediately half-reared, then crow hopped and bucked. As Claybourne struggled to get the horse back under control he heard the sound of laughter as the horse continued to buck around the yard.

Finally, he was able to calm it down. He glared at the Morgan then said angrily, "I'll make you the same deal as I tried with your pa..."

"Pa wouldn't sell an neither will I!" She interrupted as she brought her rifle up and aimed it at Claybourne, adding, "Now turn around an get the hell off my land!"

"Miss Jenric.......you will regret this ," swore Claybourne loudly, Pausing, "This is not the end." He snarled angrily, his dark eyes glaring at Morgan as he turned his horse around as he and his men left at a gallop.

"I think I need to bring the boys down from the gap." Garret stated worriedly, as the three watched the riders leave.

"No." Stated Morgan angrily as she watch the men disappear behind a ridge, "they need to stay up there with the cattle. We can deal with this ourselves."

Chapter Seven

The sun was just rising, casting a golden glow onto the cliffs above the valley when McCord opened his eyes shivering.

"Hell." he thought to himself, as his teeth chattered, "don't it ever get warm up here." As he rubbed his hands together he picked up small pieces of wood and dry grass then stoked the fire.

Taking his knife he hit the corner of a piece of granite, as the sparks flew, it caught. Moments later flames hungrily burned the dry wood. Standing near it he warmed his hands.

Walking to the small steam that ran through the valley he dipped the pot that Charlie had given him into it's icy water. Even though it was mid summer, the stream, fed by mountain runoff was still frigid.

He took the pot and sat it on the hot coals of the fire, next he opened the sack and pulled out a pouch of coffee and poured some of it into the now boiling water.

He checked the fishing line he put in the night before. Pulling it in, he felt weight on it and then saw the trout. As he pulled the fish on to the bank, he heard a rustling not far from him, looking up he saw a large buck, it's antlers just knobs of felt.

Slowly, he reached for the bow he had made, his movement slow and deliberate, his eye's never leaving the deer, he reached for an arrow, slowly he fit the arrow into the bow, drew it back, then aiming for the animals left side, he let the arrow fly!

Right on the mark, the animal took a step forward, then sank to the ground dead. He took his knife and approached the animal carefully; many a man had been gored and trampled by an animal they had thought was dead.

Approaching it from behind, he jumped and landed on the animals back, pulled the head up then cut it's throat, he waited for a moment then began to skin it. Slicing into the hindquarter, he cut a steak and threw it into the fire.

The smell of coffee filled the air. As he poured himself a cup he heard the scream of an eagle then he watched it dive close to the stream, as it rose, in it's talons was a struggling fish.

"Looks like we both eat today." He thought as he raised his cup skyward in a salute.

As the venison cooked, he made quick work of the carcass then raised the meat high into a tree not far from the wikiup he had built.

He had been there now for over a month. For the first time since the beating he had taken, he felt almost normal. The wikiup was small, but it gave him shelter from the winds and driving rain that would come up almost daily. The blankets Charlie had given him were on one side along with his clothes and extra supplies.

He pulled the venison out of the fire then ate it along with some pheasant eggs he had found. When he was done, he walked down to the stream. Gutting the fish, he cut it into strips and put them on a rock to dry.

"Not even Carrie would know me now." He thought as he stared at his refection.

Splashing his face with the cold water, he shivered as it coursed down his chest. Taking out his knife he laid the sharp edge against his face and began to shave off the whiskers.

Then took a dried piece of hide and tied back his hair. As he looked at his reflection, a white scar showed prominently against his tanned face. Anger rose inside him.

"Its been long enough." He thought angrily then he stood up and stalked angrily back to the fire.

Raising his fingers to his mouth he whistled for the stallion. The horse slid to a stop just short of hitting him, then lowered it's head and nudged him. Smiling, McCord straighten the animals forelock.

He saddled and bridled the animal then picked up his bow and the arrows he had made, along with a can of what looked like black tar. Knowing it was easily a days ride from here he mounted the stallion and left headed toward the range of the Double Diamond.

The sun was well up as he heard the sound of cattle just over a ridge. Dismounting, he crept cautiously toward the top of the ridge. There were over a hundred head and four riders kept the animals together.

Backing down quietly, he remounted the stallion then headed down a ravine toward the main ranch house. He took pieces of a shirt and tied them around the stallions hooves.

"You can't track what you can't see." He snarled quietly, his teeth clenched, his jaw hard, his eyes like ice as he turned the stallions head toward the ranch house.

Nearing nightfall, he pulled the stallion up in a ravine a half mile from the Double Diamond ranch house. Taking his bow and arrows and his Henry, he climbed to the top, where he sat in the cover of a large boulder overlooking the ranch. He had waited for a moonless night like this and tonight was it.

As the night enveloped him, he watched as men came and left, he saw the two men, Kincaid and Stanford inside as the oil lamps were snuffed out. He pulled out his arrows, dipping them in the can then struck a match, the end burst into flame, then he let the arrow fly!

The first one hit the side of the house with a thud. The second broke a window and he saw the curtains catch fire , he sent a third, this one landed inside the house.

Within seconds the inside of the house was engulfed. As men came streaming out of the bunkhouse to fight the fire. McCord aimed his rifle and began shooting. Immediately three men went down, the rest ran back inside and began shooting from the bunkhouse. Then he saw Kincaid!

Aiming his rifle, his shot was not to kill, just to keep him inside. He sent round after round into the house. From underneath he heard footfalls in the leaves below him and knew he had been there long enough.

The ranch house was burning as he made his way to his horse. He mounted the stallion then raced up the ravine. The horse half reared as he turned, the fire illuminated the night.

"You bastards," His blue eyes like ice, his jaw clenched hard, he snarled through clenched teeth, "you shoulda' made sure! He kneed the stallion up the ravine and back to his camp.

In the days that followed Claybourne sent men out daily, looking for sign. When none of them could find him, Claybourne sent a wire to a man named Vaughn Thomas. A man he had been told could track a bird if you had enough money.

Two weeks passed without any sign of Thomas or McCord, some of the men working for Claybourne left scared.

"Where is that son of a bitch you hired!" Swore Claybourne furiously as he glared at Kincaid.

"That son of a bitch you are talking about, would be me." Said a voice from outside, "Mr Claybourne I presume? I am Vaughn Thomas."

Stepping into the light, Kincaid and Claybourne had their first look at this man Thomas.

He was dressed in buckskin, his hair was black, long and snarled, his face, lined and deeply tanned was leathery, a large scar ran from above his left eye to the length of his face.

From atop his horse he glanced around at the damage. The main house was nothing but charred embers.

"One man did all this." He remarked as his horse moved beneath him. Seeing bandages on the hands and arms of the two men he was looking at. The man Claybourne, his face blistered and red. Kincaid had similar wounds.

"Gents, my price just went up." He said quietly. As Claybourne and Kincaid stared angrily at him.

"I don't give a damn how much it'll cost," Snarled Kincaid, "just kill him. Thats what we hired you for!"

"So tell me about this McCord." He said as he dismounted and sat on a hay bale. "I need to know this so I can know the man." Pulling out a cigar he lit it as he studied the men infront of him.

Later that night, Thomas sat by a fire, as it's light danced along the walls of the rocks that surrounded him, he thought about this man, McCord.

Kincaid had said, "he thinks and acts like an Apache. He hunts you, then like the other night, he shows up where you would least expect him to be." Claybourne had remarked "He led a group of renegades called The Outriders back in Arizona, and he was known as *"El Cetan Nagin, the Shadow Hawk"* more Apache than white. Just like the Apache, he disappears like a damn ghost, and leaves no trail."

He remembered hearing stories of the man known as *"El Cetan Nagin, the Shadow Hawk"*. His exploits had been near legendary. At the campfires of his friends the Commache, he had seen the fear in their eyes at the mere mention of his name. This was a man to be reckoned with.

"Ol' son," he said to his horse, his dark eyes gleaming with anticipation, "looks like this one will keep you in oats this winter an me in whiskey." As he turned in he whispered, "We start the hunt in the morning."

The sun was just rising as Claybourne sat at the table in the barn. Angry and sullen, he stood up and walked out into what was left of his ranch. He picked up a rock and threw it into the charred wood of his ranch house.

"It was that girls fault." He thought angrily, as he picked up another rock and threw it hard at a fence post. He put it together that she had somehow found McCord and helped him, otherwise as Kincaid had said, how could he have survived!

Knowing McCord, he knew if something were to happen to Jenric, he would come to find her. His eyes glowed with hate as he thoughtfully built a cigarette then lit it as his eyes looked toward Storm King Mountain.

The mountain dominated this part of the valley. Within it's foothills was the J-Bar, a ranch he had wanted since he came here. Somewhere up there was a place called Windy Gap. For months he had tried to find it, but no one knew where it was except for a select few and they were not talking.

There had to be a way to lure McCord to them. Knowing Thomas was looking for McCord, still he thought, taking the J-Bar would be like icing on the cake.

He threw the cigarette into the dust and crushed it with his boot. Turning he strode into the barn and woke Kincaid.

"Get the boys, we're goin' after J-Bar!" He said angrily. When Kincaid looked at him Claybourne added, "If Thomas does not get him, McCord will come after that bitch."

Within an hour he had twelve riders ready. Remembering the last time, he realized they could not just ride in. It was mid morning as they entered J-Bar land. He stopped and looked at Kincaid.

"Take five men and come around the ranch house from the North." He told Kincaid.

"Take four men and come up from the South." He instructed another.

"I'll take the rest. Remember we want the girl alive!" He stated as his horse moved beneath him.

"Alright, lets go." He said, his eyes dark and angry.

Morgan was sitting on the fence of the corral when Garret rode into the yard. Tipping his hat he rode up to her.

"Mornin' Miss Jenric." He said as he dismounted and stood looking up at her.

"Mornin' Garret, how are things at the gap." She asked as she looked out into the trees that surrounded her ranch house.

"Got the men fixin' the fences, other wise everything is good." He replied.

"Garret, Morgan." Said Charlie as he came up behind them.

"You hear what that damned McCord did." Fumed Morgan angrily.

"Yeah, setting' the Double Diamond on fire!" Laughed Charlie loudly.

"Yeah, heard about that, wonder what his beef is with them." Said Garret as his face broke into a grin and then laughed.

"Don't know, and I don't give a damn." Stated Morgan angrily, her eyes flashing. Adding, "All I know is that his actions could hurt this valley."

Without warning a shot broke the stillness of the day as the bullet hit the post next to her. Within seconds the three ran for cover as another shot hit the ground infront of Morgan. Racing to the house, she grabbed her Winchester as Charlie ran to the bunkhouse and Garret to the barn.

As she stepped outside. Strong arms encircled her, struggling she heard the voice of Kincaid say, "Jenric, you best just give it up."

As Charlie ran to the bunkhouse, he was suddenly knocked to his knees. Then something white hot burned into his back the last thing he knew was the dust as he fell dead into the dirt.

Garret raced into the barn, running inside he was hit hard by a fist and knocked to the ground. His arms were pulled behind him and tied. Roughly he was jerked to his feet and shoved hard out the door. He was knocked to the ground as he tried to get to Morgan. She struggled with Kincaid a moment later Kincaid balled his fist and hit her hard. Within minutes, the men took hay and spread it around the ranch house. He and Morgan were forced onto a horse. As they left, he turned to see the ranch house and barn engulfed in flames.

"Take them to the draw just north of here. If he comes, we'll get him." Said Claybourne his eyes glowing with hate.

"What happens if Thomas gets him." Asked Kincaid. "What are we going to do with them then."

"Like you said Roman, theres a thousand different trails to drop bodies up here." Was Claybournes answer. Turning their horses, they headed toward the draw under Indian Peak.

For days Thomas followed tracks leading into an obscure canyon of Storm King. At first it had been relatively easy, now tracks were nowhere to be seen.

He scoured the gullies and ravines for signs of the man he hunted. He figured McCord would not be far from the Double Diamond, yet each day he went further into this broken canyon.

However, as each day passed, he began to respect this man named McCord. He could not find one bent blade of grass, nor overturned rock, broken twig, hoof scar on the rocks. Nothing!

At times, he felt he was being watched as the small hairs on the back of his neck would rise. He would look around, using his field glasses he would scan the sandstone cliffs for any sign of the man. He disregarded these feelings and thought that what he had heard about McCord was just getting to him.

He followed a trail leading under the massive walls of rock. Above him the early afternoon sun was just hitting the inside of the canyon walls. As he rode deeper into it the air was cooler. Hugging a trail beneath mammoth walls of limestone and granite he looked for any sign of the man he hunted.

His horse plodded slowly down a rock strewn trail leading towards a turbulent river. He could hear the river long before he saw it.

The water was running fast and high. It's force so strong, he could hear boulders being carried under the water. The roar, amplified by the massive walls of rock, was deafening.

He pulled up suddenly as he thought he glimpsed movement on the ridge across the river. Taking his field glasses, he scoured the rock laden side and again came up empty.

"Where in the hell are you." He swore as he put the field glasses back into his saddlebag.

Continuing down the trail into the depths of the canyon, he found a place where the river split into a fork. Kneeing his horse into the turbulent river, he crossed to the other side.

Reaching down into his saddlebag he pulled out his field glasses again as the horse moved restlessly beneath him. Again nothing. He guided his horse up a steep brush covered ravine when he saw a flock of birds suddenly take to the air.

"Well," he said to himself, "might that be you McCord?" As he continued up the ravine, he noticed a recent rock slide. Dismounting, he approached the area carefully. He saw a slight indentation of a boot, it was fresh! Standing up, he pulled his gun.

"I know your somewhere around here McCord!" He yelled, his voice echoing along the walls of the canyon. For a moment he stood with his gun pulled. Re-holstering it, he mounted his horse.

Somehow the tables had been turned and he had become the hunted! For the first time he felt fear. Knowing he was now a target, he turned the animals head back down the trail and across the river.

He glanced nervously over his shoulder as they came to the river. He was getting tired of playing McCords game. Realizing he was the hunted his plan now changed. Now, he would somehow have to make this man McCord come to him.

As the sun began to set, he looked for a campsite. Rounding a bend in the trail, he found what he was looking for. A cave lay nestled among the rocks, a remnant of a long ago catastrophe. Several large blocks of granite had fallen together leaving a small space, just big enough for a man.

As he dismounted, he felt someone or something watching him. Nervously, he unsaddled his horse, then built a fire, all the while, his senses alert, he waited.

McCord watched from high above as the man below set up camp. He had been following him for the last few days. A faint smile crossed his lips as he knew it was a set up.

As the darkness enveloped the canyon, the only light to be seen was the fire, save for the stars above.

McCord had changed from boots to Indian leggings. Catlike, he moved noiselessly from rock to rock edging closer and closer. He flattened himself against a boulder as he studied the cave now infront of him.

He saw what he was looking for, a darker shadow moved within the cave, as the light from the fire danced along the walls of the rock.

Moving away from the campfire, he circled back around, then worked his way silently down toward the cave from above. There were a series of ledges leading down toward the cave.

Noiselessly he approached. He pulled his gun as the man stepped out of the cave into the light of the fire.

"Stand right there Mister," Stated McCord evenly, adding, his voice low and deadly "who are you, an what do you want with me." At the sound of McCords voice, Thomas froze . He was amazed that he did not hear his approach. As McCord entered the campsite, Thomas got his first look at the man he was looking for.

McCord was taller than he had expected, his arms were well muscled, his face tanned save for a newly healed scar. Like Thomas, he was dressed in buckskin, with Indian leggings. But it was his eye's that drew his attention, he felt chills run up his spine as he felt the penetrating ice cold stare of McCord.

Motioning for Thomas to sit on a rock, McCord, his eyes never leaving him, came further into the light.

"I asked you, who are you and what do you want with me." Stated McCord, his voice soft and quiet.

"McCord," remarked Thomas casually, "I presume you are him." adding, "my name is Thomas, Vaughn Thomas."

"I am." Was McCords reply.

"Ran into a couple of friends of yours," stated Thomas, "name of Claybourne an Kincaid." Then he added, softly, "they seem to want you dead real damn bad."

"So they hired you; put your hands behind your back!" Snarled McCord angrily.

As Thomas obeyed. McCord quickly tied his hands then tied his feet.

"Mr Vaughn Thomas," he said to the man, "my fight ain't with you, it's with the men you know as Claybourne, his real name is Stanford, an Kincaid," adding, "I am giving you a choice Thomas, you best leave, because if you don't, then I will not hesitate to kill you the next time we meet."

As he turned to leave, McCord looked down at Thomas, snarling in Apache, " NE *t DA he*" translated it meant "death to all intruders. Thomas knew what it meant and he recoiled in fear.

McCord reached down and picked up the rope holding Thomas's horse, as he turned to leave he looked down at him and smiled.

"By the way, think I'll take your horse." He said, Adding, "it's a hell of a long walk out of here back to the Double Diamond, it'll give you time to think about what I said."

Through out the night, Thomas rubbed his hands against the sharp edge of the rock he was laid against. The sun was just coming up as the rope finally broke and his hands were free. He rubbed his wrists, seeing the rope burns he felt anger rise, shivering from the cold he quickly untied his feet.

"I will get you for this." He swore angrily underneath his breath, his dark eyes flashing as he stood up. Knowing the long way he had to go, he started back up the trail leading out of the canyon.

It was early afternoon, as McCord rode the stallion toward the Double Diamond. As he crested a ridge, he could see black smoke rising from just below Storm King.

Panic hit him! He slammed the spurs into the stallion and raced toward the plume of smoke.

As he approached the ranch house his stomach was in knots. The barn was gone, nothing was left. Glancing at the house, it was just charred embers.

A man's body lay next to the water trough. Dismounting he knew immediately it was Charlie. Angrily, his eyes like steel he gently rolled Charlie's body over.

Under the hot sun, McCord dug a grave beneath an old cottonwood, taking Charlie's body, he laid it inside, then started filling in the dirt.

"I promise you, I'll find her Charlie." He vowed as he piled rocks on top of it, his narrow blue eyes turned ice cold as he looked around. He saw the tracks of at least ten horses. The tracks were fresh. As he crouched next to the tracks leading out he saw two of the sets were deeper than the rest. He knew immediately two of the horses were carrying double.

As he stood up, his blue eyes cold and hard, his jaw set, McCord mounted the stallion, he slowly followed the trail that led toward a deep red mountain known as Indian Peak, just north of the Double Diamond.

Between him and the mountain was a valley. The valley was a flat open plain, dotted with small bushes, brush, cedar and scrub oak.

To the left of a cut in the mountain he saw sunlight reflecting off of field glasses, flashing from the top of a cliff on both sides of a notch. Knowing he could not cross during daylight, he had to find a place to wait for the sun to go down.

Laying flat, he crawled to where he had left the stallion then circled around toward a stand of pine trees not far from the ridge overlooking the notch. He left the stallion amongst the trees then crawled toward a large slab of rock. Here he waited until nightfall.

"Boy's," Stated Kincaid, "just keep on your toes."

"Mr Kincaid," remarked one of the men, "how sure are you he'll come.

"Damned sure" he said as he walked to the tree where Morgan was tied up, he pointed to her, he'll come for her, I know it's been a few days but if Thomas hasn't gotten him, he will be coming here." He stated loudly.

"When." Asked another.

"I'm giving' Thomas one more day, if he don't come back here with McCord, we'll take these two up into Storm King." Was Kincaid's reply, adding "if he is still alive, he will come. Just keep alert."

As the night grew darker, McCord saw the light of fires from behind a series of rock formations.

Silently, he crept to the mouth of the cut. From his vantage point, he saw Garret tied to a tree, his left eye swollen, dried blood had spread from a cut on his head. His eyes hardened as he saw what they had done to him.

He could just glimpse Morgan, her blouse was torn, her hair was snarled and lay in strands, her right eye was swollen from where Kincaid had hit her, her face was streaked with dirt and tears. Enraged McCord felt for the handle of his gun, thinking better of it he withdrew back to the safety of the night. The horses were inside a rope corral toward the back of the cut.

Silently, he crept toward the tree Garret was tied to. Although the only ones who knew him by sight, were Kincaid and the man known as Stanford he also knew the men they had hired would question any one they did not know.

At the sound of breaking twigs and a rustling not far from him, he faded back into the darkness of a cliff.

"Keep your gun handy." Stated one of the men.

"No telling' where he might be." Said the other one.

Smiling to himself, McCord eased silently toward the tree that Garret was tied to.

"Don't turn around Garret." He whispered. Garret, felt the ropes holding him loosen, then felt the cold blade of a knife in hands.

"Just wait." McCord whispered lowly into Garrets ear, "when the horses run this way, get Morgan."

Giving just a slight nod of his head, Garret heard McCord slip behind a bush as a man walked past them.

McCord slipped silently to the horses. One of the horses snorted loudly, wild eyed it tossed it's head as it tried to back up. Quickly he slipped into the pen whispering softly, within seconds the animals calmed down.

"Easy," A man said to the horses as he walked up. Pulling his gun he looked around.

"Jake, where are you." asked a voice lowly.

"Over by the horses." was Jake's quiet reply, "thought I heard the horses acting up."

"Every thing's OK though." He added, his voice low, as he reholstered the gun.

"We're all a just a might jumpy Chet." Said the other. "Hell who wouldn't be with this gent McCord comin' an nobody knows when."

McCord waited as the men left, then he untied the rope holding the horses. He grabbed the mane of one and kicked it hard. The horses lunged forward as one, racing out toward the cut. McCord leaning low grabbed another by it's reins, then screaming, he raced toward Garret and Morgan.

Pulling the animals up to a sliding stop, he threw the reins of one to Garret and stretched his arm out to Morgan. For a moment she paused, glaring at him, then grabbed his arm and he pulled her onto the back of the horse.

Slamming his heels into the animal, it lunged forward toward the cut. The horses had scattered the campfire, hot embers were thrown into the brush and now it was on fire!

Men scattered as they tried to escape the now billowing clouds of thick black smoke as dry brush seemed to explode into flame! Sparks flew as the panicked horses ran.

Coughing and choking from the thick smoke, the men ran out as McCord, Garret and Morgan burst through!

The flames leaped high illuminating the darkness as the three riders made it into the shelter of the trees. Above a ridge McCord raised his fingers to his mouth and whistled, a moment later the stallion raced up the slope to meet them.

Sliding off the back of the horse he had been riding, he gave the reins to Morgan and leaped on to the back of the stallion.

"We've bought a little time, they'll be after us in a short." Remarked McCord panting, "Lets move!"

"Damn it to hell," raged Kincaid, as he realized they were gone. "Get after em!"

"Can't," said one of the men angrily, adding, "he stampeded the horses Mr. Kincaid!"

"Get after the horses then!" He screamed as he angrily kicked the tree where Morgan had been tied up.

The trail up to greenhorn was difficult to say the least, heavy rains had cut the trail in several places, more and more, the three had to dismount and lead the animals around the breaks. Heavy thick brush grabbed at their clothing, seeing the tiredness in their faces he knew they had to rest.

"Wait here." He said, "going to check the back trail." Nodding their heads tiredly, McCord took the stallion back down the trail they had just come up.

In the early dawn, he pulled the stallion up then used his field glasses and scanned the horizon to the east. In the distance he saw a cloud of dust. He knew he had to somehow block the trail.

A large boulder teetered precariously along the edge of the trail. He figured if he could just move it slightly it would fall and take down half the side of the gully with it.

Looking around he found what he needed from an old sturdy thick cedar he used his ax and cut down a long thick branch.

Digging a shallow hole underneath the boulder, he placed the branch into the hole and leaned down on it hard. His muscles bulged and the rock started to move! In the distance he could now hear the fast approaching hoof beats as the men were coming closer.

Again he leaned on the branch, putting his weight on it, it bent but did not break! The boulder moved slightly then gritting his teeth he pushed with all his weight on it; the boulder teetered on the edge then fell! The sound was like thunder as half the gully fell with it burying the trail in rock, trees and dirt.

"There he is!" Yelled a voice as the men pulled their horses up sharply almost within the cloud of dust and dirt of the avalanche. Bullets flew and ricocheted off the face of the boulders as he leaped into the saddle.

His face stung as shards of granite sprayed him, a bullet burned his arm as he leaned over the neck of the horse! As the stallion raced up the trail, it lost it's footing on the shale, going to it's knees several times as McCord urged it on with voice and hands.

Topping a ridge, McCord turned around, dust lay heavy in the air from the slide, but now there was now no way for their pursuers to continue tracking them.

Morgan and Garret were waiting for him as he rounded a bend. His face was streaked with blood, dirt and sweat. The stallion's knees were bloody from where it had fallen.

He dismounted and uncorked his canteen, using his neckerchief he wiped the blood and dirt from his face then worriedly washed down the stallions legs, it's legs seemed to be ok, as he remounted he turned to the others giving them a hard stare.

"Let's move." he said as he headed the horse west toward his valley.

Chapter Eight

As night began to fall, they entered a strange world; a ghost forest of long dead cedar. In the twilight, their silhouettes shrouded in a white mist, stood as eerie sentinels, they were, as if in testament of the desolation and unforgiving nature of this land.

The stars littered the night sky and the moon glowed a bright white as they came to the lava fields of the long dead volcano known as Blowout Mountain.

The going was treacherous, the lava was slippery and fragile and sharp fragments made the going slow. He made camp under the rim of the long extinct volcano and they tiredly sat down. Within the shelter of a lava tube, McCord built a fire with wood from the cedar and scrub oak now growing into the lava. No one spoke as they sat; each lost in thought.

"You OK?" asked McCord as he looked at Morgan. Her face was streaked with dirt and dust, her hair was in tangles and a bruise was on her face from where Kincaid had hit her.

Giving him a look, she glared at him without saying anything. Not understanding why, he stood up then strode angrily toward the rim of a sink hole, the remnant of the explosion of long ago. In the darkness a mountain lion screamed, it's scream seeming to echo the anger he was feeling.

"Morgan, what the hell is wrong with you, that man there just saved yours an my life."stated Garret angrily.

"If he hadn't come here Charlie would still be alive!" She snarled back as her violet eyes flashed hatefully.

"No Morgan, this didn't start with his coming here," Stated Garret hotly, "it started with Claybourne an his bunch killing your pa, your just looking to blame him for everything."

Giving him a look, tears welled up in her eyes as she stood up and walked into the night. Looking up into the dense dark sky, she saw a bright glowing object fall from high above, then disappear. The wind began to blow, gently stirring the branches of the pine tree she was standing under.

Sitting down, she let the tears fall. She began to think of everything that had happened to her in the last six months. First her pa, now Charlie, but most of all everything she and her pa had worked for was gone, the J-Bar was gone. Feeling an arm come around her she looked up at Garret, tears ran down her face as she sobbed into his arms.

"It ain't his fault." restated Garret gently as he held her close to him. She just looked at him, with Garret's arms around her, they both walked back to the fire.

McCord looked up as they came into the camp, pulling out some of the deer jerky he had made, he poured water from his canteen into a large piece of clay he had found. It was shaped like a bowl with a deep indentation, within a few minutes the water was boiling.

With the hot water and jerky they ate in silence. He had built the fire underneath an overhang of lava, he placed several small pieces of basalt into the fire. The rocks would keep the fire hot and easy to start in the morning. The heat of the fire was reflected by the walls of the lava chamber and would keep them warm throughout the night.

As dawn fingered the sky in the east McCord awakened the pair. Overhead, a hawk dived and soared as the early morning sun tipped the tops of distant cliffs gold.

"Let's move." Stated McCord, "should be at the valley in a few hours."

Cresting a ridge, he pulled out his field glasses. There were no signs of pursuit. He headed the riders single file down a little used trail to the cut in the cliff he had discovered.

The entrance was hidden with trees and thick bushes, their branches lined with thorns grew in front of a giant wall of granite. The cut was just wide enough for a horse and rider to pass through.

"Ain't much," he said, then added, "it'll do for a short time." as he led them into the valley and the small wikiup next to the trees.

"Nice place you have here." Remarked Morgan sarcastically.

"Here," he said, ignoring her remark, as he handed her a pair of jeans, and a shirt. "you might want to put these on."

As he turned to leave he pulled a gun from a sack and handed it to her, "know how to shoot one these."

"McCord," she remarked dryly. "I was raised with one of these."

"Just don't shoot me by mistake," He added as a wry smile crossed his face.

"McCord," she said, her eyes flashing with anger, her voice low and even, "I make no mistakes."

Motioning for Garret to follow him, they rode toward the cut, "We can't stay here long. But she needs to rest up." Remarked McCord, adding, "The best chance of keeping her safe is getting her to Defiance, a friend of mine is there, his men will keep her safe."

Nodding his head Garret agreed. The two men set about destroying the tracks leading to the cut.

With a fallen branch, they worked hard erasing the tracks of the horses. They piled rock and dirt making it look natural. Then retreated to the safety of the valley.

For three days they let the horses rest and graze in the valley. McCord hunted with his bow and fished, with fish drying on rocks, he cut venison into strips for jerky, while Garret kept lookout from the ridge above the cut.

"So when am I going back." Demanded Morgan walking up to McCord.

"You're not." Was his terse reply.

"Oh yes I am." Retorted Morgan, her violet eyes flashing, "you can't keep me here."

"Now Morgan," said Garret, looking from one to the other, "you need to listen to McCord!"

"No!" she replied angrily, "I want to go to the J-Bar!"

"J-Bar is gone." Stated Garret gently.

"Then......then …." she said, her voice choked with emotion, "I can go to Castle or to the… Running M, George and his men will help me."

"No!" snapped McCord, "if I have to Miss Jenric, I will flat tie you down!"

"Morgan," pleaded Garret, "you got to listen....they went after you once, you go back there, they will go after you again."

"Shannon," She snarled furiously, "you know I can ride and shoot with the best of them and you don't think I can take care of myself!"

"That's not the point." Said Garret, as he started to lose patience, "you are a target now."

"That's why we have to get you somewhere where it's safe." He added angrily, "them ranchers are counting on you.....you don't have a choice!"

Angrily she looked from one to another, turned around and stormed into the wikiup. She stomped her feet, she turned and glared at McCord. With a toss of her hair she walked out and away from the two men.

The next day, in the distance Garret noticed a cloud of dust. Using his field glasses, he saw a group of riders coming slowly toward the cut.

He ran down into the valley, and raced toward the wikiup looking for McCord. Turning around he saw McCord near the stream.

"There comin' Travis." He exclaimed loudly.

The two rode to the ridge. Grabbing his field glasses McCord saw Standford, Kincaid and leading them was Vaughn Thomas.

"See you throwed in with them." He sneered then with an angry scow, his face dark with anger his eye's turned to steel. If it had just been Standford and Kincaid, they would have been safe, but with Thomas leading them McCord knew they would be found.

Riding back to the wikiup, he quickly grabbed a sack threw in a pot and stated, "best fill your canteens." Adding, "we leave now!"

"You coming'." He stated, giving her an icy stare. Morgan just looked at him then with a curt nod of her head, they headed to the corral.

They saddled the horses, took the jerky and filled all the canteens and they began the treacherous climb up a trail that cut into the side of the cliffs toward the red rim rock of the Canyon of the Grand.

Thomas led the men slowly toward the cut. For hours he had tracked the faintest of trails then nothing. No rocks overturned no scars of hooves.

As sweat poured down his face, his eyes never leaving the ground. For an hour he criss crossed the area still nothing! Taking off his neckerchief, he wiped his face dry, then his eyes spotted a shadow deep within a thicket and behind a large fallen granite wall.

Kneeing his horse into the cut, a smile crossed his face as he entered the valley. Turning around, he motioned for the others to follow. They rode to the wikiup.

"They were here less than an hour ago." He stated to Kincaid. Working his way around he found the tracks of horses leading into the rugged upper canyon country.

Much like the desert, a dry desolate place of steep cliffs, deep ravines and dry washes. A home for rattlers and scorpions.

"They went up there." Said Thomas, pointing up into the rugged red sandstone cliffs leading into the desert like rim country of the Canyon of the Grand.

"Damn him to hell," swore Claybourne. As he stared hard at the trail leading into the cliffs, he said hotly, "I can't believe he'd take a woman up there."

"You going' up there?" questioned Kincaid, as he stared at the trail.

"No, but we now know where he's headed." replied Stanford now known as Claybourne.

"Defiance?" Questioned Kincaid.

Nodding his head, Claybourne's eyes never leaving the trail, he stated evenly, "set men at the river crossing. If he makes it down that'll be our best chance to get him."

"And if he doesn't." He added with a smile, "that country up there will have done us a favor."

Thomas gazed at the trail above the valley. As the others turned to leave, Kincaid turned to Thomas.

"You coming?" He asked?

"No." Was his reply, "he will come back here, I feel it. and when he does," paused Thomas, "I will be here to greet him."

"You think they'll make it then." Stated Kincaid evenly.

With a curt nod of his head Thomas watched three riders disappear behind a wall of rock.

"Yes Mr. McCord," he thought to himself, "we will meet again."

As they headed into the high canyon country, McCord worriedly watched the sky as ominous black clouds began to build on the horizon. The wind picked up and thunder could be heard crashing in the distance.

Lightning split the sky overhead, he noticed a cave just to their left. The cave was large enough for the horses as well as themselves. Motioning for them to follow, he dismounted and led his horse inside. The others followed suit.

Thunder crashed as lightning seemed to explode all around, the walls of sandstone shook as thunder crashed. The rain began, gentle at first, then fell hard. With the wind driving the rain, it came down hard and fast. The horses tossed their heads nervously, as water began to pour into the cave from the ceiling.

Rivulets of dirt and mud streamed down walls of the cave. Morgan angrily glared at McCord as mud dripped down her hair and on to her shirt. Her eyes narrow she fingered the gun he had given her then thinking better of it, she moved to where the water and mud was not as bad.

From above came a deeper rumble and the ground began to shake! Rocks loosened by the rain began to fall and the roof of the cave began to collapse! A large block of sandstone missed McCord by inches.

"Get the hell outta here!" Screamed McCord to the others as he ran to the horses.

Grabbing the reins, he wildly waved them out of the cave into the pouring rain. As the three ran out they were hit with the full force of the storm.

Rain pelted them, the wind almost drove them backwards! A thick smell of ozone hung in the air as the rain loosened earth fell! A raging torrent of mud, trees and rock rushed down the trail toward them!

They were standing in a dry river bed! Grabbing Morgan, McCord forced her up a rock slide and the two men scrambled up behind her and out of danger as a torrent of mud rushed by!

The cave they had just left was no more, as the mountain side fell! Huge blocks of sandstone now lay where the cave had been.

Knowing they needed shelter, McCord fought his way through the wind and driving rain to a stand of Aspen. Motioning for them to follow he led the way.

Buffeted by the wind and with the rain pouring down, he used his knife and cut first one slender branch then another. He shook his head as water dripped into his eyes, then he cut the bark into several long pieces.

Being wet, they bent but did not break. The wind whipped through their clothing, shivering with cold they watched as McCord took the pieces and tied them together then pulled several trees together, their branches intertwined making a shelter of sorts.

He saw Garret looking at him questioningly, "learned this from the Apache," he explained, adding, "we came this far north a few times."

Taking his knife he dug into the trunk of a pine tree. As a black tar like substance slowly welled around the hole, McCord scrapped it on to his knife, then spread it on to several wet branches.

Taking his knife he dried it off, then dried off a rock, taking the knife, he hit the knife against the rock, as sparks flew on to the pitch it started to smoke, seconds later he had a small fire burning then slowly he piled small sticks on to the fire. Within minutes they felt it's warmth.

"Your just full of surprises." Stated Morgan dryly, as she glared at him. Her hair lay in mats full of dirt and mud. Her face was streaked with dirt. She was wet, shivering and miserable as she sat next to the fire.

The rain continued throughout the night. As the sun rose, McCord went looking for the horses, finding no sign, he walked back to the camp.

"Looks like we go on foot from here." He stated.

"You know McCord, if it wasn't for you and that damned private war of yours." she snarled as her eyes flashed with anger, "maybe we wouldn't be in this fix." she spat angrily.

He looked at her questioningly, as she continued, her faced twisted in anger, her eyes flaming in anger.

"Yeah we heard all about your attacking the Double Diamond, how you set the ranch on fire."

"You killed Charlie! She snarled angrily, her voice choked with emotion then she spat, "You may not have pulled the trigger but because of what he and I did for you he's dead!"

McCord looked at her angrily, then at Garret as he stood up. Without saying anything he walked into the cold night. Her words had hurt, he was angry with himself, in part because he knew she was right.

"What in the hell is wrong with you." Screamed Garret, his voice trembling with anger, as he turned Morgan around to face him.

"He saved your hide....he didn't have to come back!" He screamed at her. As she glared at him he continued angrily, "If he hadn't we'd both be dead." He said, his voice full of emotion. Adding, "maybe it's time for you to look at yourself and quit blaming him for what has happened and maybe put the blame where it actually needs to be."

"Don't it bother you," she snapped back. "that Charlie's dead, an....an and that I....that I lost my ranch!" She said angrily, her voice filled with emotion.

" Ma'am." he started sarcastically, then snapped "this gent has saved your ungrateful hide! You best stop and think about that!" He angrily retorted.

McCord deep in thought, walked to the rim of the canyon, with the sun just rising, he knew with their horses gone, that meant no food or water. Without water they would have no chance to survive up here.

"Come on, we'd best we leave now while it's cool." He said as he woke them up.

As the sun rose, it beat down on them unmercifully, the wind that blew was like a furnace, the hot air seemed to draw moisture out of their bodies with each step. McCord reached down into the dirt then handed them several small pebbles.

"Put them in your mouth." he said hoarsely, seeing their questioning looks he added, "it'll help." As they both put the pebbles in their mouth, they felt saliva build inside their mouth. He knew they needed rest.

"I'm going to look for a way down." He said to Garret as he left and walked toward a steep ravine. Garret sat next to Morgan, leaning against a rock, he closed his eye's then glared at her angrily.

"What are you Miss Morgan," he snarled, then added, "you ain't got no right to keep being angry at McCord. Adding, "your acting like a spoiled brat, not getting your way, and your layin' all the blame on him!"

He got to his feet and stalked angrily toward the rim of the canyon. Looking down, all he could see were the tops of pine trees and from a distance, he heard the roar of the river far below.

Above, he saw an eagle soaring high in the cloudless sky. The sun beat down on on this arid landscape, the red dirt was more like sand than dirt and the rocks themselves were hot to the touch even the scorpions and rattlers were staying out of sight.

The two sought out any shade they could find. Sweat darkened their shirts as they waited for McCord to come back.

As McCord scouted the rim, he thought about Charlie and about what Morgan had said, Angrily he kicked the dirt, angry at himself and the thought of Charlie's death. Then he thought about what Morgan had said.

"Just one more reason." He thought, as he picked up a rock and threw it at a tree in the distance.

He watched as a herd of bighorn bounded away from him. Their hoofs seeming to stick to the side of the cliff. Looking down he watched as they bounded from ledge to ledge.

"That's it!" He thought, then he tracked the sheep to an outcrop. As he looked down, he saw a series of ledges, and an ancient rock fall. He watched the sheep jump from the ledges to the rock fall, and down to a trail below.

"There is a way down." He thought, "downright dangerous;" but it was there. Now he just had to convince the other two.

Turning around, he walked back and found Garret and Morgan then motioned for them to follow. Taking them to the outcrop, as Morgan and Garret looked down, he could see the fear in their faces.

"It won't be easy," he started, then Morgan interrupted him, "what the hell McCord," she said disbelievingly, her eyes wide with fear, added, "You really think we can climb down this." Then said, with a slight smile, "You must have me confused, I ain't no damned mountain goat."

For the first time, he smiled at her words then nodded his head, he said, "I'll go first, then Garret, you stay up top while Morgan climbs down."

"You've got to be kidding." Breathed Morgan as her voice shook with fear.

"I don't see where we have a choice," added McCord quietly, then said added somberly, "There's no water up here, no food....... if we don't do this," he paused and with a deep breath he added, "we will die up here. You game?" He asked as he gave her a hard look.She gave a quick nod of her head, her eye's wide with fear.

McCord started through the maze of rock and brush from a long ago slide, slowly working his way to a ledge just underneath the rim. Once there, he looked up at Morgan.

"You ready?" He asked. As she nodded her head He added, "Garret take her hand and help her down to me."

Seconds later she stood next to him, clinging tenuously to the side of the ledge. As Garret came down. McCord sat down with his foot braced on a large boulder, he told Morgan, "now take my hand and I will lower you to that boulder there," Pointing to a large boulder just below them.

She gulped, closed her eyes for a moment, took a deep breath, then took his outstretched arm, holding on, she used rocks to steady herself as she made her way to the boulder.

"Garret your next." He said. Garret worked his way slowly toward Morgan seconds later he stood next to her.

Now it was his turn, he slowly lowered his body over the edge, his muscles bulging, he worked hand over hand toward the boulder, then dropped, landing hard on his shoulder.

"Not exactly what I had in mind." he said with a half smile as he slowly stood up, dusted the dirt from his shoulders and jeans.

He pointed down to a series of ledges leading to a ancient rock slide, this was the trail of the sheep. Slowly they made their way down, at times going on all fours, backward over the rocks. Every once in a while a loosened rock, would nearly miss them as it fell, bouncing down, toward the roaring river down below.

For what seemed hours, under the intense sun, they manipulated their way down, sweat darkened their clothing. They went slowly as they knew each step could be their last. Finally, they were standing on a trail. It hugged a tall limestone cliff on one side and a sheer drop of a thousand feet into jagged rocks below on the other.

The trail was nothing more than an animal trail that had been cut by the mountain sheep over eons of time. Standing on the trail, all three looked up from where they had come.

It looked impossible! Nothing but jutted cliffs of limestone and granite, and rock slides, yet they had made it!

As they began the steep descent the going was hard as the trail was narrow, working their way around the red cliffs and granite outcroppings they finally spied a valley nestled high in the canyon. A crystal blue lake seemed to hang down from the cliffs above.

"Heard about this place," breathed Morgan, "my pa told me about it a long time ago. Adding, "they call it hanging lake. I thought he was telling me a story."

Morgan went to take a step and heard the distinct buzzing sound of a rattler as it lay curled,

next to a rock in the center of the trail.

"Do not move!" Said McCord quietly, as he saw the snake ready to strike!

Moving slowly, as not to provoke the attack he carefully took his arm and moved Morgan very slowly away from the angry snake. As he took her place, he started weaving back and forth!

The attention of the snake was transfered to him. It's eye's followed his movements. As the snake seemed to be hypnotized as it began to mirror his moves. Slowly it swayed back and forth, suddenly McCord grabbed it by the head and tossed it over the edge!

"Where in the hell did you learn to do that." Breathed Garret, his eyes wide, as McCord took Morgan into his arms and held her as she trembled with fear. Holding her close, he led her to a rock and let her sit down.

"The Apache." He stated quietly, as he looked at Garret, Adding, "I was raised by them."

As they entered the valley a herd of deer bounded quickly away. It was an amazing place.

The lake was fed by a waterfall that fell from a hole high in the wall of the rim rock canyon. It was a brilliant blue and acted like a mirror, reflecting the azure blue sky, white clouds and the glowing, golden cast of the setting sun on the red sandstone rim of the canyon.

Picking up sticks and dried moss, McCord dug a small pit with his knife, then inserted the moss taking his knife blade, he hit a rock several times watching the sparks from the knife fall into the moss. A few minutes later, the moss caught, and began burning as he started feeding the fire, He looked up at Morgan. His blue eyes had a gentleness in them she had not seen before.

"You did great today." he said gently

"You said we didn't have a choice." She remarked quietly.

"I'm sorry." She said quietly as she stared into his eyes. Adding. "it's just..."she stammered, "my ranch, and Charlie are gone." her voice choked with emotion, "then Claybourne killing' my pa."

McCord took her in his arms and held her as she buried her face in his chest and cried. Looking down at her, he kissed her lightly on the forehead and wiped her tears away with his finger, as she looked up at him her face streaked with dirt, sweat and tears he held her close.

"I'm taking you to Defiance," He stated, "I have a friend there who will keep you safe." His lips gently kissed her forehead, then he led her to a rock and sat her down.

"You rest here," He said, his voice soft and gentle, as he let her go he added more wood to the fire, then started to the lake.

"Raised by the Apache." Thought Garret, shaking his head as he watched him go to the lake. It answered a lot of the questions he had, his knowledge of the wildlife and survival techniques he had witnessed, then he began to collect wood for the fire.

McCord cut a long branch off of a sapling. then scraped off the bark while sharpening the end to a point.

Feeling it for balance, he went to the edge of the lake. While he waited he thought about Morgan. Shaking his head he knew he was not ready. But she had stirred something deep inside him.

"Maybe," he thought then remembering Carrie he shook his head, staring hard at the canyon wall he thought, "no one else will die because of me or what I do."

A fish jumping in the lake caught his attention. Seconds later one swam up just a foot away. Raising his spear, he jabbed and pinned it to the lake bed. Within a few minutes he had four more. Picking them up, he walked back to the fire. Morgan glanced at him, took the fish and gutted them. McCord then took each fish and wrapped it in wet grass, then covered it in mud and threw them on to the hot coals of the fire.

That night with the tensions of the day gone and the first full meal they had in three days, they sat around the campfire as Travis laid out his plan to them.

"They will probably be staking out the canyon," started McCord then Morgan interrupted him saying, "Or, they might have figured we died." For a moment they sat silenced then McCord laughed and agreed.

"We should move only at night," he began, "that way we can see the fires and as black dark as it gets in the canyon, we'll see them before they see us; we'll have the advantage."

That night as Morgan and Garret slept, McCord crept out of camp toward the rim of the canyon. Beneath a clear moonless night, the stars littered the sky, carefully he crept along the trail through the dense undergrowth and rocks. The lower he went, he began to go through thick forests of pine and aspen as he made his way down toward the river below.

Topping a ridge, he crouched down and saw fires dotted along the river. It was going to be harder than he thought.

"Maybe there's another way." He thought, turning around he glanced up at the imposing red rim of the canyon then he hiked back up the trail into the valley.

As he sat by the coals of the fire, he mulled over what he had seen. The fires indicated they were all by the river no one was up in the cliffs. There had to be a way through the cliffs to get around the men that were waiting for them near the river.

He thought of Morgan, if it was just him he would not have a problem but it was her. He smiled as he remembered how she had climbed down like, as she had put it "a damn mountain goat."

He finally fell into a restless sleep. Then awakened with a start pulling his pistol, squirrels were chattering loudly and a herd of deer stood like statues. Following their gaze he saw a bear slowly walking by the lake. Holstering the gun he waited for the bear to leave then walked down to the lake.

He rinsed his neckerchief in the cold water of the lake. He wiped his face, wincing as water hit the cuts on his face. The cold water revived him. Walking back to the fire pit, he stoked the still hot coals with dry wood.

As the others awakened and made their way to the fire, he told the them what he had seen the night before. He outlined his plan about crossing high under the cliffs.

"I don't see any other way." He said his voice soft and low. Adding with a smile, "looks like your gonna play mountain goat again Morgan."

She half smiled at the statement and knowing she had no other choice, she nodded her head in agreement. Garret and Morgan spent the day in the sunshine of the valley as McCord scouted the route underneath the massive cliffs.

For two hours he looked then found it, nothing more than a path, it lay high up, directly beneath the monster cliffs and was just wide enough for them to move single file. The trail paralleled the cliffs, on one side the cliff on the other a fall into the rocks below.

It would be a treacherous descent, however, he saw the prints of deer and elk and also the claw marks of bear and mountain lion, to him it meant it was an active well used animal trail.

Returning to the valley, he laid out to them what he had seen. He went into detail as how it could be done but would be treacherous. Tired, he laid down and tried to sleep as did the others.

As twilight approached they left, headed down the trail to the path he had found. Finding the trail during the day was difficult but at night it was near impossible!

As night grew darker, they found the path that hugged the rim rock. Carved through the centuries by elk and deer it was treacherous! For hours they hugged the walls of the cliffs and slowly made their way across.

As the moon rose, it's white light guided them above the first two fires. Staying within the shadows of the great cliffs, they went undiscovered.

For most of the night they slowly worked their way along the scant trail as it curved and cut it's way through the cliffs. More than once, they stopped to take a deep breath and then continued foot by foot.

The two men helped Morgan over the deep trenches carved into the trail by the rain. As the moon began to set, the path began to descend and widen out. The jagged rocks gave way to a gentle slope as it began to widen. It was here they could smell smoke of a fire.

It was almost dawn, exhausted, their clothes dark with sweat, they began to slowly climb down toward the churning river, just a few hundred yards away.

Travis held up his hand and motioned for them to get down. The thick smell of a cigar announced the presence of a man not more than ten feet away.

Leaving the others McCord stealthily approached him. Just as he was getting ready to grab the man, another voice surprised him, he faded back into the cover of a bush, as the other man approached.

"Hear anything Sam?" asked the first man.

"Just mountain sheep an deer." Grinned Sam.

"Just keep on the lookout." Laughed the first. "I think they're dead, ain't no way in hell they could have gotten past us." He added as he walked away from Sam.

"Check back with you later." He said as he walked back down toward the river.

Taking his knife, McCord again approached Sam. Sneaking up from behind, he grabbed Sam, placed his hand over Sam's mouth, and stabbed him, he let the body fall and motioned for Morgan and Garret.

"Let's go, they're gonna know soon enough where we are." He whispered, nodding their heads in agreement, they quietly made for the river.

Chapter Nine

As the sun began to rise. McCord found a cave hidden deep in a rock slide. Walls of limestone lay scattered around the rocks. Within one was a cave hidden from view of the river. They all sank, exhausted to the ground. As Morgan leaned her head against the wall of the cave, Garret and Travis took turns standing watch.

Voices suddenly filled the air. Knowing that the body of the man named Sam had been found. They lay still as men began to hunt for them. The cave was well hidden, it was covered with brush and rock and they went undiscovered.

The last rays of sunlight glinted gold against the walls of the canyon when McCord shook Garret awake. Quietly, so as not to awaken Morgan, they walked to the entrance of the cave.

"The way I see it," Whispered McCord, "one of us has to swim this river and get into the town of Defiance."

"What the hell," Garret said halfheartedly, "I'll do it. I think you should stay with Morgan."

"I agree." Stated McCord, adding, "When you reach the far bank, stick to the shadows go to the hotel up on the hill to the west. When you get inside, ask for Doc Holliday." He saw the surprised look on Garrets face, adding "we're old friends" stated McCord softly. Then he whispered, "Now go."

Slowly and quietly, Garret worked his way through dense brush and trees to the bank of the Roaring Fork River. As he entered the water, he gasped as the frigid water surrounded him.

He swam slowly across, his body numbed by the cold water did not want to work! Still he went on, something dark floated toward him. It was a log, blindly he reached for it and grabbed on.

The current was swift, but with the log he was able to maneuver it toward the bank on the other side. Finally, he felt ground beneath him. He crawled up the bank and collapsed, exhausted, he laid still, his body quaking as he shivered from the cold.

The cold night air along with his wet clothes chilled him to the bone. Dazed and exhausted he laid still then forced himself to his feet.

Keeping to the shadows he finally saw the oil lamps leading to the hotel built at the base of a mountain.

His legs numbed by the cold did not want to work. He stumbled several times as he worked his way up the steep steps. He flung open the door and fell inside.

"I.......I.....need....Doc Holliday!" He stuttered to the man at the desk.

"I think not." Was the man's reply as he looked at him. "We don't......" started the man then he saw the gun that somehow materialized in the man's hand.

"Look you Son of a bitch," swore Garret, his voice low and deadly, "I've been shot at, I just swam that river an I need Holliday now!"

"I am Holliday." stated a voice from behind him.

Turning around, he saw a well dressed man in black standing with two others holding a gun aimed at him.

"Please drop your weapon." He said in an authoritative voice. Then the man named Holliday told the man at the desk, "do not worry Henry, I have this under control."

"Need to talk to you alone." Stated Garret as he looked at the other two others suspiciously.

"Anything you have to say can be said in front of my two friends here." Said Holliday matter of factly. "Now why are you here!" He demanded.

"The names Shannon," He started, adding, " A friend of yours, named McCord sent me"

"Get this man a brandy." Ordered Holliday loudly as he and the other two men helped Garret to the couch.

"Henry, bring this man a brandy and a blanket....now!" Ordered Holliday loudly.

"Drink this" he said, holding the brandy to Garrets lips, As he did he felt it's warmth course through his body as they put a blanket around him.

"Now," asked Holliday, "what about this man McCord."

"Told me to come find you." Stated Garret tiredly, "him and Morgan Jenric of J-Bar Ranch are across the river. As he tried to stand, he was pushed back.

"They got men up and down the canyon looking to kill them," He said as he attempted to stand but could not.

"You are in no condition to go with us." Stated Holliday, then turned to Henry, "bring our horses here now."

Nodding his head Henry ran out the door to the livery, a half hour later he returned with three saddled horses.

"Where are they." Asked one of the men, he was tall, over six feet, his hair was dark brown, his eyes, blue-gray, almost the color of steel.

"It's alright as they are friends of his as well. This man is Logan Teel and the other is Chad McKinley." Said Holliday as he saw Garret's questioning look.

"They're on the other side of the river, right where it forks, behind the buildings on the east side of town." Was Garrets reply.

As the men walked out, Garret closed his eye's as the warmth of the brandy and the blanket began to take effect.

"Henry, get that man out of those wet clothes, you can give him some of mine." Said Holliday as he walked outside.

"How do you think he will react to you being here Logan." Asked Holliday as they mounted the horses.

"No idea." Was Logan's reply, smiling, he added, "told you he threatened to kill me the last time we saw each other."

"Yeah." Replied Holliday dryly, as they headed toward the river. Scanning the far bank Logan looked for a sign. A flash caught his attention.

"There they are." he quietly exclaimed pointing toward the bank.

Riding their horses into the frigid water, they worked their way across to a line of trees. As the horses climbed out Morgan and Travis walked up to them.

"Something told me you'd be here Logan." Smiled McCord, as he grasped his friends hand in a warm handshake. Adding, "Sure glad you are"

Helping Morgan up behind Holliday, Travis climbed up behind Logan. Handing Travis a rifle," Logan said, "From what I hear, you may need this yet." From out of nowhere, gunfire exploded all around them.

"Hold on," Screamed Holiday as he spurred the horse back into the river with Morgan clinging to him.

"Chad, cover us!" loudly yelled Logan, as he spurred his horse.

Jumping off the horse, McCord threw himself back onto the bank then went to one knee rapid firing the Henry. Within seconds, Logan came back firing his rifle into the bushes where the gunfire had come from.

As Travis stood up, something white hot burned into his leg. Holding on to the horse for support, he saw Logan return fire and a man screamed in pain. Grasping his friends outstretched hand he swung up behind him.

Crossing the river amid a hail of bullets they quickly escaped into the safety of the town. Reaching the hotel, they dismounted, as Travis slipped off the back of Logan's horse, his leg buckled and he lost his balance and fell hard into the street!

"He's been shot! Someone get the Doc over here! Yelled Logan.

A moment later, Logan and Chad helped McCord up the stairs and into the hotel. They eased him into a chair. Logan was shocked at his friends appearance. His hair was long, he had a scar on his cheekbone, his face was gaunt and white.

"Been a long time Logan," panted Travis as his face twisted in pain. Pausing, "I found them, Stanford's calling himself Claybourne." They were interrupted as a man walked inside the hotel.

"Where's the gent that got himself shot and ruined my night. Only Holliday could a got me up outta' my bed at this late hour." Stated a tall gray haired man with a smile as he closed the door behind him.

He looked around then saw McCord, walking over to him the Doctor was all business. He slit the pant leg with his knife then looked at the hole in his upper calf, then on the other side was the exit wound, the bullet had gone completely through, he then reached into his medical bag and pulled out a bottle of whiskey.

Taking the whiskey, he poured it on the open wound. The pain was intense. Gritting his teeth, McCord slammed his fist down on to the table. Then glared at the Doctor.

"What in the hell do you think your doing."He swore angrily as pain knifed through his body.,

"Son," replied the Doctor matter of factly, "you got yourself shot. An this here whiskey is good for your innards as well as your wound."

"Don't be walking on that leg for at least a week." He said as he placed a bandage on the wound. As Travis started to argue, the doctor raised his hand then walked away.

"Oh thought I'd leave that bottle for you, from the looks of you, you might need it." He said as he turned and walked out.

His body shaking McCords hand trembled as he poured himself a drink. Downing it in one gulp, he poured another. Finally, with a combination of whiskey and exhaustion McCord passed out. With Chad's help, they took McCord to a room and laid him gently on to the bed.

"How is he." Asked Morgan worriedly, as she stood outside the door.

"With rest he'll be OK." Said Logan, then he held out his hand, "Miss Jenric, I am Logan Teel a United States Marshal. I am here as a response to your letter to the Governor."

`Shaking his hand she said with a smile, "I wrote the governor a few months back, I didn't think anything would come of it."

"Miss Jenric," Said Holliday with a smile. "please allow me to introduce myself, I am John Henry Holliday, folks know me as Doc and I am at your service. You can stay as my guest, if you need anything just speak to Henry here, and I am sure he will do what he can to accommodate you. Isn't that right Henry?" As Henry nodded his head he gave Morgan a key.

"Ma'am," We have a room available just up this hallway to your left. The number is 271, I am sure you will be comfortable there."

Tiredly she nodded her head and went to the room. Looking in the mirror, she was horrified! Her face was stained with dirt, her blouse was torn, her hair lay in mats and filled with mud and dirt. She asked Henry where she could clean up and find new clothes.

A moment later, he returned with new clothes and a helper poured warm water into a wooden bathtub. She had heard about them while she had been in Denver several months ago. It was a new invention just now coming here to the mountains.

The sun shone brightly through the window as McCord opened his eye's. His head felt heavy and had a dull ache, his mouth was dry and tasted like cotton. As he sat up, he felt pain stab through his leg.

Painfully he stood up and limped to the door. He could smell food cooking, hungry he limped down the stairs to the restaurant inside the hotel.

Seeing Morgan, Chad and Logan with Holliday, he limped over. He eased himself painfully into a chair and took the coffee Logan handed him. It had been a long time since the coffee tasted this good. Then a plate of eggs, bacon, sausage and potatoes materialized in front of him.

"Morgan's been filling us in on what has been happening." Stated Logan as he sipped his coffee.

"Doc," explained Travis, "I brought her here for your protection. She's a target now." Travis said as he put a fork full of potatoes in his mouth.

"She is welcome to stay as long as she wants too." Said Holliday as he sipped his cup of coffee.

"Logan, what are your plans?" Questioned McCord as he took a bite of the food. "and how did you know I was here."

"I'm here because I was told to come by the governors office in Denver." Replied Logan, his blue-gray eyes hard as granite; "Travis I'm here to eliminate this situation, and," pausing, he leaned forward, "to get Stanford and Kincaid back to Arizona to stand trial."

"The man you know as Sam Claybourne is actually Clay Stanford, he and Kincaid escaped from the prison in Yuma two years ago." He explained as he saw her questioning look.

Hearing his words, McCord looked down at his plate, suddenly not hungry, he shoved the plate angrily and stood up. His eye's like ice, he glared angrily at the men seated at the table.

"Logan I told you once what would happen if you tried to interfere." He said, his voice low and threatening. As the others sat in silence he added, "I do not need, nor do I want your help with this. this is my fight and mine alone." Pausing, he gave Logan a penetrating stare, then added his voice soft and low and threatening, "Don't get in my way."

With that he limped away from the table and back to his room. Taking his fist he slammed the wall hard. Leaning against it, angry, he closed his eyes for a moment.

"Damn you Logan." He whispered, his teeth clenched, his blue eye like steel. Turning to the window, he looked out toward the mountain known as Hardscrabble. Covered in a mist, it looked foreboding and angry, seeming to mirror how he felt.

He turned, grabbed his holster and buckled it on. Pain knifed down his leg as he tied the holster down.

Limping out of the door, he worked his way down the series of steps to the dusty street and toward the livery.

Sweat beaded on his forehead, lightheaded he leaned against the wall of the building for support. Gritting his teeth against the pain he forced himself into the livery.

"Can I help you?" Asked a man then he stated, "Say ain't you the fella that come in last night."

"Need a horse." Growled McCord, ignoring the man's question.

"Mister, don't think you're in any shape to ride." Said the man with concern in his voice as he saw McCord leaning against a stall.

"Just get me a damned horse." McCord demanded, his teeth clenched, as he gave the man a penetrating stare that seemed to go through him, then pulled his gun.

"Alright Mister," stated the man fearfully. Raising his hands in the air.

"This one's already saddled." The man said nervously as he handed the reins to McCord.

He watched as McCord fruitlessly tried several times to mount the animal. Finally, through sheer strength, he pulled himself up on to its back. leaning over its neck, gritting his teeth against the pain. He closed his eyes for a moment.

"Mister." started the livery man with concern.

"Don't even." said McCord through clenched teeth, as he glared at the man, grimacing in pain he turned the horse's head toward Hardscrabble, kicking it he headed out of town.

As McCord left, the man ran for the hotel. Rushing inside, he looked around and saw Holliday at the table with two others.

"Doc" he yelled as he ran to the table.

"That man you brought in last night....he come to get a horse an he left." Stammered the man.

"What in the holy hell." swore Logan jumping to his feet.

"I tried to stop him.....but them damned blue eyes of his, it was like I wasn't there, he just looked right though me." Stated the livery man as he shook his head nervously.

"Not many would have tried to." stated Logan quietly. Motioning for Chad to follow him he got to his feet.

"So," said Chad as he gave Logan a hard stare.

"We go after him." Said Logan as he grabbed his guns from behind the chair and buckled them on.

For an hour they tried to pick up his trail, finally Logan pulled his horse to a stop. Looking at Chad he remarked angrily, "how in the hell does he disappear like that."

"Ain't no sense trying to find him. He'll find us when he's ready." Said Logan, his gray-blue eyes, hard as steel as he shook his head angrily and the two rode back to town.

Seeing Morgan's questioning look, Logan just shook his head. Then stated angrily, "We leave in the morning for the valley."

CHAPTER TEN

As the sun rose in a cloudless sky, Logan and Chad finished tieing the packs to the horses. As they turned to leave. Morgan rode up.

"Now Marshal," She said with a smile, "you wouldn't be planning to leave without me now would you."

"What in the hell do you think your doing Miss Jenric." Stated Logan angrily.

"Why Marshal, I'm riding with you." Was her reply, as she pulled her horse up beside him.

"NO! Travis brought you here for a reason. And Miss Jenric, you will stay here if I have to place you in custody!" Was Logan's heated reply.

"I either ride with you Marshal or I ride alone." She stated defiantly her violet eyes flashing in anger. "You know Marshal, those ranchers up there are a curious bunch. They don't like or trust outsiders. They know me, they know whats at stake and my being there will help you." She said.

"Besides that..." she stated, her voice choked with emotion, "they killed my pa, they killed Charlie and they took my ranch!" Then defiantly she added, "And you expect me to just stay here and do nothing; I will not!"

He thought about what she said, his eyes hard, his jaw set, he said in a sharp voice. "Then let's move out."

The walls of the canyon loomed large even at this distance. Cathedral cliffs reached high into the sky, their rims glowing a reddish gold as the light of the early morning sun hit them.

They traveled slowly through thick brush and over dead falls, the trail, at times took them perilously close to the raging river that had cut this canyon eons ago.

Churning and turbulent, it's sound was deafening, late afternoon found them half way through, pausing within the walls of the canyon, they stopped to rest the horses and set up camp for the night. Logan rolled a cigarette then lit it, as the blue smoke swirled in the slight wind that blew he looked up at the incredible spires of granite and sandstone cliffs that surrounded him.

It was a place of amazing beauty but at the same time a rugged unforgiving place that had for centuries killed many men who dared to enter it's heart.

It was an untamed place, where at any time, rocks the size of buildings could fall, where rain falling miles away could instantly turn the river into a raging torrent of death and destruction. The color of the river was a deep reddish hue. The Spanish named it *el Rio Colorado;* the red river.

Many had died here caught in rock slides, or drowned in the rivers rampage. He saw the evidence, huge walls of rock lay in the river, even now, small rocks danced down the steep slopes and splashed into the river.

In awe of the canyon, Logan stood transfixed gazing at castle bluff, so named by the Spanish explorers who, besides the Ute and even the Apache, were the first to see this place. They too had stood in his place, to them, this sandstone formation reminded them of the huge castles of their homeland.

Next to it stood battlement mesa, where legend had it one tribe of Ute had held off a force of over one hundred Blackfeet. As light began to fade, they set about making camp. Morgan saw Logan standing by the river and looking at the incredible spires of sandstone.

She came up from behind him and for a moment they just looked at the star littered night sky, a brisk wind blew cold around them.

From up above, small pebbles danced down the steep side of a cliff and from behind them came a thud as a rock tumbled down the steep slope and fell just behind them!

"Its the ones you don't hear, that kill you." Stated Morgan quietly, as she stood next to him.

"So, tell me about you and Travis." She asked quietly.

"What," Said Logan chuckling as he looked at her, " that's he's as wild and unpredictable as that black stud he rides. And if he don't start thinkin' he's gonna get himself killed."

"Why is he like that." She asked as she placed her hand on his shoulder.

"Did he say anything to you about Carrie?" He asked giving her a hard look, as she shook her head no.

"Figured he wouldn't." He said quietly. "She was his wife.......but not just his wife..... but his best friend, ...his companion and she was his life...... as his life was hers."

"When they killed her," he said angrily, his voice choked with emotion, "they took his life. Least ways that's what he thinks."

"You see, we had just returned from catching rustlers in the northern end of the territory.

we were not that far from his ranch so I told him to go.

When I got back to the office, I found a wire from the warden at the Yuma territorial prison stating that both Kincaid and the man you know as Claybourne, his real name is Stanford and two others, the Ault brothers, had escaped and the Indian trackers had lost the trail at the Big Sandy."

"It was Travis and his testimony in court that put them there." Logan said, his voice almost a whisper, as he stared into the blackness of the canyon. I immediately organized a posse and left headed to his ranch. We were too late." He said his voice quiet and full of emotion.

"I was there," he said his voice raspy, "I saw what they did to him. He nearly died, the doc didn't hold out much hope but he survived."

It's the anger inside him thats kept him alive and it's that same anger that may kill him. He takes chances knowing he could be killed, but I don't think it matters that much to him. Getting these two is his goal, and has been for two years now, and Morgan, he won't quit, not unless they kill him."

"When they killed her, I don't think they had any idea what they would unleash." He growled angrily.

"Heard from a marshal up in Utah that he just walked in on the

Calhoun gang, called out the Ault brothers then shot them in front of Calhoun!

Later when they went after the gang in the hole in the wall, they shot Calhoun, just before he died he told them 'bout this marshal that just walked in on them. Said he had the eyes of a devil".

"He's dangerous Morgan, to them and to himself." He said, as he looked hard at her.

"He's worse now than he was even with the Apache." He said, as he looked at her. "Did he ever talk about that?"

"He told us up at the valley he had been raised by them, but thats all," She said nodding her head.

"He was just a kid and had been out hunting. he explained, When he came home, he found his folks dead. He tracked the sign to the village of Black Feather a chief known to be friendly to whites. His folks knew Black Feather and Travis had spent time in his village.

Black Feather allowed him to challenge the ones who killed his parents. One by one he killed them." then added quietly, "He was just twelve years old!"

"Black Feather adopted him as his son, said he had the courage of a mountain lion, known as the tiger of the desert. But even though he was the son of the chief he still needed to learn the Apache way.

The women of the tribe are the worse. They would go after him with sticks and rocks, they treated him as if he were a prisoner.

But, being white, he has always felt he had to prove himself. He was never fully accepted by the Apache nor by the whites. Later, because he was white he was the one they would send into the camps to spy on the "white eyes".

They had a name for him "El Cetan Nagrin; the whites called him "Shadow Hawk." They knew him as a renegade.

When I first met him the thing that struck me was his blue eyes," then he added as a smile crossed his face, giving Morgan a look, "those damn blue eyes of his, its like staring at ice, unfeeling, cold and ruthless."

"When I first met him he was stuck under a dead bull buffalo." He said as a smile crossed his face. Seemed he was part of a hunting party, he was challenged, his position with the tribe was at stake.

He got too close, the bull gored his horse, as the horse went down, he was thrown on to the back of the bull and slammed the spear into the animals heart, as it went down, he tried to jump but the animal turned and threw him to the ground then it sank dead on his leg.

I was out chasing renegades when I came up on him." Pausing he looked at her, "the only thing white about him was them damned blue eyes of his. So I pulled the bull off him, his leg of course was broke, and the whole time he just stared at me.

I butchered the buffalo then took him and the buffalo to his village. They gave me the buffalo robe and made me his blood brother.

A few years later, I started hearing talk of a white man riding with the Apache. A white man like the Apache, he would give no quarter in a fight, they called him a renegade. People were afraid of him. Just the mention of his name would terrify most Indians and whites.

I was working for the army as a scout and had ran down some renegades that had been raiding ranches on this side of the Mexican border. They had me pinned down inside a church just outside of Nogales. Thought I was done for, when over a ridge he comes flying down with about twenty braves an they ran them off.

Shortly after that we began riding together. Since I already was working for the army, he began to help me with the scouting.

The army never really trusted him because of his rep. Fact is the first time he rode in with me, they swarmed all over him and put him in irons, then threw him in the stockade!

Took a fair amount of talking to get him out. Finally the commandant, Brigadier General Thomas Devin, a friend of mine, released him." Logan laughed, "took all of my persuading and arguing for him to not kill the soldiers that put him in the stockade.

We worked with the army for a while scouting, then we were both recruited by the Arizona Marshals." Logan explained with a smile, "guess they thought if we were part of them they wouldn't have to chase us all over the country."

"That," He stated quietly. "was a long time ago." Adding, as he took a deep breath, His voice soft and low, he said, "I hadn't seen him for over a year until the other day when I set eyes on him. And, for the first time, I felt the fear others have felt, looking into his eyes," he paused adding, his blue-gray eye's like steel, his jaw hard. "Morgan he's changed. He's like a wounded animal, he's more dangerous now than he was in the past."

"The Apache have a name for this they call it *"go de,"* a black spirit that haunts your mind. They unleashed that devil inside him the day they killed his wife." He growled through gritted teeth, his eyes narrowed as he looked down at Morgan then he turned and walked back to the fire.

Tears glistened in her eyes as she had listened to Logan. Thinking about what he had said now made it clear to her. The feeling of emptiness she felt each time he looked at her. The haunted look in his eyes that she had seen many times.

How, at times, he looked like he was lost and alone. Then the name Carrie. Her thoughts were interrupted as she heard Logan say, "Got an early start to the valley tomorrow best turn in now."

As she laid down and closed her eyes, she remembered the kiss at the lake, she remembered how he looked at her and she had seen gentleness in his eyes when he looked at her. and the soft kiss on her forehead.

She remembered how his arms felt around her as he held her close to him. Most of all how she remembered how he made her feel, safe and secure.

Chapter Eleven

The sun burned down hot, the air was filled with dust, as people walked across the street trying to stay out of the way of the wagons as they rumbled past. Claybourne sat looking out the window. He was sitting in the chair behind his desk when Kincaid walked in.

"Heard from the boys in Defiance, Teel and McKinley are headed here an that Jenric gal is with them." Stated Kincaid as he walked to a chair and heavily sat down.

"What about McCord," Questioned Claybourne as he continued staring out the window.

"Heard he took off up to Hardscrabble" Replied Kincaid as he poured himself a drink.

"If he goes back to the valley, Thomas will get him." Stated Claybourne quietly, although not as sure as he could have been.

"Clay," began Kincaid hesitantly, "maybe we should just call it quits here an leave."

"Roman," began Claybourne quietly, turning to look at him he gave him a hard stare, his dark eyes flashing with anger. "if we leave now, you know damn well they will follow us, theres nowhere we can go where he won't find us." pausing he fingered the shot glass in his hand, then looked hard at Kincaid, and added, "No, this time we half'ta stay until it's finished."

"You say that Morgans with Teel and McKinley." Stated Claybourne thoughtfully, as Kincaid nodded his head. He poured himself a drink then looked at Kincaid with an evil smile and said, "Then lets give her a welcome home party, get the boys together."

As Kincaid strode out of the room, Claybourne turned back to the window and gazed at the imposing peak known as Hardscrabble Mountain.

"If your up there McCord, your a dead man." Snarled Claybourne quietly.

For days Thomas had been watching the upper trail for McCord. He had heard that McCord had made it through to Defiance. With McCord leading them, he had known they would. Even though he respected him, he also hated him for what he had done to him.

It had taken him almost two days to get out of that canyon, he had found his horse just outside its walls. It angered him that he had been bested by an Apache. He had always thought of himself as part Comanche. Throughout their history, the two tribes had always been at each others throats.

Thomas, having come from a similar background, also practiced the "the art of the enemy". Knowing his enemy and how he would react. Knowing McCord, he knew he would return here. On the fifth day he saw a rider entering a stand of Aspen high above the valley.

"Welcome home Mr. McCord." Thought Thomas smiling to himself.

For two days, McCord had followed a trail up into the rugged country of Hardscrabble, the mountain had been named by the pioneers who claimed "it was a hard scrabble to go over it".

The mountain lived up to its reputation, with steep draws, deep gullies, thorn laced bushes and the ever present danger of rock slides.

Finally, he saw the valley below him, as he pulled into a stand of Aspen, he sat looking at the trail. As a warrior, he had been taught to know the enemy, become your enemy, think like your enemy. From the age of twelve this had been ingrained in him and had been a big part of his training as an Apache warrior.

With this knowledge, he knew Thomas was waiting for him. But where, mentally he went over the trail and knew the best place would be down past a huge wall of rock where the trail opened up.

Rubbing his leg to ease the pain, his eyes were like cold steel as he scanned the trail looking for for any sign of Thomas.

McCord felt he was being watched as he sat in the shelter of the Aspens. Taking out his rifle he thumbed shells into the magazine and laid it across the pommel of the saddle.

Not knowing whether it was the pain in his leg or that he was just tired of the cat and mouse game they had been playing, he had decided to bring it to a head. Knowing he was still out of range, he kneed the horse down the trail, his eye's scanning for the tell tail sign of Thomas.

In the distance, sunlight flashed on the bluish tint of a rifle barrel. A split second later, McCord fell off his horse on to the rocky tail as a bullet tore through the space he had been in moment before!

"I finally got you, you son of a bitch," Thought Thomas triumphantly as he mounted his horse, and rode to where McCord had fallen.

The sun burned down and the ground was hot as McCord lay face down amid the rocks and dirt of the trail. From a distance he heard the sound of hoof against stone. Tightening his grip, his thumb cocked the rifle, pulling it into position while he lay perfectly still. His hand on the trigger; he waited.

Thomas saw the body of McCord laying in the trail. Riding his horse to the body, he smiled as he dismounted. McCord rolled over on his back, brought the rifle up and pulled the trigger!

Thomas's face registered surprise as he felt the bullet tear into him, his legs folded as he fell to his knees then into the hot rocks in front of McCord.

"Thomas, you were good, just not good enough," Snarled McCord angrily through clenched teeth, as he stood over the body with the rifle by his side.

He rolled the body of Thomas over and took his knife, and shells. He pulled the saddlebag off of his horse. Inside it he found a pot, beans, coffee, jeans, shirt and socks in his stash.

In the early evening, it was still hot and he was sweating, but at the same time his teeth chattered. He built a fire just off the trail then painfully limped to the stream, he undressed, leaving everything on the bank, then jumped into the icy cold water.

The frigid water surprised him, he gasped as the cold water hit his wound. He forced himself to stay in the water. After a few minutes, shivering, his teeth chattering, he stood up and limped to the bank. He put his clothes back on then grabbed Thomas shirt.

They were almost the same size, as he buttoned the shirt and rolled the sleeves up he put the socks on then the jeans and finally the boots. He buckled on his gun belt and tied it down.

Limping, McCord went to Thomas's horse and took the horse to where he left Thomas, he picked up the body, laying it across the saddle, he then tied the mans arms to the stirrups then he did the same with the dead man's feet.

He knew he was running a fever, the Apache had a treatment, it was the leaves off a birch willow. For an hour he scouted the trees, then he found what he was looking for. In a stand of Aspen, he found the willow. Using his knife, he cut several branches and carried them to the fire.

He sat down and heated up the beans and poured himself a cup of coffee. As he drank it, the warmth of coffee helped. He stripped several of the leaves off the branches then chewed them.

A moment later, he took the blanket and laid down. As the pain eased, his eyes burned and his head ached. Closing his eyes, exhausted, in pain, he fell into a fitful sleep.

It early morning when something woke him. Hearing a rustling in the trees, he rolled to his right, pulling his gun, then saw his stallion Raven walk hesitantly toward him.

Reholstering his pistol, he stood up with a smile and limped painfully to the horse. Somehow Raven had been able to get his bridle off as well as the saddle. His legs were bloody and there were marks on it's haunches.

The stallion allowed McCord to feel it's legs and the deep cuts on it's haunches. The marks looked like that of a mountain lion.

Taking his neckerchief he washed the animal's wounds. The wounds were not as bad as he had thought. He whispered, "looks like you tangled with a lion boy," the stallion tossed it's head as if it understood.

Taking the saddle off the livery horse, he placed it on the stallion's back. Taking off the bridle he let the livery horse go and put the bridle on the stallion.

Grabbing the reins of Thomas horse, he limped back to the fire, using black charcoal he mixed it with water and with a stick he wrote on the back of Thomas shirt, "He wasn't good enough".

Pleased with his handwork, his eyes narrow, his jaw set, he headed the stallion out of the valley toward the Double Diamond and Stanford and Kincaid.

It was mid afternoon as McCord approached the outskirts of the range of the Double Diamond. He looked for a place to leave the horse. Just outside the gate, next to the road, he left the horse grazing in the grass.

He turned the stallion and left headed up toward the crossroads of Derby Junction a half a days ride from the valley.

It was late afternoon, as four riders made their way up the road to the Double Diamond. As they talked about the weather, and cattle, and McCord, one of them spied a horse grazing in the meadow off to one side of the road.

"Say," said one of the men, "what do you make of that." As he walked his horse toward the other he suddenly pulled it up.

"It's that gent Thomas." He said as he backed away, his face white, "he's dead." He breathed.

"He was suppose to be the best." Said another with fear in his eyes.

"Yeah," stated the third, then he pointed to the shirt and read the message. His eyes wide with fear he looked at the other two.

"That's enough for me," said one quietly, "man I got me three kids and a wife," adding, "she don't need to be no damned widow! I'm collecting' my time then calling it quits!" As they saw the message scrawled on the dead man's back.

"Best take him to the ranch." Said another with fear in his eyes. Three of the four agreed as they gathered the reins and headed for the ranch house.

"Men," greeted Kincaid with a smile, watching the men approach it was Nick, Jake, a man named Twitch and Calhoun. Then he saw the fifth horse with the body draped over the saddle.

"What happened here." He demanded.

"Found him on the road just outside the gate Mr Kincaid." Said the one named Twitch, then he added, "Mr Kincaid me, Nick and Calhoun we....we... want to collect our time."

"See whats writ' on Thomas's back." Said Nick, explaining, "I got me a wife n' kids."

"Just collect your time then get the hell outta' here." Retorted Kincaid angrily.

"He killed Thomas." Stated Kincaid angrily to Stanford as he slammed his fist hard into the wall next to the door. Adding, "then he leaves this message- *he wasn't good enough!*

Already lost three good men." Fumed Kincaid angrily as he pounded the wall again with his fist. Stanford was furious, everything they had worked for was falling apart.

"Find that bitch Jenric." He stormed, "we get her... we'll get him."

"Mr Kincaid," said a voice from behind, "turning around he saw the man named Jake leaning in the doorway. "there's some kind of a meeting going on at Morrison's spread. Heard riders talkin' about it."

"When." questioned Kincaid, "tomorrow night with them marshals," said Jake, "bet that Jenric gal will be there."

"Let the boys know, we wasn't invited." Smiled Kincaid, "now get."

Needing supplies, McCord headed up into Greenhorn Mesa toward the crossroads named Derby Junction. The junction was not much but a saloon, and a general store. As he rode, he kept to the shadows finally he pulled up behind the store.

By this time, he figured, they probably new he was back. He still was running a fever, his leg still hurt, not wanting any confrontations he gritted his teeth against the pain as he quietly dismounted, and limped into the store.

Seeing him come in, the man behind the counter offered him coffee. Taking it he also told the man what he needed. The man glanced down and looked at his leg and the blood spotted jeans, then at McCord's pale face.

"Hunting accident." Remarked Travis dryly as he saw the man looking at him.

"Been a lot of them round here lately," remarked the man candidly, as he continued to stare at McCord, "you wouldn't by chance be that gent that's causing all the hell for the Double Diamond would you."

" 'Cause, now I'm not saying' you are," Travis's eyes turned to steel as reached for his gun, as the man continued, but if you are him, we got Double Diamond riders coming up here all the time, got a pack horse out back ready to go if you are him. But," giving McCord a knowing look, he added, "if your not, then I won't tell you not to use the old stage road."

"Thanks friend," Smiled Travis as he reholstered his gun and gingerly stood up and grasped the mans outstretched hand.

"You was never here." Replied the man with a smile.

Following the mans advice Travis took the reins of the pack horse and started down toward the valley below. As he was riding, he heard voices laughing heading towards him, he pulled his hat low over his eyes and the men passed without incident.

Chapter Twelve

Knowing the area he was in, he found a cave well hidden in the rocks. Dismounting, he unsaddled the stallion then unpacked the coffee, beans, hardtack, and blankets the man had given him.

That night as he sat watching the light from the fire dance along the walls of the cave. It reminded him of nights long ago. He remembered his parents, Noah and Aggie McCord.

When he was eight years old his father lost their farm in Ohio and they joined a wagon train headed into the west. For months they traveled eventually his father was given land in the Arizona territory.

He was ten when they started farming the land, it was obvious to his father, that this land was better suited for grazing than farming. Beyond the river lay an Apache village, within days of their arrival, the Apache, led by Black Feather surrounded their home.

At first, it looked like they would be killed, then one of the Indians approached and offered his father a horse in exchange for blankets and food. Travis was invited several times to the village and developed a friendship with several boys his age.

For two years, he and his parents lived in harmony with their Indian friends. As he turned twelve his father had given him a rifle. He had gone hunting and when he returned, he found both his parents murdered!

Having learned from the Apache how to track, he tracked four horses to Black Feather's village. He found the horses the men had ridden and went to Black Feather. He then issued a challenge to the four who had murdered his parents. The only weapon he was allowed to use was the knife. One by one, he took them on and killed them. He had been wounded several times, having watched him fight, and Black Feathers wife, Song of the Willow had given him daughters, Black Feather adopted him as his son.

The Apache believed the spirit of their ancestors came down at night and would dance with the fire along the walls of the caves. He remembered Black Feather, his adopted father, who had taught him the way of the Apache.

He remembered back to when he turned sixteen and was for the first time able to ride with the men of his tribe on raids.

To become a man in the Apache tribe, he needed to be skilled with the knife, the ax, the warclub and the long bow. Black Feather schooled him in the art of fighting, how to use the knife when killing his enemies and taught him the skills he would need as a warrior.

Black Feather told him, you must either kill or be killed; he also said to him, "You, my son, need to know *what it is to be Apache.*"

He learned by fighting others of his age and rank. They would hold wrestling matches, horse races and knife fighting was taught with wooden knifes as was the lance.

By the time he reached sixteen, he could not be beaten and was taken by his uncle Spotted Horse to a ceremony, here he and four others were given the scratcher and a tube of water. He was not allowed to drink the water, just carry it with him. This was done to teach the young warriors discipline.

During each successful raid, the warriors would use the scratcher and scratch his shoulders. At the end of the fourth raid, he achieved the honor of becoming a warrior in the eyes of his tribe.

It was on the fourth raid, the tribe was under siege by the white eye solders. Taking the uniform off of a dead solder, he had walked into their camp, no one noticed him as he made his way to the horses.

There were too many to fight alone, instead, he cut the ropes to the horses then mounted one and screamed as he rode and stampeded their horses through the camp, he shot several as they tried to stop him.

For two years he fought, side by side with Black Feather against the invading armies of the white eyes, defending their homeland.

"You are like hawk my son, his father told him after having seen him fight, "you have fought with it's courage, like the hawk you are cautious and stealthy, and you are a great hunter."

"The hawk knows it's prey, it plans it's attack, it stalks silently, it is a master of hiding, and it is a master of deception.

My son, this is what I have seen of you. You are the shadow of the hawk, you have put fear into those you have fought! Your courage will strike fear into the hearts of our enemies, they will tremble when your name is told to them, they will pray you will not come into their villages, as like a spirit, they cannot defeat you, you are *"El Cetan Nagin, the Shadow Hawk,*

As he thought of Logan, a wry smile crossed his face as he remembered the last time he saw his friend. Remembering the look on his face as he had tied him up saying, "We've been friends for a long time Logan, but this is something and I have to do alone."

The first time Logan and he met, he was trapped under a dead bull buffalo. He and several of his friends had been hunting.

From the top a ridge, they looked down at a seething brown ocean of buffalo. His friend Stone Eagle had laughed at him and dared him to go alone. His other friend, Walking Bear cautioned against it but knowing his standing with the tribe was being called, as he was the son of the Chief, he knew he had to show them.

He took his bow and arrows along with his lance, he kicked his horse and raced it down the ridge toward the buffalo! As the herd started running, a bull turned away from the others and stood for a moment watching his approach.

Swinging it's massive head from side to side, snorting and bellowing, it rose on it's back legs, then it stomped his front hooves, it slid to a stop in a cloud of dust as it dug it's massive horns into the dirt, it bellowed loud; then charged!

Seeing the enraged bull coming at him, he attempted to guide his horse as close as possible, with just voice and knees, his horse went directly at the charging animal! He fit an arrow into his bow, aimed and fired!

His arrow hit the bull just behind it's left leg and went deep into the the animal. This enraged the bull more! Screaming in pain, it swung it's massive head toward the horse. It's left horn went deep into the horses stomach!

The horse stumbled forward, as it fell to the ground, he jumped directly at the enraged animal. Somehow, he found himself on it's back! It threw itself into the air, screaming with anger and pain, as he stabbed the animal repeatedly with his knife before he was thrown off!

He hit the dirt hard! In a cloud of dust, the bull slid to a stop and turned around! To his left was his lance. Scrambling to it just as the enraged animal, snorting and bellowing loud, charged him again!

As it lowered it head, he sidestepped, took his lance and jabbed it hard into the animals underbelly. The bull narrowly missed him, screaming in pain, in a cloud of dust, it turned to come at him again. It's small red eye's were glaring with pain and hate as it lowered it head again, and charged!

He scrambled to his feet, his eyes locked on to the buffalo, he stepped aside as the animal flew past, then with all his strength he stabbed his lance again only this time it hit it's mark.

As it fell, its body pushed up against him and knocked him into the dirt; underneath the belly of the buffalo, he tried to roll out, but his leg was broken and the animal fell dead on top of it.

The others, seeing him thrown from his horse, left to go to the village and bring help, but the village was hours away. For what seemed an eternity, blinded by pain, and not able to move he lay trapped under the dead animal.

Hearing a noise he saw a white man approach, a young man of maybe eighteen years just a few years older than him. His eyes gleamed with hate as the man approached him on the horse and just looked at him.

"Kinda' got yourself into a fix ain't you." He had said as he half smiled down at him.

"Let's see if I can help you." Said the man, as he dismounted. Taking a rope he put it around the head of the beast and then tied the other end to the horn of his saddle.

Mounting the horse he kicked it, slowly the horse pulled the buffalo off of him. Dismounting the man came back. He saw his leg was twisted at an odd angle.

"It's broke." He remarked quietly as he sat on his knees beside him. Looking around he found several thick branches.

"This is going to hurt like hell." He told him, then handed him a piece of rawhide, "bite into this."

The pain was intense, but he refused to give a sound as the man straightened his leg then with the branches made a crude splint and finished by tieing the splint together with his rope.

"The names Logan," he said holding out his hand.

"I am Gray Eagle, my father is Black Feather of the White Mountain tribe." He replied as he shook his hand.

"Whats your white name." Logan had asked quietly.

"I am Apache!" He had said defiantly.

"Not with them blue eyes you ain't." Logan had said laughing.

A smile crossed his face as he remembered how angry he had become at Logan for telling him he was white. He then watched as Logan skillfully skinned the buffalo, then quartered it and put it on a makeshift travois.

That night, by the fire, he had wondered why this white man did not kill him, but had helped him instead, or was it because he knew he was white.

The next day, Logan helped him to the travois. Then began to pull it, headed north toward his village. His village was well hidden inside a deep canyon in the red cliffs of the white mountains.

For several hours they traveled, suddenly the horse stopped as screaming voices could be heard. Moments later they were surrounded by men from his village. Black Feather walked to his side and grasped his hand.

"It is good to see you my son." He had said. Seeing what this white man and done for his son he walked up to Logan.

"Come," He had said, "you will come to my village with us and celebrate Gray Eagles return." he stated, as he mounted his horse.

When they entered the village, they were immediately surrounded. Song of the Willow ran up to him, with tears falling, she grasped his hand, as Black Feather opened his village to Logan.

That night, with the beating of the drums, they celebrated his return and then Nep *ot on je diyi,* Bear Watcher, the medicine man took Logan's arm and his arm, and with a knife he sliced first his arm then the Logan's, taking both he held them together, as their blood mixed, he looked at them both, as Black Feather announced, *"skee-kizzen"* welcome brother, *"bhaava crunatus"*you are now blood brother to *"qual bith tsa cho"* gray eagle. you will be known to us as *"shoz litz ogue"* yellow bear, you have saved my son! You and my son's blood are now mixed; you are now brothers"!

At eighteen, he left his village with five others to ride with the Apache War Chief Geronimo, he proved himself many times.

His ability to track, his cunning and his stealth, and his knowledge of the white eyes, drew the attention of Geronimo and he became one of his lieutenants. His exploits became almost legendary. It was his tracking and his fighting that drew Geronimo to him.

He, like the Apache gave no quarter, yet he used his intelligence, knowing when to run and when to fight. Frequently, they rode into Mexico and would destroy village after village. When Mexico asked the United States for help, it became the Seventh Calvary's job to stop them.

As the conflicts with the Seventh Calvary became almost an obsession to Geronimo, Travis and twenty other braves split and went off on their own. They raided farms for horses and food, they attacked the scouts for the army. Killing them and then driving off the horses and stealing their food.

He was leading a splinter group of renegades when he saw Logan again. At twenty three, he and his followers were raiding the compounds of the forts, driving off the horses of the soldiers and had become a force to be reckoned with.

For days he would go alone to scout the soldiers, he would chart their positions, he would find the weakness and he would lure them into traps and when the time was right he and his warriors would attack. He would have his warriors dig in and wait as the army would unknowingly become surrounded. Then when the time was right, they would attack from all directions.

The army had taken to calling him and his group *"The Outriders"* as they were not a part of any group and rode by themselves. After one attack the army lost almost twenty men. They had put a bounty on his head.

They were raiding forts in the southern part of the state near the town of Nogales, he had heard of a white man trapped there. His spies had told him this man was *"shoz litz ogue"* yellow bear, the man he was blood brother to.

He and his braves stormed the renegades and ran them off and freed him. As they met again, Logan persuaded him to join him. He had convinced Travis the whites were coming like an unstoppable ocean. To continue fighting, would be suicide.

He had heard that Geronimo had fled deep into Mexico and Sitting Bull and Crazy Horse of the mighty Sioux Nation had surrendered to the hated white eyes just a year before. In order to preserve the culture of the Apache, he ended up riding with Logan, using his reputation as a weapon.

He also was becoming a legend as a fast gun. This almost became his downfall as any town they entered, men would call him out.

In Winslow, he and Logan had stopped for supplies. He was in the saloon as Logan was getting the supplies they needed. Three men came in and started to harass him as he stood silently at the bar.

They had run into them earlier on the road, and for some reason they chose to start a fight with him. Trying to avoid the confrontation, he stood there but when one grabbed his shoulder, he turned, like lightning, and grabbed the man's neck in a headlock, and pulled his left arm, up behind him and threw him back into the other two!

As he turned to leave he heard the slapping of leather, turning he saw them start to pull their guns, his gun materialized in his hand, fanning his weapon, a moment later they lay dead.

He shot a look at the others in the saloon, his gun still smoking, as no one moved, he turned and walked out into the sunlight.

They had left Winslow and entered Camp McDowell, headquarters for the southern part of the territory, the fort was commanded by new general, a man by the name of George R. Crooke, a man Logan had just met but knew he wanted Apache scouts.

He had heard of this man and knowing Travis's reputation and that he had bounty on his head, he felt that this man alone would be the one to help them.

As they went into the post, the solders recognized him and he was dragged from his horse, handcuffed and thrown into the stockade.

He remembered the small cell he had been put in and how sitting in it for three days was almost more than he could bear, finally Logan was able to get him released but only if they would continue scouting for the army for another two years, as Devlin had put it, "I need an Apache to find an Apache"!

They had be asked to help find the village of War Chief Mangas Coloradas, the army was looking at trying to capture him as Coloradas hated the white man and his warriors were the most vicious of the tribes.

On the first day, they stumbled on a wagon train that had been attacked. There was very little left except for two women who had managed to hide, as they were escorting them back, when they were attacked by Coloradas's warriors. Logan fell with a bullet wound in his leg, not able to run, Travis fought for all of them.

For two days he and the two women fought them off. On the third night, he crept into their camp. From the war lances, he took the feathers and broke them, scattering them on the ground.

He went to the ponies and picked four, and the rest he stampeded through their camp and screamed in Apache, *za stee*! Its meaning was Kill! The next day they were gone and Travis was able to get Logan and the women to the fort.

The army wanted Coloradas stopped, he was called into Devlin's office and was asked if he would deliver a message to Coloradas.

Devlin knew of his reputation and had been impressed with his knowledge of the tribes and knew that he had been able to stop many of the confrontations with the Apache Tribes and the army. Coloradas's warriors were known to be brutal and savage, and had been attacking the settlements. Many of the outlying ranches had been attacked and each time the army would lose them in the rugged deep canyons in the southern part of the territory.

General Devlin asked him to deliver a message to Coloradas requesting a meeting to discuss a treaty, McCord accepted the job and left headed into the red rock canyons where Coloradas was known to be.

For days he had searched for his village, he knew he was being watched, he also knew they would allow him into their camp. Finally he climbed a ridge overlooking a layered red canyon, in the rocks, built into the canyon, he saw the wikiups.

As he started down, into the canyon, he was surrounded by the warriors of Coloradas, they took his knife, his gun and his rifle. Their faces were painted black around the eyes and wearing the red bandannas they ushered him into the village.

Surrounded by the warriors, he was escorted to the wikiup of Coloradas. Coloradas knew him to be *El Cetan Nigrin,*, and knew his fearsome reputation. He set a meeting for later that night. He was taken to a wikiup where he waited. Knowing he was the one called *El Cetan Nigrin* he was treated with honor and respect, true to his word Coloradas met with him.

As he explained what he wanted, Coloradas had told him, "If you can beat my best warrior in a wrestling match, then I will go with you to meet your white eye, but if you lose, you will be my prisoner and you will be killed".

The next day, he was escorted to a circle on the outskirts of the village. Inside it he saw a tall, well built man, he was a head taller than McCord and ten pounds heavier, waiting for him. As he entered it, Coloradas was seated at the head of the circle, surrounded by his lieutenants.

As they circled each other, McCord searched for his opponents weakness, the man threw a left punch at him, he blocked with his right arm, his right hand closed over his opponents hand, digging his thumb into the back his hand McCord brought his left arm up and drew his opponents arm back, throwing the man off balance, using his legs, he twisted his body and brought the man down, as he laid his knife against the man's throat, he defiantly glared at Coloradas.

A moment later, he stood up breathing heavily, reaching down he grasped the warriors hand and helped him up along side of him.

Coloradas was a man of his word, within two days McCord, Coloradas, along with his lieutenants, rode into the fort, expecting to meet Devlin, instead, Coloradas and his lieutenants were taken prisoner immediately.

This was not what he had been told and had agreed to. He remembered how angry he was as he argued with the commander but it was of no use. Devlin refused to let them go.

McCord took off the blouse the army had given him and threw it on the ground in front of the Commander. Then walked to the stockade and looked at Coloradas, grasping his hand, he had said *Ka Dish Day,* farewell/until we meet again".

He remembered how Coloradas had looked at him and said, *hi-disho* it is finished, and put his hand on McCords shoulder as he put his other to his heart. His dark eyes stared intently at McCord as he was led away in irons. A year later he heard that Coloradas had been killed while trying to escape back into his canyons.

For a year he and Logan traveled the Southwest and never scouted for the army again. It was during this time, they met Holliday in Tuscon.

Holliday recognized the danger these two men represented and not wanting trouble, instead he offered them jobs working for Virgil Earp as his deputies.

While working as deputies, they had numerous fights with both the Clantons and the McLaurys, regarding stolen horses and cattle.

Within six months they were both approached by Zan l. Tidball, head of the Arizona Marshal service, and were recruited for the service. A smile crossed his face as he remembered Logan slapping him on the back.

"Partner, guess they don't want to half'ta try to come after us." He had said with a smile.

His face turned hard as he remembered how he had met Stanford. How as a marshal it had been his and Logan's assignment to catch Stanford, while trying to stop the range war taking place in Pleasant Valley up in the Tonto Basin country in the northern part of the territory.

A local man Fred Wells had lost most of his cattle to hoof and mouth disease and had gone into debt trying to buy cattle from Standford, Stanford wanted him to join forces with another man Fred Brunham, when he refused Wells began taking his cattle into the Muggyowns above the Tonto Basin.

Stanford sent him there to bring back the cattle but he instead worked a plan with him to get Stanford and Kincaid. Logan also was bartering a truce with Wells and Bunham and with their help they got enough on Stanford to bring him and Kincaid to trial.

Stanford did not know McCord was a Marshal and when he went in to testify against them, Kincaid tried to turn against Stanford but it did not work as McCord had enough on him as well.

His reputation as a fast gun, and his years as a renegade helped him as Stanford thought of him as an outlaw. In no time he had worked his way into Stanford's trust.

For two years he worked as a cattle boss for this man while gathering information against him. Again he saw Stanford's face, twisted with hate and anger as he testified in court against him and his partner Kincaid.

He knew it was the testimony he gave to Circuit Judge Peel in Phoenix that resulted in his sentencing him and Kincaid to twenty years hard labor at the territorial prison in Yuma.

A smile crossed his face as he remembered the first time he saw Carrie. Carrie was the daughter of Simon Brookledge, a well respected cattleman and the owner of a large ranch.

His ranch sat on the outskirts of Apache Junction just outside the Superstitions, a range of mountains in Southeastern Arizona, the town lay in the foothills of the mountains.

He and Stanford had ridden to his ranch to look at his cattle and his land, as Stanford was looking to buy the ranch. Also he was involved with Carrie.

As they rode into the yard Simon and his wife Corinth came to meet them. Their daughter Carrie had just returned from school in New York. She had just turned twenty two, her eyes were green, her hair was dark brown and tied back with a ribbon.

As she came out and stood beside Stanford, he could not take his eyes off her, as Stanford introduced him, he nervously shook her outstretched hand. When Stanford went inside with her father, she remained outside with him. A smile crossed his face as he remembered, he had been so nervous that he nearly had fallen off his horse.

For weeks after meeting her, he took every moment to be with her. Her parents thought of him as just another cowboy and forbid Carrie to continue seeing him. They had wanted her to marry Stanford but the two of them worked out schemes to meet. Many times he had wanted to go to her father and explain but he could not.

As their love grew, Stanford became angry and hostile, as he had thought of Carrie as his. The final straw came as Stanford was going to send him to Mexico to bring up another herd when he, Logan and twelve others including Chad and Tidwell, arrested him and Kincaid.

He and Carrie were married four years later. He remembered their wedding, Logan had stood up for him as his best man. The day had been bright and as they had returned to his ranch, his village came to greet them.

He smiled as he remembered how Carrie at first was frightened, then as the women of the tribe presented her with a painted pony and a beaded dress, she accepted their friendship. That was the day Black Feather, gave him Raven. Logan gave him his gun with the silver hawk's head engraved in the handle as a wedding gift, "Just so you don't forget." Logan had said as he smiled.

Closing his eyes, again he felt the pain of missing her as tears came to his eyes and he whispered, "I really miss you my darling."

He eased his tired body down on the blankets given him by the man at Derby Junction and thought of Morgan, her violet eyes, her stubbornness, he smiled as he remembered the kiss at the valley and how she did not complain throughout the climb down from the cliffs.

Shaking his head, thinking of Carrie, and how she had died, he shook his head at the thought.

"I can't and I won't," he thought his eyes hard, glistening like steel, "I will not let that happen again."

Wincing, as pain shot down his leg. A smile crossed his face as he thought of the man at Derby Junction, and the conversation, Closing his eyes, he fell into a fitful sleep filled with images of his past.

The sound of horses coming up the draw, worked it's way into McCords sleep. He awakened with a start. Quietly, he crawled up the rocks above a little used road. He saw a wagon heading his way.

Moving quietly, he crawled behind an outcrop then lay flattened on a ridge, watching the wagon approach. One man drove the wagon the other two men were on horseback on either side.

"So Jake," said the driver, "heard they're gonna try taking the Jenric gal tonight."

"Yeah," said Jake, "there's some kinda' meeting going' on at Morrison' running M ranch tonight."

"We're meeting' the bosses outside that ranch." He added nervously.

"Wish we could find that McCord fella." Added the third man.

"Hawley," growled the driver, "you gotta be crazy! After he what he done to Thomas and the bosses;" adding, you really want to meet up with likes of him!"

"It ain't him I want," replied Hawley with a laugh, "it's the twenty thou-sand I want."

"In order to get that cash Hawley," Replied Jake with a laugh, "you gotta bring him in and I don't think you wanna try."

"What the hell Logan, what were you thinking." He thought angrily As the wagon rolled out of sight.

"Damn you Morgan! Thought McCord as a slight smile crossed his lips as he remembered her telling him "when are you going to understand I do what I want." He remembered her defiance toward him, even after he had rescued her and Garret, then as a smile crossed his lips as he again remembered kissing her at the valley.

"Guess you didn't have a choice Logan." He thought as a smile crossed his face as he tightened the cinch.

The running M was a good half a days ride from here. The sleep had done wonders, feeling almost one hundred percent and knowing he had to warn Logan, and also, now to protect Morgan, he mounted the stallion and headed toward the ranch that lay on the other side of Rifle Gap.

CHAPTER THIRTEEN

As daylight faded, ranchers began arriving at the running M. Morgan greeted each one then pointed them out to Logan. Pearly Hawkins of the G bar H was the last to arrive.

"George, Pearly, Don, Noah, Ben you all know me," Said Morgan, as she stood up, "you knew my pa Carl, you know I would not have called you here away from your ranches if it were not necessary."

"Pearly, you had one of Claybournes visits." She said hotly.

"Made me an offer an I laughed at him," Said Pearly, adding, "he offered me beans for my land." Said Pearly as he stood up. "then he ups and threatens me," The room buzzed as the other ranchers confirmed what Pearly had said.

"This here is Marshal Logan Teel......." She said, before she could continue Chad ran in, his face hard.

"Logan, we got riders coming!" He interrupted.

Taking Morgan and Chad aside, he told them, "take the families into the back of the house." then said to the men, "grab your guns."

As gunfire erupted, three men carefully made their way behind the house toward the door. One motioned with his arm to circle around to the other side. He waited a moment, as the other man silently stepped onto the wood planks, he motioned for the others to follow.

Taking a deep breath, he kicked the door in and stepped inside with his gun pulled. Seeing Morgan, he grabbed her! A man raced to her defense, one of the others waiting outside, slammed him with the butt end of his gun, bringing it down hard on his head!

Knocked to his knees, he was struggling with another, when he was hit again by the barrel of a gun, and was knocked to the floor, almost out, he laid still! From seemingly far away, he heard one of the men say. "Get her up to Fords Crossing."

Morgan fought her attackers, she kicked one of them, swinging around, she punched another, pulled from behind, a man grabbed her arms, pinning them as the one she had kicked, quickly put his hand over her mouth, she tried to bite him, as the other tied her arms behind her. Then they stuffed a bandanna in her mouth and tied it behind her head. Over her head they placed a black sack.

As she struggled, they dragged her to a horse, as another, breathing heavily, picked her up and put her roughly onto the horse.

"Get her outta here an up to Fords Crossing." Said the one as they mounted the horses and left going back behind the house and into the blackness of the night.

"Dammit, I'm too late." Thought Travis as he heard the sound of gunfire. He pulled the stallion to a sliding stop, as it half-reared he pulled his rifle then dug his heels into the snorting stallion and raced it toward the house.

McCord leaned out of the saddle and began to fire the rifle under the neck of the running horse. A trick he had learned well as an Apache and used when he was a renegade.

Men bolted away from the charging animal, then began firing at McCord. As the stallion raced into the yard McCord leaped off the back of the still running animal!

Amid a hail of bullets he jumped over the water trough, landing next to Logan. Then turned around and fired back into the night at muzzle flashes.

"Travis, damn glad to see you." Remarked Logan with a smile.

"Couldn't let you have all the fun now could I." Smiled Travis as he pulled the trigger again aiming at a muzzle flash.

"By the way, came to warn you." Said Travis with a grin.

"A might late aren't you." remarked Logan casually, as he fired another round.

"Is Morgan here." Questioned Travis worriedly as he shot into the night toward a muzzle flash

and was rewarded with a scream of pain.

"Yeah, she's in the back of the house with Chad, why." Was Logan's reply as he shot his rifle.

"Heard they're gonna try to take her." Was his reply.

As quickly as the gunfire started it stopped. As the ranchers stood up, they all gathered around McCord. Not use to this attention, McCord tried to back away from the throng of men, he looked at Logan for help, as Logan stood smiling at him.

"So your the one that's been a thorn in the side of them varmints" Remarked Pearly with a smile. Slapping him on the back.

"Uh...yeah." He replied nervously with a half smile, looking around he saw Logan with a smile on his face, giving a look to Logan for help, as one by one they grabbed his hand and shook it.

"Since you been here," Said George laughing, "they ain't had time to bother the rest of us."

"Yeah," remarked another laughing, "they been too busy chasing you to come after us.

"Wheres Morgan and Chad?" asked Logan as he looked around worriedly. Hearing a noise, Logan looked in the doorway and saw Chad barely able to stand, holding onto the door for support, blood flowed freely from a wound above his eye and his hair was matted with blood from where he had been hit.

"They took her Logan," Gasped Chad, as he leaned weakly against the door, "They....they came through the back."

Travis and Logan rushed to their friends side as Chad's legs gave out and they half carried him to a chair while the other ranchers gathered around.

"I....I tried, tried to stop them. He gasped as he closed his eyes, "They thought they knocked me out. But I heard them say they were taking her to a place called Fords Crossing. I tried...." He breathed then fell unconscious.

"Get him to a Doc." Stated Logan angrily, his eyes like granite his jaw hard as he looked into the darkness.

Fords crossing lay between Rifle Gap and Dowds Junction, high in the broken land of the flattops. A land of steep cliffs, deep ravines, and wash outs. It was barren with hardly any cover save for stands of Aspen and pine. A posse would be seen from miles away.

"Lets go." Said Logan angrily.

"Logan," stated McCord quietly, "they'd spot you coming with a posse a mile away."

"He's right. I know that area well. It's just bare rocks, pine, an aspen up there." said Morrison.

"I'll go." McCord stated quietly, his eyes hard and cold, "sides it's me they want, not her."

"No." Said Logan shaking his head emphatically, Adding, "I'll go.

"Logan," said McCord adamantly, "you going makes no sense. I know this country, you don't." then added as he went to the stallion, " 'Sides your needed here."

"You want this now." Said Logan , as Travis mounted the stallion, reaching up he put a badge in Travis's hand.

"I resigned Logan." He said hesitantly. Fingering the badge, he looked down at Logan, Then he handed it back stating quietly, "Not ready yet." Kneeing the stallion he left toward Rifle Gap and Fords crossing.

For what felt like hours, they rode. Blindfolded Morgan knew they were headed into the mountains as she felt the coolness of the night air. Her arms ached; her legs were tied to the stirrup of the horse she was riding.

They rode silently though the night. Finally they stopped. She felt the ropes cut and her legs were free, she tried to kick at one of her attackers as she was pulled roughly off of the horse and pushed forward.

Stumbling over rocks, she tried to slow them down then was pushed roughly again, this time she fell to the ground!

She was jerked to her feet and shoved forward again. She kicked at the sound of a voice as she was shoved down some stairs and fell head first into the dirt. From the smell she figured it was a root cellar. A moment later, a knife cut the ropes holding her hands together and the blindfold and gag was taken off.

It was s black dark inside the cellar, the air was stale and the smell of rotting vegetables was thick in the air. She felt a breath of fresh air as the door opened then closed again. Feeling around, she felt for anything she could use as a weapon.

She felt a wooden handle. Sitting down next to it, trembling angry and afraid, her eyes clouded with tears as she started to cry. Defiantly, she stood up, as she wiped the tears from her eyes; angry at herself.

"I will not let them win." She growled quietly, as she clenched teeth in anger.

The moon shone full and bright as Travis went up the trail from the running M. His eyes were cold as he searched for some sign of the riders.

He found broken branches from the trees, below him, he saw the white of hooves chipping the rocks, even with just the light from the moon, he could see their trail as they had hurriedly gone up the mountain.

It had not taken him long to find the trail the men had left. Walking the stallion slowly, McCord's eyes scanned the trail for the slightest sign, a misplaced rock, a leaf turned wrong, broken branches, several times he dismounted and crouched near the trail. The sign was leading him further into the broken country of the Flattops. From the tracks he knew he was less than an hour behind them.

Targe Calahan paced back and forth in the small cabin they were in. He kept looking out the window at the root cellar, then turned and paced again. He had been fired by Morgan several months before. Angry, he started for the door as a man stepped in front of him.

"Where you goin' Calahan." He remarked as he blocked Calahan.

"That damned Jenric, she fired me! He swore loudly, as he slammed his fist into the wall. His face dark with anger, he pushed the man out of the way and walked into the dark, toward the root cellar.

"Calahan you best leave her alone." Argued the man, as he followed him out the door, standing in the doorway he shook his head and walked back inside the cabin and closed the door.

Ignoring the man's outburst, Calahan marched through the rocks and strode angrily to the door of the root cellar.

The tracks were leading him towards the top of a ridge, in the air he could smell smoke from a fire. Knowing he was close, he left the stallion and went up the ridge on foot. Pulling his gun, his eyes like ice, he quietly crested the ridge and could see the cabin in the trees.

For what seemed an eternity, she sat and waited for someone to open the door. As her eyes adjusted to almost no light, she felt her way around. The walls were made with layers of rock. The ground was dirt. There was nothing in here save the wood handle.

She figured if she could not see it neither would anyone else. She heard the sound of voices then a rush of air as the door opened. For just a moment she glimpsed a large man coming down the stairs toward her! She grasped the handle tighter, as she backed away from him and into the back wall.

"You ain't so high n' mighty Miss Morgan Jenric now are you." Said a familiar voice. She recognized it as belonging to a man she had fired several months ago, his name was Targe Calahan.

"Targe," she said, as her voice quivered, "you don't want to do this."

His big burly arms reached for her but caught her blouse instead. The fabric ripped as she pulled away from him!

His breath was foul as he leaned toward her, she sidestepped then with all her might, she swung the handle and knocked him backwards into the stairs, dazed, he sat for a moment then lunged at where he thought she was. Again she swung the handle and this time it connected and she knocked him out.

Sobbing, with tears streaming down her face, her eyes wide with fear she ran up the steps, praying the door would open, as she hit it, it opened!

Desperate for cover, she rushed out into the cool night! Fearfully, she ran as hard as she could toward a ridge that loomed close and away from the cellar and Targe Calahan! Moments later, she heard men screaming as they saw the open door.

"Dammit anyway!" exclaimed a man angrily, "how in the hell did she get loose."

"That damned Targe! He let her go!" Exclaimed another.

Trembling with fear, not knowing what to do she flattened herself behind a large boulder. Her breath coming in short gasps as the men started looking for her. As they approached, she heard a noise behind her. As she opened her mouth to scream, a hand covered it.

"Shh! It's ok, I'm here now." Whispered the familiar voice of Travis in her ear.

She threw herself into his arms, burying her head in his chest, she sobbed uncontrollably as he held her. Getting herself under control, she looked up at him and saw the concern in his eyes.

"She couldn't have gotten too far, hell it's almost dawn give it another hour. She can't go nowhere." Said one, stopping not far from the boulder.

"An Targe you best hope we get her or your the one to explain why and how she got away. I don't think Kincaid's gonna be real happy!" He stated angrily, as the men turned and went back to the cabin.

As the men's voices faded, Travis helped her to feet, and with his arm around her they crept silently down the ridge to his horse. He picked her up and placed her in the saddle then swung up behind her.

Daylight was fast approaching, knowing they had little time, he searched for someplace safe. Traveling up a dry wash, they entered a stand of Aspen. Their leaves a bright gold. Further up was a stand of pine in front of rock ledges.

Here centuries before, a massive earthquake created an uplift of giant rock formations. It was these formations he headed to.

Inside one was a natural bowl, riding through a notch in the rock, he dismounted then helped Morgan down.

She threw herself into his arms, shaking from fear, she sobbed quietly into his chest as he held her, then he gently kissed her forehead, and wiped the tears away with his finger.

"It's ok Morgan," he said quietly as he caressed her hair and held her close to him, her body trembling as she sobbed in relief that is was over.

"I'm sorry Travis I should have stayed in Defiance." She sobbed, with tears streaming from her eyes.

"No reason to be sorry, 'sides I'm kinda glad your here." He said gently, as a smile crossed his face. Turning around, they walked arm in arm to the cave.

"Should be safe here till nightfall." He said quietly and kissed her again. A smile tentatively crossed her face as she looked up at him.

"Did they hurt you." He asked softly, as he saw her cuts and bruises for the first time. Anger welled up inside him at what they had done to her.

"No." she replied, then added, her voice quivering, "but I hurt them!"

"Thats my girl...." He said as he smiled and gave her a hug. Holding her close to him, he lifted her face to his and his lips gently caressed hers.

"You rest up," He said softly.

Her face, stained with tears. she nodded her head then tiredly made her way into the cave for sleep.

It was late afternoon when she made her way out of the cave, looking around she saw him sitting on a boulder not far away, cleaning his gun.

"Feeling better." He asked, looking up as she walked up and sat beside him. Adding, with a smile, "you look terrible." He put his arm around her and held her close, his lips gently touched her forehead, as a slight smile tentatively crossed her face.

"You know Morgan I was married," he started slowly, "her name was Carrie." Taking a deep breath, his voice choked with emotion.

"She wasn't just my wife," He stated quietly, as he looked toward the clear sky overhead. Taking a deep breath, he added, "she was my best friend."

"She would've loved it here." He said quietly as he picked up a blade of grass. "She planted damned wildflowers in the desert. Then she made me dig a well so she could water 'em.'" He said as tears welled up in his eyes, his voice choked with emotion.

"When I asked why, she said it made it feel more like home. She could ride with the best of 'em an she could rope almost better than me."

"I said almost." He stated as a slight smile crossed his face. "She was my life." He whispered quietly, "and they killed her....Morgan they killed her for what I do."

"Logan and I are both Marshals......" He said, seeing her questioning look, adding, "I put em' in prison at Yuma. When they escaped, they came and found our home."

"The night she died, I promised her I would find the ones who did it and that they would pay for what they did to her!" He said through clenched teeth. Taking a rock, he threw it hard into a bush. Tears glistened in his eyes as he looked out over the peaceful and tranquil clearing.

"Your becoming very important to me." He stated softly. "and I want you outta this valley." As he turned to look at her he said softly, "I'm afraid....I'm gonna....lose ....you ...too."

Their conversation was interrupted by the sound of hoof striking stone and the sound of voices coming up the trail toward the notch.

Pulling out his gun, he quietly scaled a ridge. He flattened himself as he saw three riders slowly approaching from the east tracking them. Sliding down, he ran to the cave. He saddled the stallion then placed her on it's back. Ravens ears flattened as he shook his head.

"Morgan.....you ride outta' here when I give the word, find Logan, Raven here will get you outta' here. Won't you boy." He said, as the stallion tossed it's head and he reached up gently brushing her face with his hand. "Now Git!" he said softly. Turning around he went back to the front of the cave.

He thumbed cartridges into the cylinder of his colt, then snapped it into place. His eyes narrowed, his jaw set, he waited. Hearing the retreating hoofbeats of Raven, he found cover behind a large granite wall.

"I can't believe she got this far without help." Said one as he scanned the ground.

"She had help Jarvis, an it's gotta be McCord." Said another.

"Best keep your hand on your gun then. 'Cause you know he ain't gonna leave without her, an theys only got one horse." Said Jarvis.

As they came around a curve, he fired! The man Jarvis, clutched his chest and fell into the dirt, as his bullet found it's mark. The others ran to the cover of the rocks.

Seconds later the peace of the clearing was shattered, as gunfire exploded. Bullets careened off the granite all around him. One man ran to the cover of a boulder as McCords shot missed!

"He's over there." Screamed one, pointing to the boulder as four others, hearing the shots, came riding quickly to the clearing. From above a rifle exploded, the shot narrowly missed him!

McCord rolled on to his back firing the colt! A man fell! Then quickly rolled on his stomach and shot again! His bullet found it's mark as another man fell into the rocks in front of him!

As he started to get up, he heard the ominous click of a revolver from behind him, a man said, "go ahead McCord, your worth twenty thousand dead or alive; your choice."

Like lightning, he rolled to his right throwing his knife! The mans shot went wide as the knife found it's mark. The mans legs folded as he sank to the ground dead, infront of McCord.

He quickly grabbed his knife, then ran back into the rocks as he heard footfalls coming up toward him. Crouching behind a boulder, he waited as the man approached.

Taking his knife, he waited one more moment, then lunged at the man from behind, his left arm went around the mans neck as his right arm stabbed the man in the chest. Breathing heavily, he faded back into the rocks as another approached him.

"Jake." He whispered as he paused to look around.

"He ain't here." Growled McCord as he came from behind, grabbing the mans head, he pulled it toward him as his right arm slammed the knife deep into the man's torso.

A few moments later, he heard the remainder of the men leave. Picking up his rifle, he moved silently through the night as he followed them.

Keeping to the rocks, trees and bushes, he was nearly invisible. In the moon light he saw the ghostly outline of a ridge. Silently he dropped to his knees and crawled to the top. From there he saw the cabin with four horses.

As he backed down, he was tackled from behind and slammed into the ground! Rolling to his left, he brought the butt end of the rifle into the mans face, then felt another grab him, he threw the barrel into the other mans chest and pulled the trigger! The blast from the rifle, threw the man backward into two others.

As he jumped to his feet the other four gang tackled him and knocked him to the ground.

His arms were roughly pulled behind him and tied, as he was yanked to his feet.

"You son of a Bitch!" Growled one, as he stood in front of him breathing hard, he balled his fist and slammed it hard into McCords stomach. Followed by a right cross to the jaw. This knocked him backward into another of the men.

Pushed from behind, he fell into another man who spun on his heel and slammed him hard in the kidney's!" Blinded by pain, he fell to his knees gasping for breath. His head roaring, he could not avoid being kicked in the chest! As he fell backward, his head hit a rock, lights flashed as he faded into unconsciousness.

Morgan sat on the stallion and watched with horror as Travis was mobbed by the others. Tears fell as she saw him knocked unconscious. Angrily she turned the stallion back toward the cabin.

Reaching the ridge, she dismounted, taking his knife and rifle, she quietly crept toward the far wall. Keeping to the trees, tears fell as she watched them drag his limp body through the dirt and tying him up next to a tree.

It was dark when McCord flicked open his eyes, his vision blurred then cleared and he saw the campfire burning in front of the cabin. As he moved, he gasped as pain shot through his ribs. one of them stood up and glared at him. By the light of the fire he saw the man's eye was nearly closed.

"You know McCord, you killed a few of my friends today." Calahan snarled as he walked over to him and kicked him hard in the ribs.

Calahan gave him an evil smile as he turned to leave, then turned on the balls of his feet kicking him again, this time hard in his side and walked back to the fire.

As McCord lay writhing in pain, he felt the rope around his wrists loosen, then drop off.

"Calahan, you should be damned glad we got him otherwise Kincaid would've had your head." said another one of the men, as he added wood to the fire.

"Whens he suppose to be here." Said Calahan as he drank a cup of coffee and glared at McCord.

"Soon." Was the reply.

McCord felt the cold barrel of a rifle slide into his hands. Slowly, as to not to attract attention, he pulled it to him. As he felt the stock he brought the rifle quickly to him and rapid fired it.

The first bullet knocked the man Calahan backward into the fire, before the others could react, he fired three more times, in seconds the other three lay dead, as each bullet found a mark.

Turning around he saw Morgan, her eyes wide, he saw the horror in her face of what she had just witnessed.

"Thought I told you to leave." He snarled through clenched teeth, as he thumbed cartridges into the magazine.

"I told you to get hell outta here Morgan,... I mean it! I don't want you here.... Kincaid will be here anytime!" He growled, his blue eyes blazed as he stared hard at her.

"Come with me Travis." She begged as she touched his arm.

"I'm gonna finish part of this when Kincaid gets here." He snarled through gritted teeth, as he threw her hand off his arm angrily, glaring at her, his eye's like ice, he spat, "Will you just get the hell outta here!"

Stepping back from him, she saw for the first time the anger inside him, she now knew how others had felt looking into his cold, emotionless eyes. Her stomach was in a knot as he glared angrily at her and for the first time, she felt fear of and for him and now knew the fear others had felt, as he gave her a look with his penetrating, cold eyes.

"You know McCord," she spat angrily, "I could'ave left. Then where would you have been!"

Ignoring her, McCord took the rifle then ran back to the ridge overseeing the cabin. Morgan watched him then turned on the balls of her feet, stalking angrily down to the stallion.

Grabbing it's reins she mounted it, turning she saw McCord laying flat on the ridge, angrily she kicked the animal hard and raced toward the trail out of the valley.

For what seemed hours he waited, thinking about what she had said. Shaking his head angrily, he picked up a rock and threw it into the bushes.

It was near dawn when he heard the sound of hoof striking stone and the familiar voice of Kincaid as he called out of the darkness to the cabin. When no one answered he rode in flanked by two others.

"My God," breathed one, "what happened here." As they saw the bodies of the four dead men laying around the glowing embers of the fire.

"McCord." Growled Kincaid, as he glanced around worriedly and backed his horse nervously out from the light of the fire, for a moment he was illuminated by its dull red glow.

A shot shattered the night! Kincaid was knocked from his saddle to the ground. As men gathered around his crumpled body they heard the sound of steps retreating up the ridge.

"Go after that bastard." Yelled one as he checked Kincaid.

"Kincaids still breathing." Stated another.

"I'll help you get him to town." Added the first.

"The rest of you get after the bastard that done this!" Angrily snarled the first man.

McCord ran hard up a draw, breathing heavily, each breath torture, holding his ribs he looked quickly around. The night was fading fast as the sun began to rise. Hurriedly, he looked around, his only escape was to climb up the steep angled wall of the draw.

The soil was like white chalk, a mixture of sand and gypsum. His hands and feet sank deep into the unstable soil. Crawling on all fours, he used the bushes and rocks to pull himself up but the going was hard.

"There he is." Someone yelled as a shot buzzed by his head. Moments later, bullets peppered the slope around him.

Half way up the slope a tree had fallen over, it's roots sticking high in the air, he threw himself behind it, as shots rang out.

Panting, he looked down the slope as he thumbed cartridges into the magazine of his rifle, taking quick aim he fired! His bullet dug dirt infront of one of the men. Bullets slammed the tree trunk he was behind, showering him with small pieces of wood.

There was a lull as the men reloaded, he quickly moved further up the slope as he dove for cover behind a boulder, a bullet burned it's way deep into his side.

"I got him!" Screamed one of the men.

Knocked into the dirt, he lay dazed for a moment, knowing he had to move he gritted his teeth and forced himself up to a ledge just below the ridgeline.

Blood from the wound flowed through his shirt leaving red drops on the white slope of the ravine. His side was on fire, his hand bloody, he lay still as bullets peppered the ridge around him.

From above him came a rope. Glancing up he saw the worried face of Morgan just a few feet above him. Slipping the opening of the lariat around his body, he nodded his head and was jerked up the slope to the cover of bushes above.

Stumbling forward, he saw Raven with the rope around the horn of the saddle. The horse was nervously prancing as Morgan rushed to him. Putting her arm around him, she helped him to the horse, then into the saddle and climbed up herself.

Turning the horse's head up the trail, she kicked it hard and the horse raced up the slope toward the mist covered base of Devils thumb.

A land scarred through time by intense wind and sand storms. Carved through the centuries, by hurricane force winds, and sand storms, Devils Thumb, dominated this land, standing alone above this scarred land of deep chasms and ravines, blasted by the ever blowing wind, sand and rain.

It was a land of broken spires of granite and tall weathered sandstone cliffs with it's scattered broken rock, eroded through time laying at the base of these cliffs. Small bushes were the only sign of life here. It was the perfect place for the rattlers and scorpions to call home.

They rode through scattered forests of juniper, pine and scrub oak. This was the broken land of the flattops. The horses hooves echoed on the slick granite of the trail.

It was nearing dark, a full moon had risen, bathed in it's light, it gave an eerie, ethereal look to this broken and treacherous landscape.

Tears coursed down her face as she saw the blood dripping from his side. Knowing she had to do something to stop the bleeding, she pulled the horse up on the lee side of a ridge. She dismounted then helped McCord down, putting her arm around him she guided him, stumbling to a large boulder and gently laid him down.

Going to the horse she took the canteen and his bedroll. Helping him take his shirt off, his face grimacing with pain, she worriedly looked around.

"Thought...I...told...you ...to ….leave." He panted through clenched teeth.

"When are you gonna figure it out McCord, I do what I want!" She snapped angrily. Taking his knife she cut the shirt into pieces.

"This is going to hurt like hell!" She said quietly, as she poured water on to a piece of the shirt and gently washed the wound. He gasped as the water entered the wound.

Looking around, she found moss. She cut several large pieces. Then pulled handfuls of grass. Mixing the grass with dirt and water she first applied the moss to stop the bleeding. Then the mud and grass to seal it.

Tearing a sleeve off her blouse, she made a bandage of sorts and wrapped it around McCords waist. She leaned back tiredly as McCord's eyes closed.

The warmth of a fire was the first thing McCord was aware of as he opened his eyes. Weakly he struggled to sit up as he did, he gasped as pain knifed down his side.

Hearing him, she ran and sat down next to him and held the canteen to his lips.

Barely able to swallow, water ran out of his mouth as he gasped for air. As he laid back down, she covered him in the bedroll.

The light from the moon was the next thing he was aware of as he opened his eye's . It's bright light was nearly like day. He saw Morgan standing near the rim of a canyon. This time the pain was not as bad and he cautiously stood up and walked to her side.

She had taken one of his shirts from the bedroll and had put it on. A smile crossed his face, as he noticed how large it seemed on her.

"Thank you." He whispered as he pulled her to him. Gently he touched her forehead with his lips and held her tight against him. For a moment she stood still then pushed him away.

"What in the hell is wrong with you Mister Travis McCord." She growled angrily. Seeing his questioning look she added hotly, "Twice I came back for you. I expected you to leave. But...but you didn't." Adding, "You said I was important to you. Obviously," she said quietly. "not as important as your killin' Kincaid."

He saw the hurt in her eyes, her penetrating gaze unnerved him. Turning away, he walked back to the fire. She strode angrily after him and sat down beside him.

"You are also important to me Travis." She said softly, her violet eyes filled with tears as she rubbed his shoulder. "I understand you lost something. But so have I." She quietly added, "I....I lost my pa to a murderer, I lost Charlie. I lost my family too Travis. I know you loved Carrie, but the way your acting it's....it's like your tryin' somehow to kill yourself. I don't think I could deal with that."she added as tears fell.

Seeing the tears rolling down her cheek, he pulled her close to him., His lips gentle touching her forehead as he gently wiped her tears away. He put his arm around her and held her close to him, leaning back, his eyes teared up.

"I want you out of here, your too important to me and they know it." He said quietly. Adding, "They will try to hurt you to get to me." For a moment he was silent then he added his voice choked with emotion, "I......I ….can't let that happen again to someone I care about."

Then he pulled her to him and pressed her body against his, as he kissed her hard on the lips. They sat embraced in each others arms for a long while, neither spoke, pulling her close, his lips lightly kissed hers, then he passionately kissed her hard, his tongue probed its way into her mouth as he felt the tip of hers, he pulled her body to his as he held her tightly against him.

For the first time he felt things he had not felt since Carrie. With his arms around her, he laid her head gently on his chest, and caressed her hair as he watched the moon disappear behind low white clouds.

Her eyes welled with tears as she laid still, listening to the beating of his heart as he held her body next to his. As the wind began to blow, he walked her to the horse. Cupping her face in his hands, he lifted her face to his and kissed her gently.

"Take care of her Raven." he said quietly, as he placed her in the saddle then slapped the stallions hindquarters and watched as they disappeared into the darkness, headed down the mountain.

His side aching, he walked to the rim and saw the fires burning below. Thinking about what she had said it had hit a nerve, he sat for a moment thinking about her and his feelings about her.

"When this is over." He thought as he crouched next to the fire and angrily poked it with a stick. Clouds had moved in and a light rain had begun to fall, his side aching, he stood up and started down the trail toward the fires below.

Chapter Fourteen

The sun was just coming up as Morgan rode through a dense forest of pine trees, she was wet, cold and miserable, it had rained most of the night, shaking with cold, she could not wait for the sun to come up. The stallion suddenly stopped and snorted, tossing it's head.

From the trail below came the sound of horses and voices. Pulling the horse back into the cover of the trees, she leaned over it's neck to make herself look smaller. A moment later, Logan and ten other riders came into view. With a grin she raced down to meet them.

"Is that Raven your riding." He said in a disbelieving voice. Adding, "I've never seen anyone but Travis ride that black devil." He added quietly.

"Where is he." He asked worriedly.

"I don't know Logan." She said quietly. "I turned around and he was gone."

Nodding his head he turned the others around and they started back down the trail into the valley and up toward the Sweetwater.

"Morgan," he said, "the best place for you and the other ranchers and families are with a friend of mine up on the Sweetwater.

"The only ranch up there is owned by a man we know as Diamond Jim Brady." Said Morrison.

"His ranch is nothing short of a fort." Remarked Saunders, owner of the Cripple Creek ranch.

"He's got a damned army up there and they are the best at what they do in the valley." Added Stark of the Roaring Fork ranch.

"What better place; I know he likes fine food, beautiful women and fine horses." Said Logan with a smile.

"Why Mister Teel, did you just call me beautiful." Morgan said with a smile, her violet eyes dancing.

"Guess I did at that." Said Logan as his face flushed red while the others laughed.

Laying in the foothills, the Sweetwater as it was known, was a valley nestled beneath three huge mountains. To the north was Chinamen Hat, in the center was a perfect triangular mountain the early Spanish explorers had named Contessa. Dominating the valley to the west, rose *Monte de la Santa Cruz*, The Mount of the Holy Cross.

Chinamen Hat, named by the pioneers because it's slope climbed to a point then fell gently back to it's foothills, laden with dense forests of Aspen and Pine.

In the center was Contessa, it's peak etched high into the clouds. It's crevices still glimmered with the snow of winter. Thick forested foothills reached far into the valley.

To the west, rose the third and most spectacular it was the *Monte de la Santa Cruz*, The Mount of the Holy Cross. It's massive slopes of gray black granite glistened with quartz in the sun, it is a rugged unforgiving place, it's slopes scarred with ancient rock slides and cut by deep ravines and gullies. Rock slides and avalanches were common here, trees were sparse. It's massive slopes dove down into a river boiling beneath it.

This was gold country; its peak towering high above the others, and across its face, glimmering in snow were the crevices that looked to be a cross.

First seen by the Spanish Monks, It's crevices glowing white against the gray black peak, it looked to them, like a cross. On the other side of this massive mountain was Leadville, known as the gold capital of Colorado.

The valley lay surrounded by cliffs of red and pink sandstone, layered with white limestone, glimmering with quartz, the rocks seemed to glow in the late afternoon sun. A river slowly wound it's way across this valley.

The valley was named by the pioneers because of the water; it ran cold, clear and sweet throughout the valley. At Derby Junction, the river emptied into Brush Creek, then fourteen miles down stream it emptied into the mighty Colorado river that through the eons of time, had carved the Canyon of the Grand.

It was a full days ride up to the Sweetwater and the ranch owned by Brady. Cresting a ridge, Logan stopped. Beneath them lay the Sweetwater valley.

Thick stands of fir, Lodgepole pine and Aspen lay long the valley floor. Juniper bushes dotted the landscape.

Wheat, corn and barley grew here by the acre as well as lush grazing for the hundreds of cattle owned by the ranch. Toward the back of this valley lay the ranch of Diamond Jim Brady.

A man known for his love of gambling, his affinity for beautiful women and his love of racehorses. He had brought several to his ranch in hopes that he could breed a racehorse with a bigger heart and lungs that would dominate the sport of horseracing. Toward the back of the valley lay the ranch they were looking for.

"He might get nervous if a bunch of us ride up at one time." He said as he pulled the men up then added, "Morgan you come with me."

Carefully, they started the trail into the valley as the sun beat down on them. They rode through a forest of Blue spruce and Lodgepole pine, and small forests of Aspen, their leaves quaking in the gentle wind.

The ranch lay in a bowl up against the foothills of Chinamen Hat. Built with the red rocks of the cliffs and in the style of Mexican haciendas, the name of the ranch was *"la Hacienda Del Sol,"*; the House of the sun. As the sun was beginning to set, the ranch seemed to glow a light pink as they approached. Several riders rode out to meet them. They were vaqueros from Mexico.

"Buenas Diaz." said Logan then added, *"Donda Esta Los Senor Brady."*

One gave him a hard look then remarked suspiciously, *"donde es casa."* Brandishing their rifles they surrounded the two. Then escorted them into the grounds of the ranch. A very large man, well dressed in a black shirt and a silver studded vest and wearing black pants came out to meet them.

"Well as I live an breath," He said with a smile, "if it ain't Logan Teel, been a helluva long time since we saw each other, last time Tucson two maybe three years ago wasn't it. Say wheres McCord, you two still ridin' together ain't you" Then he spied the stallion and Morgan.

"Ma'am," He said as he lumbered down the stairs to greet them, his eyes locked on the stallion. "That your horse." He murmured as he started to walk up to them.

"No." she replied with a smile, "he belongs to a friend of mine." then added as the ears flattened and the stallion snorted, "He does not like strangers."

"Where are my manners." he said, clearing his voice, "welcome to *Hacienda Del sol,* "please come inside out of this heat."

Behind the walls, the home was open with trees, shrubs, flowers, hanging baskets and several fountains. It was like walking into a garden.

A large table made of mahogany was in the center of the garden. As he sat down, he motioned for them to sit down as well. A young woman came with four large glasses of wine.

"Jim," said Logan, "let me introduce you to Miss Morgan Jenric, owner of the J-Bar Ranch.

"Sorry to hear about you pa Miss Jenric, I new him well." said Brady, his voice soft and gentle.

"Jim, there's more, I have ten more men on that ridge. They are all ranchers and until this mess is settled down in the valley," he said leaning forward, "I need a safe place for them to bring their families."

"Logan, bring them in, been awhile since I had guests." His said with a loud voice, as his face broke with a smile ." Then he said, *"to mar Esta Señora a la Salle DE,"* to the young woman she nodded her head then walked up to Morgan.

"Come," she said with a smile, "the senor has said to show you to a room." Taking Morgan by the hand, she led her through a hallway then into a room.

The room had closets and a dresser with a mirror, there was a large four poster bed draped in white satin, with blue flowers sewn in. Inside the closet she found dressing gowns and clothes of various sizes.

As she passed a mirror, she was horrified at her appearance. Her hair lay in strands and matted with dirt. Her face was streaked with dirt and sweat and the shirt, the one she had taken from Travis 's bedroll was stained dark with sweat, dirt and blood.

"Would you have a place where can I wash up? She asked as she looked at the girl embarrassingly.

Smiling at her, the girl grabbed her hand and took her to a room with a bathtub. She took several pails and brought them back with warm water. For the first time since being in Defiance she was able to clean up.

Logan stepped outside and motioned for the others to come down. Turning he went inside and with Brady he waited for others to come in.

"Claybourne been around here," He asked.

"He came around."Brady answered, then added softly giving him a hard stare, "I pay my men well to keep vermin like him away."

The others walked single file into the house, they made plans to bring the families to the safety of Brady's ranch.

As the day turned to night, clouds built on the horizon, and the wind began to blow. Lightning flashed over head, thunder crashed, reverberating against the surrounding cliffs, rain started to fall, at first it sprinkled, then fell with a vengeance! Lightning exploded almost continually against the black dark sky, thunder cracked, its deep rumble shaking the house.

Morgan stood watching the drops of rain run down the pane of glass, she thought of Travis out there somewhere.

Tears welled up in her eyes as she remembered how he had looked at her, how he kissed her as he put her on the stallion, she brought her hand to her face and remembered his hand gently touching her face as he sent her away.

There was a knock at the door, "It's open, she said quietly, a moment later Logan came in.

"Do you think he's alright." She said, her voice catching as he came up behind her.

"Yeah I think he is Morgan,..." he paused, then in a quiet voice, " he ain't like you an me, he's a surviver." Taking a deep breath, his voice quiet and low, he said "He's had to be, from the death of his parents, the Apache and the army."

" Right now," He said as he put his arms around her, "he is fighting everyone, you, me, Stanford and Kincaid. She looked up at him as tears fell from her eyes.

"He has fought his entire life," he added, his voice low and gentle, "his will to survive is what has been and is keeping him alive now. He's fighting himself right now, his feelings for you and the anger that is inside him. It's that anger that will not let him quit." He held her close and looked deep into her eyes.

"What you and I think of as hell..... he calls home," he whispered, his eyes hard as steel, he added, "Right now Morgan, he's living right on the edge, he will not allow anything to stop him," he paused and took a deep breath, as he looked at her, softly adding, " until he kills them, or they kill him, nothing will stop him, including his feelings for you."

As tears fell, he pulled her to him, holding her close, they both looked out into the darkness, each of them thinking about McCord.

The rain fell lightly among the forest of Aspen and pine as McCord made his way down the mountain. Smelling smoke, he paused, checking his gun he spun the cylinder and snapped it into place. His eye's like ice, his jaw set, he stepped out of the bushes and walked into the camp with his gun leveled at them. The three men froze as he stepped into the light of the fire.

"I"m sure you know who I am," he started, giving them a hard penetrating stare, as he placed his foot on a rock. Leaning over, his gun aimed at them.

Seeing a pot of beans boiling on the fire, with his free hand, he grabbed a plate, his eye's never leaving the men. As he took a mouthful, one of them moved his hand toward his gun.

"Mister, move that hand any closer to that gun of yours and you will meet your God!" he said, his voice deadly quiet.

"Now gents," he stated amicably, "you might just toss those guns of yours over to me," he added, his voice soft and quiet, "but you best do it slow. First you", he said to the one who had tried to pull his gun.

"Now you," he said pointing to another, then just moving the barrel of his gun he pointed at the last man.

"Now take off your clothes." he added with a a half smile as he took another bite. As they just looked at each other.

"Start with your boots." He demanded,his voice soft, low and deadly, one by one they did what he told them and their clothes came off. As they stood infront of him cold, wet and shivering, Travis half smiled.

"Good beans." He said as he put the plate down on the rock.

"You there," he said pointing to one of the men, "pick up those things an toss 'em into the river!"

"But Mister......" said one pleadingly, McCord cut him off his voice soft and deadly, "You came after me. Now let me tell you what your gonna to do. Think maybe you three should head to town." Adding, his voice deadly quiet, "my fight ain't with you, but if you come after me again, I will not hesitate to kill you. An since I need a horse," he added, "and you three don't, think I'll borrow one and take the other two."

Moving to the horses he untied them then mounted one, his face glistened with sweat, as he picked up the reins of other two, he left headed down into the valley toward a town. The three men stood shivering in their skivvies as they looked at each other, in the cold night air.

"Did you see them eyes of his." Said one softly. "It's like lookin' at the devil hisself."

"Did you hear him? I sure as hell didn't. I wanna know how the hell he got into camp without us hearing him." Said another as he shook his head.

"Damn, he's like a ghost." breathed the third. Then added, "ain't no way in hell I am comin' after him again!"

The other two nodded their heads in agreement. As they began to walk, shivering in the cold night air and the rain, they stumbled over rocks and sticks in the trail toward the town of Dowds Junction several miles away.

It was raining harder, lightning flashed overhead as thunder crashed, his side felt like it was on fire. Closing his eyes against the pain, half conscious he weaved in the saddle. Leaning forward, the rain poured off his hat, as he struggled to stay in the saddle.

From out of the fog, the soft glow of oil lamps could be seen. The street was empty as the horse plodded slowly through the rain. He pulled the animal up infront of a saloon.

Shivering, he nearly fell out of the saddle then stood a moment using the animal for balance. Pushing off, holding his side, he staggered into the saloon and collapsed in a chair.

"The names John," said a heavy set man as he walked up to the table. "You have got to be McCord." He stated quietly. As he nodded his head. John added "Folks around here call me Big John; come on mister McCord lets get you outta' sight."

John helped McCord to his feet then they went into a back room. Laying him down, John heard someone walk in. He came out of the room wiping his hands with a towel and went behind the bar as if nothing was wrong.

"Get you something. Mister." He said as he wiped the bar with the towel.

"Whiskey." replied the man, adding, "wheres Tandy.

"Who?" Asked John as he put a bottle and a shot glass in front of the man.

"Tandy, the man that owns that horse outside." Was the reply.

"He's in the back room," said John, thinking quickly, he added with a smile, "he's had just a might too much to drink." Then added with a knowing smile, "you know what I mean."

"Yeah, know what you mean." said the man as he chuckled.

"When he comes too," He added, "tell him Kenny was here looking for him.

As the man Kenny left, John went back to the room.

"You don't look so good." he remarked to McCord as he noticed how pale he was. Then added, "Double Diamond riders is combing them mountains for you mister and after what you done to Kincaid, they're looking under every rock and stick for you."

"That's..why... I'm here." He breathed, his face twisted in pain, his teeth clenched, he added, "figured they wouldn't look for me here."

"Need a doc." He gasped as pain tore through him.

"Think you can stand?" Asked John worriedly.

He nodded his head, his teeth clenched, with Johns help McCord shakily stood up then went out the back door of the saloon to the office next door of Doc Clemins. John knocked on the door, a moment later an older man with white hair opened it.

"Get him inside quick," Clemins ordered. As he worriedly looked around.

"Take him to that room back there." Said Clemins quietly, pointing to a room with the door open.

"Set him down over there." Said Cumins pointing to a table. As McCord sat on the table Clemins started to examine the wound in his side.

"You know McCord, you are him, right." Stated Clemins as he took the makeshift bandage off. As McCord nodded his head, he added, "I've been a Doc in this town for three years and I ain't ever had this much business." as cut the bandage off, he looked at McCord, then added, "Came up here to retire, looking for peace and regular doctorin'."

"That hurt?" He asked as he looked at McCord and pressed down on the wound. McCord gasped in pain, glaring at him.

"Guess it does." He chuckled as McCords face twisted in pain.

" Anyhow, you know, skinned knees," He said conversationally, "the occasional broken limb an such; an since you come here, I ain't had a moments peace, I'm thinkin' I should have staid in Denver."

"You best drink this son," he said matter of factly, as he poured McCord a glass of whiskey .

Shivering with cold, McCord's hand trembled as he downed the drink. The doctor poured a second, then a third, hearing a knock at the window he saw John and motioned him to come inside.

"John," he said quietly, "your going to have to hold him down. I have to clean out this wound, I think the bullets still inside.

"Bullets do a hell of a lot of damage to the human body." He said as he began to clean out the wound. "I just don't understand why men do this to themselves." Glancing at John, "he continued, "a small round piece of lead leads to all kinds of things, blood poisoning, infection and even gangrene.

"Here, pour a little into this cotton an hold it over his nose and mouth." Instructed Clemins, seeing Johns questioning look he said, "this is chloroform, it puts people to sleep."

"Hold him John," He said giving John a glance, as he picked up the forceps. Sweat beaded on his forehead as he felt for the bullet. "a moment later, he breathed, "got it!" he then held up the bloody end of the forceps and looked at the small bullet, turning it in his hand.

"Now hand me that brown bottle there." He ordered, taking the bottle, he opened the lid then poured a red tinted mixture onto a bandage and wiped the wound with it.

"It's iodocal, a two percent iodine mixture, hear they're usein' it back East to kill infection." He said as he saw John looking at him again. Then he added quietly, "John hand me that knife over there," pointing to a knife sitting on hot coals, it's blade had a slight red glow.

"Hold him down John", he said, his voice quiet, as he took the knife and laid it over the wound. The stench of burning flesh filled the room. McCord's body tensed then relaxed as he fell into the black void of unconsciousness.

When he was done, he looked at John. He needs to stay still for the wound to heal properly. Then added, sarcastically, "but I don't suppose thats gonna happen."

"Believe your right on that one." Smiled John. Then he walked out into the night.

The next day Clemins opened the door to the room. Seeing McCord up, he stated "from what I've heard about you I figured you be up an around this morning." He handed him a cup of coffee."Here let me look at you." He said motioning for McCord to sit down. McCord gasped as Clemins removed the bandage.

"You know McCord," he said, as he rebandaged the wound, "I generally ain't in the habit of fixing a man up just so he can get himself shot again."

"Not planning to." Remarked McCord as his faced twisted in pain and took a deep breath.

"Treated a friend of yours yesterday." Said Clemins nonchalantly as he finished re-bandaging the wound. "The name Kincaid strike a bell with you."

"Thought I killed him." stated McCord evenly.

"You tried," chuckled Clemins, "but I think his head is just about as hard as yours."

"Here, put this on, can't have you runnin' in the mountains with no shirt now can I." said Clemins with a smile as he handed a shirt to McCord. Smiling McCord winced as he eased his body into the shirt and tucked it in then buckled on his gun belt.

"Ain't no way I can stop you is there." Stated Clemins, his voice low and soft.

"Nope." Replied McCord giving the Clemins a hard stare, as he finished the coffee.

"McCord, your as close to exhaustion as I've ever see. If you don't rest up a bit, they won't have to worry about you 'cause you'll just drop dead." He said worriedly. Then added, "By the way, John has a horse behind the saloon for you."

Hearing people outside laughing he walked to the window and parted the curtain. Then he started to laugh, walking over to the window, Travis saw the three men from the camp coming into the town.

"Well I'll be." Laughed Clemins heartily, "now that's funny." Then he looked at McCord, "You do that."

"I did." He said with a grin as he winced with pain.

"Get the hell out of here before they find you." Said Clemins with a smile, then grasping his hand. He added quietly, "Go with God son."

McCord eased his body on to the back of the horse. Then following the back trail out of Dowds Junction, he headed toward the running M, the ranch owned by Morrison.

The rain from the night before had turned the road to mud as Travis rode slowly toward the running M.

"Damn, thought I killed that bastard." He thought, remembering what Clemins had said about Kincaid, as he headed the horse toward the trail Knowing men were out looking for him, he rode cautiously. Using the stands of scrub oak, cedar and pines to keep from being seen.

Ahead of him lay the rugged, rocky trail to the flattops, a rugged desolate place, a place of scant cover, only the cedar has the fortitude to grow here. It was a place of deep cuts and ravines. It's weatherbeaten sandstone cliffs, carved through the eons of time by the driving wind, sand and rain stood as solitary guardians of this hostile land.

Once tall cliffs, now broken and scattered, they served as a testament to this angry, treacherous place. The flattops posed a natural barrier to cattle and horses, as there are no grasses that grow here nor watering holes. Just beyond this arid place, in a valley was the running M.

As he kneed the horse toward the trail, he heard the sound of a shot then felt shards of wood as a tree seemed to explode next to him! Standing in the stirrups, he turned to see ten riders, coming fast toward him.

He slammed his heels into the horse. The horse leaped forward at a dead run. Leaning over it's neck he urged it on with hand and voice.

He pulled the horse to a sliding stop and looked around as it pranced nervously, seeing a trail to the left, he whirled it around then slammed his heels into it again, like a shot the animal raced down a rocky trail leading into a red rimmed canyon.

Bullets flew past him as he rounded a curve and saw before him a land of broken rock leading to an almost vertical wall of sandstone. Pulling the horse to a sliding stop, he jumped off it's back taking his rifle and his canteen and ran into the shelter of the rocks.

Chapter Fifteen

The afternoon sun glowed in the clear azure blue of the Colorado sky as a dust cloud materialized in the distance. On a ridge just above Windy gap, Morgan and Logan were waiting for the first of the herds to come in.

The ranchers had entered into an agreement with the army to supply them with one thousand head of cattle to be distributed to various Indian reservations and army posts through out the west. The buyer was to be here in two weeks.

"That's the bunch from the Three Peaks ranch," she said excitedly, as the ground began to shake and tremble, what sounded like thunder were the hooves of four hundred animals.

The ground shook as the animals passed just below them. Clouds of dust lay heavy in the air as herd after herd entered the gap.

The gap was sixty thousand acres of the best grass and water in this part of Colorado. For months Claybournes men had been trying to find it, Claybourne knew of the deal with the army, and was at a stalemate as he had been unable to find this place.

As men drove the cattle in, others were branding, cutting and roping, the air was filled with the sound of men, cattle and horses.

The last to arrive was Morrison's running M. As the dust cleared for a moment, they heard a distant rumple, like an earthquake, the ground began to shake! Rocks fell as his herd of five hundred head rolled like a living wave across the landscape, they crested the ridge and swarmed into the gap just below.

Morgan and Logan watched as the cattle slowly settled down then they started down into the Gap.

The late afternoon sun beat down on McCord as he ran into the rocks just ahead of the men behind him. Bullets careened off the the granite all around him. Falling behind a boulder, he pounded the dirt with his fist, angry at himself, he knew he was trapped.

"We got him now," screamed one as they knew he was inside a box canyon. "go get Mr.'s Kincaid and Claybourne," he added as he dismounted, then motioned for the others to do the same, as one rode his horse at a dead run toward the town of Castle.

The day was hot as the man Stanford, now known as Claybourne sat in his office. The bottle of whiskey was nearly empty, he poured the last few drops into his glass.

Leaning heavily back into the chair, he thought about McCord and then about Kincaid, the fact that Kincaid was still alive was a mystery, had the bullet been a just a little closer he would have died. He slammed his fist down hard on to the desk, as he remembered when he had met McCord for the first time.

He and Kincaid were bringing cattle up from Mexico into Arizona, there was a war brewing between ranches in Well, a county in northern Arizona. He had met a young lady named Carrie Brookledge and they were getting serious.

He remembered how much he had loved her then came a man he had hired to bring his cattle up from Mexico. A man named McCord.

McCord was tough, young and good looking, Claybourne had met him in a saloon and had watched him take on four men who had chosen to pick a fight with him. He had watched him fight the four and in the end, McCord was the one standing. The other four lay unconscious in the dirt of the street. He had approached him a day later as McCord was getting ready to leave the town.

He chose him as cattle boss because of his reputation as a renegade and outlaw. The men knew his reputation and seemed to respect him both out of fear and as a leader.

The territory has been in a drought for three years and the small cattle population was almost nothing. During this time Kincaid had worked a deal with several ranchers in Mexico, where he would buy the cattle cheap then drive them into the territory and sell them to the ranchers.

However, not all the cattle were paid for, Kincaid had been paying off those who worked for the ranches to steal many of the animals.

They were making a fortune selling them to the ranches in the territory to replace the cattle after their herds were decimated by the drought of 1870.

The Mexican herds were a hardier breed, as they had been bred in the desert landscape of Mexico. They acclimated to the landscape of Arizona quickly. The cattle though, also brought the dreaded hoof and mouth disease into the territory.

Stanford and Kincaid were selling these diseased cattle to the desperate ranchers. McCord knew this and this is how they were found out.

Unaware that McCord was a marshal, he had taken him into his confidence. By doing that McCord was able to come up with proof of what Stanford and Kincaid had been doing.

For over two years, McCord had worked with them. Finally, Stanford and Kincaid were surprised by the Arizona Marshal service, Tidball, Teel and McKindley were the one's that had caught them red handed.

But it had been McCords testimony that put both Stanford and Kincaid in prison.

They were sentenced to twenty years each in the territorial prison outside of Yuma. The prison lay deep in the desert. The small cell they had to share was nothing short of a cage.

Within two years Stanford had worked his way into that of a trustee. In that position, he could leave with guards and go into the town of Yuma for supplies from time to time. On one of these visits he heard that Carrie and McCord had been married.

He still remembered how angry he had become and vowed then to kill McCord, figuring if McCord were out of the picture, Carrie would come back to him.

He formed a relationship with another woman, Magdalena, the sister of Montoya, the guard. For months he worked to get close to her. She fell in love with him. It was with her help they developed their plan to escape. But they would need guns, ammunition but most of all water.

Knowing this Standford and Kincaid planned to escape with the Ault Brothers. Five years in the prison had changed both. Each man swore to get McCord, but for very different reasons.

It was on a moonless night they escaped. They had bribed Montoya and had crept quietly outside the buildings and worked their way to the fence leading outside to the walls.

As they had approached the fence, Montoya was there with his key and with his help, they made it outside the walls. The plan included Montoya leaving with them. Instead Standford slammed a knife into him. He and Kincaid carried the dead man to a ravine.

As planned Magdalena was waiting for them with horses and pack horses a short distance away . Knowing they had just a few hours before the Indians would start tracking them they hurriedly left.

Beneath clouds of stars they started into the desert. They moved quickly and had made ten miles before the sun came up. They had sought shelter near the hot red rocks of a canyon, they moved only at night, during the day, it was an inferno, they broiled in the sun, within days they were burned and blistered from the uncompromising heat.

Within two days the pack horses quickly succumbed to the heat, bogged down in the soft sand and one after another died.

They rode their horses into the ground, finally they were left on foot, alone in the desert. At night they could see the torches of the Yaqui tracking them just a few miles behind them.

The Indian trackers, even tracked them at night. More than once they had to leave their camps as they could hear voices.

On the eighth day, in the distance, through a heat waved horizon, they could see the ragged outline of the White Mountains shimmering through the haze.

He thought of Magdelina. He remembered hearing her scream then saw she had been bitten by a ratter. He remembered her full lips, her round breasts and how he had kissed her as he had slammed the knife into her, killing her instantly.

Days later, nearly dead, the four of them forced themselves though grit and determination to the bank of the Big Sandy river. As they collapsed on it's bank he remembered how they relished the fact they had beaten the odds and knew the Indian trackers would quit.

They had rested for a week before they left for McCords ranch. He remembered finding a ranch just beyond the river. The four men attacked it, killed the family and stole the horses. He still remembered the look of terror on the man's face, as he had shot him.

A few days later they headed for McCords Ranch. His ranch was located in the White Mountains along the bank of the Big Sandy. He remembered how Carrie had greeted him as they surprised her. Cool and distant, and somewhat afraid, it was not what he had expected. He remembered how she had begged him not to kill McCord. How she had said she would go with him if they let him live.

When he had refused, she slammed a small knife deep into his side. He was enraged and had knocked her to the floor.

For almost two weeks they camped at his ranch, it was almost twilight when they spotted a lone rider headed straight to them.

He remembered McCord coming into the yard and remembered it was Kincaids shot that knocked McCord to the ground. They did not expect Carrie to come out of the house with a rifle.

He could still hear her voice as she threatened him. But it was Kincaid who shot her, not him. `Panic drove them to leave. Knowing if anyone found out they killed a woman there would be no place safe, they headed for the mountains of Colorado where they were completely unknown.

The Ault brothers elected to stay with Calhoun. Thinking that McCord was dead, they left headed in different directions.

"We shoulda' made sure." He thought as he slammed his fist into the desk again. His thoughts were interrupted by a rider coming fast. It was one of the men out hunting for McCord. The man pulled the horse to a stop then raced into the saloon then to the back office to Claybourne.

"We....we got that McCord fella trapped Mr Claybourne." He announced as he ran inside breathless.

"Where!" Demanded Claybourne, as he stared at the man.

"Up in a box canyon near the flat tops, they call it Widows edge." was the mans reply.

As Claybourne stood up to leave, another man at the bar finished his drink and walked out, mounted his horse and rode out of the town toward the Sweetwater and Logan Teel. It was Garret Shannon!

It was mid -afternoon as all the herds now were in the gap. The cattle grazed contentedly on the grass as riders kept watch circling the herd, singing and talking soothingly to the cattle in order to keep the herd calm.

Hearing the sound of hoofbeats coming up the trail, they both turned and saw Garret riding toward them. His horse was lathered and spent.

Morgan, Logan he yelled, as he pulled the horse to a sliding stop.

"They got McCord trapped! Heard it in town," he added breathlessly, "said he's in a box canyon they call Widows Edge, just north of the flattops.

Chapter Sixteen

Having taken shelter beneath a huge block of granite, McCord rested for a moment. Angry at himself he leaned back and closed his eyes.

"How stupid am I," he thought to himself, then slammed his fist into the dirt. "A box canyon," he whispered angrily. Looking around, he shook his head knowing they had him trapped.

Bullets ricocheted off the granite every time he moved. Sweating from the heat, he took his canteen and took a drink. The water was warm, but it was water.

Keeping low, he moved from slab to slab heading for the base of the cliff. Every once in a while he would hear a bullet ricochet off the granite around him. Between the rocks were thick stands of brush.

He slowly crept through the thick brush toward a huge wall of rock, that through the eons of time, and the constant freezing and thawing had separated itself from the cliff.

As he got closer, he saw the cliff was layered, huge cracks and holes, criss crossed the face. Blocks of fallen rock lay like steps leading to the separated wall of rock. He carefully made his way up the rocks toward the slab.

The heat was intense, the sun, unrelenting. Sweat darkened his shirt as he finally reached the slab. Bullets flew as he squeezed himself into the small space between the slab and the cliff face. He sat for a moment, his side felt wet. Looking down he saw blood oozing from the wound in his side.

Closing his eye's, exhausted, he tiredly leaned back, his face streaked with sweat and dirt, he closed his eyes and rested inside the relative safety of the rock as he tried to figure out his next move.

It was late afternoon, as Logan, Chad and Garret raced their horses toward the flattops. Garret knew the way and a few hours later, they pulled their mounts up.

"From here we go on foot." He said. Then pointed up toward a little used trail on the other side of a deep ravine. In the distance, above the trail, towered a huge rugged red sandstone cliff.

"That's where we're headed, they call it Widows Edge." He said quietly to the others, as he pointed toward it and wound the rope around his shoulder.

The first thing was to cross the ravine, it was too steep to climb, plus a river boiled angrily beneath it. Logan took his lariat and tied a rock to it, twirling it above his head, he watched as the rope tangled around a branch of a tree directly across from them.

Using a boulder, he wound the rope around it and pulled it taut. Testing it, he leaned his full weight on it and the rope held. Crossing hand over hand, he slowly made his way across.

Once on the other side, he took the rope from the branch and tied it around the trunk of the tree, then motioned for the others to follow. As he waited for the others to cross he scanned the trail above.

Nothing more than an animal trail it hugged the steep cliff on one side. On the other was a drop of over a thousand feet into jagged rocks below.

For hours they climbed the treacherous trail, at times moving one foot at a time, they slowly made their way up the trail underneath the wall of the cliff and sliding ahead step by step over the loose shale of the trail.

The rock, heated by the sun was hot to the touch, the coarse sandstone cut their hands as they slowly made their way to the top, there the trail widened slightly taking them higher into the broken land of the flattops.

The cliff was now less than a half mile away. As night approached, they made camp in a clearing then stood looking back the way they had come.

"There's three ledges on that cliff," Said Garret, "If he's made up to the second ledge, then this path will take us right to him."

"Got him Mr Claybourne," Said one of the men, then turning around a he pointed at the face of the cliff. "he's up there;" said the man excitedly pointing out the slab of rock, to Claybourne as they rode into the camp just outside the rocks.

"Unless he's half mountain goat, there ain't no way he can climb out, we got men up on both sides of the cliff." The man added.

Claybourne nodded his head approvingly then dismounted and walked toward the rocks. He was nervous, they had, had him before but each time McCord had managed to escape them.

He thought of Thomas, like the damn note said, "he wasn't good enough". He glanced up and saw men high up on either side of the cliff. Every once in a while he would see a flash from a gun, then hear the sound of the shot echoing along the walls of the canyon.

"You can't stay up there forever," he thought, "this time McCord....we got you." Turning he walked back to the camp.

"Get the men together." Claybourne said worriedly. Knowing McCords reputation, and knowing what he had done in the past, Claybourne instructed the men to keep the fires burning bright and to watch for any sign that he may be trying to escape.

As the sun set, McCord opened his eyes. Looking out of the rocks he could see fires burning in the distance.

Knowing either Stanford or Kincaid or both might be down near the camp, his eyes like ice, his jaw hard, he knew he was going after them tonight. As night fell, he took his knife, then started toward the fires below.

Like a cat, he moved silently from rock to rock, working himself ever closer to their camp. Crouching down as the sound of voices came to him. As they past, he moved closer to the fire.

The smell of cigarette smoke told him a man was not far away. Crouching, he crept toward him with his knife in hand. The man was standing just a few feet away, leaning against a boulder.

McCord, crept behind the boulder, and waited for his chance. He picked up a small rock and tossed it toward a bush. As it landed, the man drew his gun and walked toward it, right infront of him.

McCord jumped the man as he passed in front of him, putting his hand over the mans mouth he slammed his knife into the man's back! He dragged the body behind the boulder and laid it down silently. Sweat beaded on his forehead, looking around, he saw another man not far away.

Leaning over, he crept silently toward him, using the boulders and the darkness he flattened against a boulder as the man suddenly turned toward him.

He flattened himself against the rock and waited, a moment later, the man turned back toward the fire, as he did, McCord jumped at him, before he could make a sound, he knocked him to the ground, bringing his right arm up, and quickly stabbed him. Taking the body, he hid it behind a boulder. He glanced around and heard the sound of horses not far away.

"He's here, get to the horses, thats where he'll go!" Screamed a man loudly as he discovered one of the bodies!

Throwing caution to the wind, McCord ran crouched over, toward the horses. Grabbing one that looked like it could run, he cut the rope holding it and jumped on it's back. Slamming his heels into it, it took off!

From out of nowhere, a man jumped for it's bridle! McCord kicked him hard in the face as another tried to grab him, he slammed his elbow into the man's neck as the horse half-reared. Another jumped at the animal. It reared, wild eyed, then jumped, heading back toward the rocks.

A shot flew over his head, then suddenly bullets flew, the horse floundered, then fell as a bullet hit it! McCord jumped! He hit hard, gasping in pain, forcing himself to his feet, he ran back into the rocks and into the darkness and the shelter of the wall.

As he made it, he slammed his fist into the wall angrily. His face sweat stained, his side bleeding again, he knew now he had no choice except to try to climb out.

If I can get up there," he thought, as he glanced up at the near vertical wall, "I just might be able to get myself outta' this mess."

From where he was, there was a ledge roughly eight feet above him. From there he saw another ledge to the right.

Just before daylight, with just enough light to see, McCord began to climb the wall up to the first ledge. The going was hard, grasping jutting rocks, he pulled himself foot by foot toward the first ledge.

Using first one rock and then another, bringing his legs up, feeling for rocks with his feet he steadied himself as he reached for anything he could use to pull himself up. He used the rocks and thick stemmed bushes as he slowly made his way up.

Just inches from the ledge, he gave one final push then pulled himself up. Breathing heavily, he collapsed. His head pounded, gasping for breath, his arms aching from the strain; he lay still for a moment.

Knowing the higher the sun rose the more likely he would be seen, he carefully crawled to a break in the ledge, looking up he saw the second ledge now less than eight feet above him.

Glancing down his stomach turned, as he saw the jagged rocks below, then he saw men scurrying and pointing.

"Ain't got a choice," He breathed, knowing if he fell, he would not survive! As he again began to climb, bullets peppered the face of the cliff all around him spraying him with small grains of sandstone.

His teeth clenched, breathing heavily, he leaned his face against the wall for a moment, taking a deep breath he continued to climb. Three quarters of the way, his foot slipped!

For a moment he hung as his foot wildly searched for something to stand on. Feeling a rock he steadied himself, sweat poured down his face as he leaned against the wall, his body shaking, his breath coming in rapid gasps.

As he reached the second ledge, gritting his teeth he used his last ounce of strength to pull himself up; his arms almost numb from the strain, he rolled on to the ledge and lay breathing heavily, shaking as he realized how close to death he had been.

He rolled underneath blocks of rock jutting out from the face. They were just wide enough for his body and offered protection from the bullets. Thirsty, his hand shaking, he pulled his canteen to him then saw the bullet hole.

"Damn it to hell." He thought as he rolled his eyes and took a deep breath. He shook the canteen and heard water inside it, he drank the last few drops, then closed his eyes and laid still as bullets peppered the wall all around him.

Waking to the sound of gunfire, the three men hurriedly scaled a ridge directly across from the massive cliff. Through out the night, they had heard sporadic gunshots. Worriedly, Logan looked at the cliff.

They carefully climbed a path of shale that led up into the cliff and a ledge. Through a thicket of thorn brush he got his first glimpse of McCord. He was almost directly across from them.

Sunlight glinted blue off the barrel of a rifle as a man stood up, Garret quickly jerked his rifle up aimed and shot, the man clutched his chest then fell.

Climbing up further, Garret took aim again as he saw another man stand with a rifle, aimed at McCord, across in the red stone of a cliff, he squeezed the trigger then saw the man fall into the rocks below.

Hearing shots that seemed close, Travis raised his head, reaching for his gun, his head pounding, his eyes blurred then cleared and he saw Logan, Chad and Garret not more than thirty feet away. A smile crossed his face as Logan threw a rope across to him.

"Travis, the ledge breaks off about ten feet from you, from there drop down to a flat rock just below. Then we can get you across." He yelled.

Tiredly he nodded his head and crawled to the break, wrapping the rope around him he started down to the rock. As he dropped down, he fell hard on his shoulder and grabbed at a branch from a pine tree growing next to the cliff and kept himself from rolling off the side.

"Grab my arm." Logan said as he reached out. Grabbing on, Travis was pulled to the other side and up to the trail.

He staggered into the red stone, breathing heavily, he turned and leaned against the red rock of the canyon wall for a moment and closed his eyes, his heart pounding.

"Bout time you got here." Said McCord with a smile then added, "got any water," adding with smile, "seems my canteens been shot." Laughing Logan opened his canteen and gave it to his friend..

"Heard shots last night." He remarked, looking at Travis.

"Yeah, I tried to leave but they wouldn't let me." Replied McCord with a smile.

"You ready to get the hell off this rock." Asked Logan smiling. Nodding his head, Travis shakily moved from the cliff and walked to his friend.

"Thanks Logan. It's been a long time." He said as he grasped his friends hand in a warm handshake.

The sun burned down on them as they made their way to the camp. Once there, exhausted from the climb, his eyes burning, his head pounding,

Travis fell on to one of the blankets and closed his eyes and for the first time in weeks he allowed himself to sleep.

His friend was in bad shape. Burned and blistered from the unrelenting sun. Dealing with the loss of blood and exhausted from climbing.

Logan worriedly looked down at Travis. His friends face was streaked with blood, sweat, dirt and was burned red by this unrelenting sun of the mountains. His shirt was in tatters, torn by the rocks of the cliff. His hands were bleeding, swollen and red from the roughness of the sandstone.

Black, ominous clouds began to hover along the walls of the canyon. Lightning flashed overhead, as Travis woke up. Gasping he got to his feet slowly, holding his side, he walked over to Logan.

"Time to go Now." Stated Logan worriedly as lightning split the sky above, seconds later, thunder cracked, then exploded, rolling along the walls of the canyon, it's sound, intensified by the sandstone cliffs that surrounded them.

Not wanting to be caught out in the open, they hurriedly made their way to an overhang just over the trail they needed to go down. Rivulets of water poured down around them as the rain fell in sheets, rocks loosened by the rain fell around them as they struggled to stay dry. Travis sent a worried look up at the cliff above as he remembered the cave in.

For over an hour they waited; finally the rain began to let up, the sun broke through the dark clouds and they started down the trail. Logan had them tie the rope around each of them.

"This way if one falls, we all do." He said with a smile.

"That ain't funny." remarked Travis worriedly as he feigned a wry smile.

Hours later, after inching their way down the trail, they came to the ravine. Seeing Travis's hands and knowing there was no way he could get across, they searched for another way to cross the now raging river, flowing red from the storm.

Walking down stream Logan found it. Here the river widened and forked. Where the river forked was a sand bar jutting out into it and the flow was not as rough.

The plan was for Logan to swim across with the rope then the others would follow. With the end of the rope secure around a boulder, Logan

entered the water, the frigid temperature was a shock! The undertow immediately pulled him under, into it's cold, icy depths.

He forced himself to the surface, gasping for air. Shaking his head, he
headed for the opposite bank. Minutes passed as he swam through it's stiff
current, shivering, his teeth chattering he finally pulled himself out on to
the bank.

The sun's hot rays now felt good, as it warmed him. Taking the rope, he
secured it around a tree then motioned for the others.

One by one they made it to other side. The cold water felt good as it
momentarily eased the pain of both the sunburn and his wound, as Travis
half swam across. Finally he struggled up the bank and sank tiredly into the
grass.

Sending Chad and Garret for the horses. He helped Travis to the shade
of an old Cottonwood.

"You ready to talk yet?" Questioned Logan.

"They killed her Logan, whats left to say." Quietly stated McCord,
pulling a piece of grass, turning it over in his hand, his blue eyes scanning
the mountains before him.

"You want me to forget about that.....Well I can't!" he snarled, his eye's
narrow and cold as he turned and looked Logan in the eyes.

"No," Stated Logan angrily his eyes flashing, "I want to go after them
as bad as you. But," Added, "your not going at it the right way."

"The right way!" exploded Travis, his blue eyes flaming angrily, " we,
you and me did this the right way, we put those bastards in prison, so whats
the point, they'll just escape....." his voice caught, "I'm doin' it the way I
was taught by the Apache;...kill or be killed!"

"Is that what your lookin' to do is to get yourself killed. We have laws!"
Stated Logan hotly, then McCord interrupted him, standing up, his eyes,
like ice.

"Where was the law that night at my ranch!" He growled angrily, his
teeth clenched hard, as he glared at Logan. The law did not save Carrie!"
He snarled angrily. "That's why I resigned, Logan. All your law does is just
gives them bastards a second chance to kill...my way doesn't." He stated,
his voice low and deadly.

Turning around, he angrily shot Logan a look then strode back to the
river. Standing up, Logan followed him.

As he touched Travis's shoulder, Travis spun on his heels, all his anger and hate directed at Logan, he slammed his fist hard into Logan's stomach knocking him backward into the mud of the bank. Surprised for a moment he lay still then jumped up throwing a right hook to McCord's jaw!

Travis blocked the blow with his left arm then slammed his right fist into Logan's jaw followed quickly by a left jab to his stomach and knocked Logan back onto the bank of the river. As McCord pressed his advantage, Logan rolled to his right, then jumped to his feet and lunged at McCord and both fell into the river.

McCord put his arm around Logan's neck, and pushed his head under the water, Logan brought the flat of his hand hard into Travis's chin! McCord's head snapped backward, for a moment his grip loosened allowing Logan's head to come out of the water, gasping for air, he slammed his fist hard into McCord's wound.

McCords legs gave out as he fell backward on to the bank, nearly para-lyzed by the pain. Logan staggered to the bank and stood over him, glaring and breathing heavily, clenching and unclenching his his fists.

"You done!"he growled, as he gave McCord a hard stare.

"Yeah," Gasped McCord as he sank back in the mud. His face twisted in pain.

"Good." Replied Logan as he sat on the ground rubbing his jaw. "Don't know how much more I could have taken." He said as he sank back into the mud.

"Where did you learn to hit like that." Grimaced McCord.

"You." He remarked with a slight smile.

"Travis the law is coming here." Stated Logan as he sat next to his friend."That's why I'm here. The Governor of Colorado, a James B. Grant wrote a letter to Governor Twittle requesting help and he sent Chad and me, they heard about the situation up here and had no one to send since the army is out chasing the Sioux on the plains, it's a real problem down there."

"The thing is," he said quietly, "I need to know if I'm gonna have to fight you as well as Stanford and Kincaid."

"Not if you keep throwing those right crosses." Smiled Travis wanely. As the two men stood up and walked back to the tree, Chad and Garret, rode in.

"Riders comin' this way! Heard one of em' say, they're headed to the gap." Said Garret nervously. As Logan mounted his horse, he reached down for Travis.

"I'll give you cover." Said McCord, backing away he gave Logan a hard stare, "Logan I meant what I said."

"Your gonna need this then." Logan said quietly as he handed Travis a rifle, taking the knife out of his belt, he gave him the knife as well.

"I'll meet you at the gap." Said Travis as he shook his friends hand.

As they rode away, he ran to an outcrop and leveled the rifle as he heard the sound of horses coming toward him.

As the horses rounded the bend, McCord rapid fired the Henry and watched as the men scattered.

He moved to another rock and fired again. Bullets fell like hail, moving back, he fired again, this time a man fell clutching his chest.

As a riderless horse bolted by him he grabbed it's mane and leaped on to it's back and rode up the trail. Then he pulled the horse up behind a granite bluff and waited.

The men charged past him, when he was sure they were gone, he turned the animal back down to the base of the canyon he had just escaped from!

"Damn him to hell, four more men dead and six injured." Thought Claybourne angrily, he was furious that McCord had escaped him again.

As he stomped angrily around the camp he looked to the mountain and calling the men together, he ordered them to Windy Gap. One of his riders had followed a herd and discovered the gap with a thousand head of cattle inside.

Without Logan and Chad, Morrison had taken over, he put men on the cliffs to watch for any sign of men coming after the cattle. One of the spotters had reported that someone was following the herd from the The Roaring Fork ranch.

With men above and others roping and branding, they worked hard getting set for the fight they knew was coming.

Claybourne's men quietly approached from two sides. Knowing the only way to get the cattle out was by stampeding them through the gap. The animals, already wary would be easy to start to run.

Four men dismounted and carefully worked their way past ranchers and the night riders to the cliffs behind the gap. The others took up position around the valley floor. With guns at ready one waved his hat and shot a round into the camp.

At the first shot, the animals began to run, the earth trembled, like a freight train, the enraged animals swept though the valley and toward the gate. Men scattered as riderless horses ran with the cattle as they broke through the fence of the gap and out into the open grasslands.

Outside the gate, men waited as the charging cattle broke through, men raced toward the front of the herd and turned the leaders toward the mountain known as Indian Peak.

It was a rugged landscape, the twin peaked mountain stood alone at the southern edge of the valley. It's foothills, was the home of Brush Creek. The creek flowed for several miles before it merged into the Frying Pan, from here it flowed another twelve miles before it merged into the powerful Eagle River. At Dotsero, the Eagle merged with the dynamic Colorado River and began it's march through The Canyon of the Grand.

In it's midst lay the beautiful Crystal Valley, similar to Windy Gap, except it was closer to Castle and the stockyards. Surrounded by sheer, weatherbeaten cliffs. it was the perfect place to hold the cattle.

Grass was plentiful, and the water was a natural barrier to keep the cattle from straying into the foothills. Claybourne and Kincaid were to meet the buyer in Dowds Junction, then escort him to the valley to inspect the animals.

Waiting at the valley were men whose sole job was to brand the animals with Claybournes Double Diamond Brand.

As the cattle streamed out of the Gap, the riders turned the animals toward the Crystal Valley. As the others kept the ranchers from following the herd.

Logan pulled his horse up at the sound of distant gunfire. As they crested a ridge, the last of the cattle were breaking out and riders were turning them. Knowing they could do nothing, they aimed for the barricaded ranchers.

Morgan was busy with those who had been shot. She watched several die from gunshot wounds Ben Coffman was the first, she saw George acting like a general directing his troops.

They had been able to keep the cattle from coming into the camp by overturning two buckboards and one of the Chuckwagons.

Morrison, using his field glasses, saw the three men above the valley, he directed several to lookout points on the cliffs above the camp.

Morgan grabbed a rifle and ran to one of the wagons. Taking aim, she began returning fire as Morrison directed the others to do the same.

Logan raced his horse, flanked by the others toward the barricaded camp. Like Travis, he had learned to fire the rifle from underneath his horses neck, protecting himself as the animal raced across the valley. Within minutes, they were inside with the ranchers.

Taking up positions, with the additional three guns, Claybourne's men began to leave, leaving just a few to keep the ranchers from leaving and retaking the herd.

As the three men entered the camp, they were surrounded by the ranchers. Seeing Morrison, Logan shook his hand and surveyed the damage. Three ranchers were dead, and dozens of their men where hurt. Morgan came up and looked at him seeing her unasked question, he turned to the fire.

Out in the valley, shots were being fired. Keeping the ranchers pinned down, unable to chase down the cattle. Taking up a position next to an overturned buckboard, Logan began returning fire as he waited for McCord.

McCord rode the horse quietly down through a maze of rocks and brush. Leaving it, he started silently through the rocks toward the camp and Stanford. In the distance he heard angry voices, one of them was the familiar voice of Stanford.

His jaw set, his eyes, like ice, narrowed as he fingered the blade of the knife. Checking the magazine of the rifle, he saw it was fully loaded. With rifle in hand, he made his way slowly toward the sound of Stanford's voice.

Hearing the sound of footfalls in the gravel around the rocks, he faded into the shadows and let the man pass. Silently he put the rifle down and took his knife, the man was just a few feet infront of him when he jumped him, bringing the knife down hard, killing him instantly.

As he crept toward another, he heard Standford's voice not far away, his eyes glinted like steel as he climbed a tall granite outcrop. Below him, illuminated by the fire was Stanford! Taking his knife by the handle he threw it at him.

As day turned to night, Claybourne mounted his horse, from out of nowhere a knife slammed into the saddle horn, just missing him! The saddlehorn exploded; showering him with pieces of steel, one hit him in the arm!

In seconds he was off the horse as gunfire exploded all around him. His eyes wide with fear he knew it McCord was out there in the dark, somewhere! As quickly as it started, it stopped, as men rushed to his aid, he glared into the black dark of the canyon.

"McCord, you will pay for this." He snarled, his face twisted in anger as he heard the sound of hoofbeats retreating in the distance.

Having seen Stanford fall, McCord began the long ride to Windy Gap. The trail was hard, the hooves of the horse slipped on the shale, rounding a bend, he could see the road and more riders.

Dismounting, he left the animal ground tied and climbed a sandstone bluff. His hands hurt as he steadied the rifle against the cliff, his eyes like ice he waited for them.

A moment later, the riders rounded a curve and McCord fired again. Three more fell dead, as the others scattered.

Crouching, he jumped down to the horse, mounting it, he rode up higher into the rocks. The trail was rocky. As he rounded a bend, a shot rang out, the bullet barely missed him. He fell to the ground with the rifle in hand, crouching low he ran to the cover of a boulder.

He heard soft footfalls coming toward him. Moving behind the boulder, he waited. Moments later a man stealthily approached him.

McCord waited until the last second then leaped at him. As they struggled, Travis grabbed the man's gunhand, he slammed it repeatedly against the cliff wall and the gun fell to the ground, McCord kneed the man in the back and with his left arm he grabbed him by the neck, twisting it hard, killing him instantly.

Dropping the mans body to the ground, breathing heavily, his side on fire, he grabbed the reins of the horse. Remounting it, he turned the animals head and headed up the trail leading toward the Gap. With the moon full up, he could see the trail easier. The horse jumped a small ravine then

Travis aimed it up the brush strewn trail into a broken landscape of ravines, gullies and draws..

He rode slowly as the trail became more difficult for the horse, cresting a ridge, the gap laid out before him. He saw three fires and toward the back he saw the overturned wagons of the men who where guarding the herd. He saw the muzzle flashes from the wagons. Then from the fires he saw where he needed to go to get through.

Chapter Seventeen

Riding down the trail slowly, he stayed within the safety of the trees, he pulled the nervous horse up. Looking down into the gap he could clearly see the fires now.

The gap was covered in thick clouds of gunpowder, it hung low over the valley floor and glowed with a red haze, like it was on fire. The air hung heavy with it's arid smell.

Logan lay still behind an overturned buckboard. His rifle in a notch. From out of the darkness he heard the howl of a coyote. Morgan slipped next to him bringing him shells.

"Damned coyote," she said angrily, "its probably going after a stray."

"Morgan, that coyote, has damned Apache accent; That's Travis out there!" He said with a smile on his face.

"Chad get up into those rocks and give him cover." He ordered. "When he gets in the clear. cover him!" he said to the rest of the ranchers.

The horse pranced nervously and tossed it's head. Talking quietly to it and patting it's neck he guided it down to the valley floor, staying in the trees, he checked his rifle then jammed his heels into the horse.

Like a shot it sped straight toward the gap as Travis leaned over the side of the horse firing his rifle from under the animals neck.

A man jumped out of the grass at them, as the horse swerved, it nearly unseated McCord! Using the butt end of the rifle he slammed it against the mans head . Another tried to jump up behind him, he swung the barrel hard into the mans neck, as the now panicked animal raced forward.

Another fell back as the shoulder of the animal knocked him backwards into the tall grass. Another jumped for the bridle, McCord kicked him hard in the chest, sending him backwards into the grass.

The wagons were now in sight! He raced the animal toward an opening, bullets flew like angry hornets as he raced toward the wagons.

The night exploded as gunfire raged. McCords horse jumped the tongue of an overturned buckboard. With bullets buzzing like angry bees, McCord leaped off it's back, looking quickly he saw Logan.

"Took your good old time getting here." Stated Logan with smile. As Travis fell next to him.

"Where are the cattle." He asked breathing heavily, ignoring the remark.

"They were gone when we got here." Logan replied as he squeezed the trigger and a man went down.

"Most of Stanford's men left." Logan added as he shot again.

"I say," said Travis as he sighted the rifle then squeezed the trigger, "we take the fight to them."

"So what is your plan?" Asked Logan.

"Coming in I saw three groups," he started, "group one is just to the east of us, group two is north of us, and group three is just past the gate. If we take three men each, we can surprise them."

Motioning Travis to follow, Logan walked toward the back of a wagon, As they approached, the ranchers all surrounded them. Several had been shot.

"So we finally get to meet you Mr. McCord." Stated Morrison grasping McCords hand firmly.

"Yeah," Said Don Stark laughing, "you was in a bit of hurry the last time we saw you." As he slapped McCord on the back. McCord gave a look to Logan as he was not use to this kind of a reception. Logan just stood and smiled.

"Nice to finally meet you." Added Morrison with a smile.

As he shook hands with him, McCord grimaced then limped to the fire. Pouring himself a cup of coffee, he eased his tired body down. his eyes burned, closing his eyes for a moment and leaned against a boulder.

"Thought you might like this." Stated Logan as he gave him a plate of beans and hardtack.

"Been so long since I've had anything to eat, my stomach thought my throats been cut." Travis said with a grin. Then he dug hungrily into the food.

"What the hell happened to you." Morgan breathed as she saw the blood soaked bandage.

"Got caught and decided to fight back." was his reply wincing, as he ate, she cut the bandage off.

"Yeah, heard about that" She replied as she looked at him worriedly.

"I'll be right back." She said as she walked away. A moment later she came back with clean bandages, a shirt and lard for his sunburn.

By the light of the fire, she could see the exhaustion in his face. His face glistening in the light of the fire was lined, his eyes red and sunken in. He looked exhausted.

Helping him to a bedroll, he laid down. He was out before his head hit the blanket. Logan and Morgan walked together back to the fire.

"Got men posted, why don't you go rest awhile. Nothing more will happen tonight." Said Logan gently as he put his arm around her.

"He'll be ok. Morgan. He's survived worse... you know that." He said as he saw her glance worriedly at Travis.

As she headed toward one of the wagons, tears welled up as she thought about the cattle, but most of all about her friends she had seen shot, Don, Nick and Pearly and those that died, Ben, Able and Murphy.

Angrily she picked up a rock and threw it hard into a bush. Logan came up from behind, putting is arms around her, he held her close, comforting her as tears fell.

"We'll get them back Morgan.....I promise." he said, his voice choked with emotion. "Now you get some rest."

"How in the hell did he escape." Thought Claybourne angrily. Not once but twice! His camp lay in ruins, his men quitting out of fear of this man McCord!

Claybourne fingered a shot glass as he thought about McCord. His thoughts were interrupted by Kincaid. His face was ashen, his head bandaged, he walked unsteady to a chair. Seeing the fresh bandage on Claybourne's arm.

"Heard he almost got you," Said Kincaid.

"You look like hell." Remarked Claybourne, ignoring Kincaid's statement.

"Feel like Hell," replied Kincaid as he sat heavily into a chair.

He handed him a piece of paper. Claybourne read it then said, "so that buyer will be here in three days."

"Yeah," replied Kincaid, as he closed his eyes.

"The cattle are down in the Crystal Valley," remarked Claybourne. "plenty of grass there an water too." He added then looked out the window.

"What about them ranchers." Asked Kincaid through clenched teeth, as he felt a knife like pain in his head.

"They ain't going anywhere, I left men there to make sure." stated Claybourne, as he poured another drink, this time he handed it to Kincaid. "You look like you need this." He remarked as Kincaid gratefully accepted it, then in one gulp it was gone.

"What about McCord." Said Kincaid, as his faced twisted in pain as he fingered the bandage around his head.

"Roman," said Claybourne worriedly, as he leaned back in the chair, fingering his glass, giving Kincaid a hard star, "I swear he's like a cat with nine lives, just when you think you got him he finds a way to disappear!"

"Yeah, but Clay," He stated evenly, his eyes glowing with anger, he placed the now empty glass on the desk, "You know even cats ultimately die. He's going to slip up and when he does.....I'll be there"

He shakily got to his feet and walked out of the office, out the door and headed toward Doc Clemens office.

The wind rustling through the leaves of the cottonwood woke McCord. His body was stiff and sore, his arms and legs ached from the strain of climbing. As he sat up, he winced from the pain.

"About time." Smiled Logan as he brought him coffee, eggs, beans and hardtack.

"Thought you was never gonna wake up." Pausing, he said concerned. "you alright."

"Yeah I'm ok, just tired as hell." he said as he accepted the coffee and food gratefully.

"You ready for this now." Logan stated, as he laid the badge on a rock in front of McCord.

"I resigned." Stated McCord softly, picking it up, he fingered the edges of his badge, giving Logan a hard stare.

"Did I fail to mention," smiled Logan, "I never sent the letter", adding with a smirk, "think I lost it somewhere in that office of mine."

"Are you." Logan added seriously.

"I....I...need to think about this." Said Travis softly as he put the star down back on the rock and stared at it.

"Travis," Said Logan quietly, as he rolled a cigarette, then rolled one for McCord, handing it to him he added, "I need you with me on this."

Picking it back up, he fingered the five starred badge, he remembered the pride he had felt as Governor Twittle had sworn them in. He also remembered the day he left, throwing it to the ground infront of Logan.

"Not sure Logan." He said quietly, staring hard at his friend.

The badge had meant a lot to him, for him it meant the law, but now it meant he would have to change his tactics, this he was not ready to do. Seeing the look in Logan's eye's and knowing he now needed his help he took the badge and pinned it on.

Yeah, I guess I am Logan." He said softly as he gave Logan a look.

"Welcome back Travis." said Logan smiling as he and grasped his friends hand firmly in his.

"I'll be back." Stated McCord to Morgan as he left the safety of the camp. With him he took a burlap sack, adding, "If Logan asks tell him I'm scouting."

A moment later he disappeared into the tall grass. An hour later he returned and walked to the fire, seeing Morgan's questioning look he just shook his head and avoided the conversation.

It was late afternoon, clouds hung heavy over the gap as Travis, Logan and Chad slipped out of the camp. In the distance they heard the sound of thunder in the distance as a storm built.

Sneaking though the grass, they heard the sound of voices not far away. Motioning for Chad, he pointed.

"You get behind that rock over there." Said Logan quietly,

"I want you to get behind them and cover me." He whispered to Travis, as he noticed Travis was carrying something in a bag.

"Somethin' to make them talk." Said Travis to Logan's questioning eyes. A moment later Travis disappeared.

Logan, his eyes like steel, his jaw hard, waited a moment then spun the cylinder of his navy colt, took the safety off then stood up with the pistol raised.

"Raise your hands boys." He stated loudly, then walked into their camp.

Taken by surprise they knew there was nothing they could do and they gave up. As Chad stood on the outskirts of the camp, Travis came up from behind them.

"Don't move that hand any closer Mister." Growled McCord evilly, seeing a man's hand start for his gun.

At the sound of his voice, the man froze. Reaching for the gun, Travis plucked it out of the holster then threw it toward Logan.

"Take your guns out of your holsters. And throw them to me." Demanded Logan. "Best do it slow."

Jamming the pistol into the mans back Travis shoved him forward, then motioned for the other two.

"We want answers." Started Logan as he put his foot on a rock, his pistol aimed at the men.

"We ain't gonna tell you anythin!" Snarled one of them as he sent a hate filled glance toward McCord.

"Oh, I think you will." Logan replied. "The man you know as Sam Claybourne is actually Clay Stanford, he and Kincaid escaped from the prison in Yuma and I am here to take them back, Now I want to know where they are hold up." He demanded.

"You can't make us talk Marshal." One of them spat.

"Maybe he can't," Snarled McCord as he stepped next to the man, "But I can." He hissed as he threw the bag on the ground.Turning his gun on Logan and Chad, he motioned for them to back off.

Looking back at the men he kicked the bag open. Seconds later three timber rattlers emerged.

"You boys know who I am." He said, his voice low and threatening, "and you know what I have done, and now," pointing at Logan, he added, "let me tell you something you don't know, you see I was raised by the Apache, I rode with Geronimo and they taught me all the ways they have of killing," his blue eyes glowed in anger as he looked at the three men saying, his voice low and quiet, "an I learned them all.

Now, the marshal here wants some answers.....and so do I." he stated, Pausing, " but if you don't want to....I think my friends here will try to persuade you." One of the men, his eyes wide with fear screamed as the one of the snakes crawled toward him.

"I'll talk!.....just get that damned thing away from me!" He screamed in panic.

Motioning for Logan and Chad, Travis turned his back and walked toward the trees. Logan raced after him. Furious, he grabbed McCords shoulder and spun him around.

His colt was aimed at McCord as he snarled, "You ever......" Then he saw Travis's colt aimed at him.

"You needed answers," snarled McCord as he stared defiantly at Logan. Lowering his weapon, Travis just looked at Logan.

"You do that again," snarled Logan, "I will put you in irons!"

Turning on his heel, he strode back to the camp. They told him the cattle had been taken to a place called Crystal Valley and the men they knew as Claybourne and Kincaid were expected to be there.

Glaring at McCord, he motioned for the three to stand then herded them to the camp.

Once there, Logan took McCord aside.

"You said you were with me." Logan stated soft and low, as the two men faced each other, with a hard look , he said, "What you did back there....."

"Got you answers, Logan. Your way would not have worked!" interrupted McCord angrily.

"I'm tellin' you what you will do and you will not go against me McCord." He snarled angrily.

Angry, McCord stood infront of Logan, defiantly he stared at him hard then knowing Logan, he angrily walked back to the camp. Logan told the ranchers what they had found out.

"That valley's quite a ways away from the stockyards in Castle." Remarked Don Stark.

"Yeah," said Morrison. "an we're gonna play hell trying to get them there in time."

McCord nudged Logan then whispered to him. Nodding, Logan's face broke into a smile.

"Travis here thinks," He said, his voice even and low, "with enough riders we can stampede the cattle right into the stockyards."

The ranchers all looked at each other then agreed. But to do this it meant some of the men had to be on foot, and they would have to move in at night then wait for sunrise. The cattle would already be wary and skittish. Plus the more they ran the less the buyer would pay.

For hours they rode through the shimmering forests of aspen and lodgepole pine, through scrub oak and stands of cedar toward the imposing mountain known as Indian Peak, it's foothills to the south bordered the crystal valley.

They entered a stand of Aspen at twilight. From here they saw the cattle grazing in the pasture. They needed to stampede the herd toward the east to the town of Castle and the stockyards.

They split the riders, half went with McCord, the other half with Logan.

The plan was simple, riders would be staged on either side of the herd. Three men would get behind the herd and start them running. The rest of the riders would be outside the valley and turn them toward Castle ten miles away.

Travis ordered three riders, Morrison, Stark and Chaney to stay in a gully, he and two others carefully maneuvered around the night riders circling the herd. As they came up through a stand of pine, he ordered Johnson, Davis and McNulty to stay in a ravine to the right of the herd.

Travis, Garret and Chad would start the herd moving. By dawn all the men were in place. Travis took off his hat.

Kneeing the stallion, he walked the horse waving his hat, the animals began to walk slowly toward the entrance of the valley. The night riders alarmed grabbed their pistols and began firing at dark shapes behind the herd.

At the first shot, the animals began to run, the earth trembled, like a freight train, the enraged animals swept though the camp, overturning the chuck wagon, scattering men, riderless horses ran with the cattle as they streamed out through the cut.

Reaching the chuck wagon McCord pulled Raven to a sliding stop, jumping off it's back he pulled a screaming man out from under the wagon.

"Where are Kincaid and Stanford." He demanded of the terrified man.

"They......they ain't here.......please mister," Pleaded the man. "Don't kill me!" Adding, "they said something about Dowds Junction an a buyer the're suppose to meet."

Pushing the man down, he remounted the stallion and slammed his heels into it's side. The stallion leaped into a dead run. The stallion raced following the cattle, he gained ground going past Chad and Garret. As he hit the cut he whirled the stallion to the west instead of the east toward Castle.

As the cattle exploded out of the cut, the ranchers turned the herd toward Castle. It was a wall of moving animals, the earth shook as the hooves of a thousand cattle broke into the open toward Castle.

Logan looked anxiously for Travis. He saw a black horse race east, away from their position.

"Damn him not this time!" Swore Logan angrily.

"I'm going after him." Yelled Logan, Chad your with me." As they whirled their horses slammed the spurs and raced toward Dowds Junction following Travis.

Chapter Eighteen

McCord sent the stallion at breakneck speed down the rocky slope toward the hills of gypsum a dry powder like dirt.

The stallion slipped in the unstable footing and slid back on his haunches amid of cloud of fine white dust, then regaining it's footing, it continued racing as McCord angled it down through a ravine then back up and across a gully!

They raced through stands of pine and Aspen, then across the flat plain and back down into a deep gully, the stallion hooves pawed the hard ground as it struggled up the slope.

Coming to a ravine, the stallion gathered itself as Travis leaned forward and it jumped, the stallions back hooves landed on the edge!

The town was now less than a mile away! The stallion ran hard, covered with foam it's hooves seemed to barely touch the ground as McCord guided it down through the steep ravines and cliffs and into more hills of gypsum, then the stallion splashed through the river just on the outskirts of Dowds Junction.

He pulled the spent horse to a sliding stop as he jumped off. Grabbing his Henry, he started quietly into the town. Keeping to the shadows he made his way into an alley.

Hearing a noise from above he flattened himself against the wall of the building. A moment later he saw the shadow of a man pacing above him.

"They're expecting me." He thought angrily, his eyes like ice. Not wanting to give away his position, he waited for the shadow to leave.

Looking around a corner, he saw three more men, one was on top of the bank, another was on top of McDonald's Mercantile, another was above Bernice's.

Walking quickly he slid back behind the buildings. Hearing voices, he stepped inside a doorway and waited for them to pass. As they went past, he came out and quietly made his way behind the livery. From there he saw the saloon.

He went inside the corral, using the horses as cover, he ran crouched over through the animals. He climbed through the rungs of the corral, and sprinted to a water trough just a few feet away! He laid still as three men walked past him. As they turned the corner, he sprinted behind a wagon and from there to the back of the saloon.

Opening the door slightly, he silently stepped inside. He flattened himself against the wall, and looked around the corner. No one save the bartender was inside. He waited until the bartender turned around then quietly he came up behind him.

McCord threw his arm around the mans neck and pressed the barrel of the rifle into his neck! Where are they!" He hissed.

The eyes of the bartender where wide with fear then he glanced up toward the stairs.

Throwing him back against the wall, McCord grabbed the scatter gun with his right hand then threw himself down, rolling to his right and fired it!

It's blast broke the upper stairs and Stanford fell to the floor. Enraged, McCord grabbed him by the shirt with his left fist, he slammed it hard into Stanford's ribs. The force knocked Stanford out of the door and into the street, McCord, his face twisted with hate, his eyes gleaming, followed.

"Sure gonna enjoy this," stated Stanford through broken lips as he glared hatefully at McCord. They circled each other then McCord lunged at Stanford, grabbing him he slammed his fist again into the mans stomach! Then again into the mans rib cage, it's force bent Stanford over and pushed him back to the steps.

Stanford saw the blood on McCords shirt, he jumped to his feet, and lunged at McCord, with a meaty fist he hit his side hard, sending him into the dirt!

Nearly blinded by pain, McCord rolled to his right as Stanford tried to kick him, grabbing and twisting Stanford's boot, McCord brought the big man down, and he fell into the dirt of the street!

They both got to their feet, circling each other again, Stanford threw a wicked right cross, he blocked it with his left arm and with his right he threw a right uppercut to his chin.

Knocking Stanford's head back and the big man fell again. Pulling him up by the shirt, he threw a combination right cross to Stanford's chin and a left jab to his midsection!

Stanford fell back into the steps of the saloon, Seething with anger, McCord breathing heavily, grabbed him by the shirt and pulled him toward him again.

"This is for Carrie!" he snarled, as he brought his knee up hard into his groin and slammed his fist into Stanford's ribs then with his left fist he drove it hard into Stanford's jaw.

The big man fell unconscious in the dirt, McCord, breathing heavily stood over him. His knuckles bleeding. Tasting blood from a cut in his mouth. His eyes glowing with hate.

"You son a bitch you killed her!" he screamed, black with rage, as he grabbed Stanford again, and brought his fist down hard against the mans jaw.

Without warning he was slammed to his knees as something white hot burned though his back.

Stunned, he tried to move, but he could not, he was hit again and he fell face first into the dust of the street the last thing he saw through a red haze, was Stanford laying in the street!

Chad and Logan swept into town just in time to see Kincaid take aim and fire and saw Travis knocked to the street.

"NO!" screamed Logan, as he fired at Kincaid!

Kincaid was knocked to the street, writhing in pain as Logan raced by him and toward McCord. He saw Stanford struggle to his feet and he fired again!

A bullet buzzed by as Stanford struggled to his feet, in a panic he staggered to a horse, he threw himself on to it's back and heading out of the town into the mountains.

Racing to Travis, Logan leaped off the back of the still running horse and fell beside his friend, as he rolled him over, McCords head lolled, limply to one side.

"Get Doc Clemens." He screamed as he held his friends limp body.

Chad pulled his horse to a sliding stop next to Kincaid. He saw Kincaid reach for his gun, he stepped on Kincaids hand, Kincaids face was twisted with pain, McKindley kicked the gun away from from him, then grabbed him by the shirt, his fists clenched.

"If McCord dies," he snarled through clenched teeth, "your a dead man!" and shoved him inside a storm cellar.

Closing the door, he put an ax handle through the two handles of the door, locking the man inside.

Racing to Logan, the two men picked up McCords limp body and carried him into the saloon.

As they laid him on a table, Clemins came running in. Shoving everyone out of his way, he walked up to the limp body of McCord.

He immediately cut his shirt off. His eyes opened in horror as he saw two wounds, both in his back. His side wound had ruptured! A bloody pink foam was around his mouth. His breathing was raspy, and irregular. To Clemins this meant one thing, he had a bullet in his lung!

Turning to Logan, he shook his head. As he started to put his bag away, Logan grabbed his arm,

"What in the hell are you doin'." He screamed.

"Logan, at this point, I cannot help him." He said, as he looked down at the man on the table.

"Doc....Doc your all we got!" Pleaded Logan, his eyes wide with fear.

"I...I...can't." Whispered Clemins. "I just can't."

"You don't have a choice Doc." As Logan, his eyes like steel pulled his gun and aimed it at Clemins.

"What in the Hell do you want me to do Marshal!" He screamed back. He looked back at the limp body of McCord, he thought for a moment, then said. "bring me hot water and bandages. There's this new procedure that I been reading about, maybe, just maybe we can save his life, Marshal."

For over an hour he worked on McCord, when he was done, he tiredly sat down and looked at Logan, "if he makes it through the night I'll be surprised." Then added, "he's got a bullet lodged between his rib and his heart. I've done what I can do."

Seeing McKindley, Logan walked to him, "where's Kincaid," He demanded.

"Got him locked in a storm cellar." He replied, then asked, "How is......." Shaking his head Logan pushed him to the side and walked out the door toward the storm cellar.

"Logan, No! Said Chad as he realized where Logan was headed.

"Your a Marshal!" Screamed Chad as Logan walked away from him.

He took several more steps, then turned around, glaring at Chad, he reached for his badge, ripped it off then threw it into the street. Turning on his heel he continued to the storm cellar.

Chad raced up to him, he pulled Logan around and pulled his gun on him.

"I know what you want to do, but Logan, your a Marshal, you just can't kill a man in cold blood! I....I...can't let you do this!" He said, his eyes wide with fear as he pleaded with him. Pausing, he said quietly, "You need to be with Travis."

Clemins was washing his hands, as Logan angrily stalked back inside the saloon, McCord lay still on the makeshift bed.

"Doc....asked Logan hesitantly.

"Don't know." was Clemins reply, adding gently, "Logan, he's got a bullet between his heart and his rib, if I go after it now......it'll kill him for sure."

Logan slammed the table with his fist. Angrily he turned and strode out into the street. He looked at Chad, "Find that son of Bitch!" he spat. Then shook his head and walked back inside the saloon.

As he sat next to Travis, he heard the sound of horses leaving. He looked at his friend, his color was gray, his breathing labored and raspy, he put his hand down on his friends shoulder then grabbed his hand and held it. Remembering the first time they met.

"Remember Travis." He said quietly, as tears gathered in his eyes, "how you was stuck under that buffalo, with a broke leg. I remember," He said, his voice in a whisper,

"I remember how you fought like hell not to make a sound," he said as a slight smile crossed his face. You were more Apache than white, or so you wanted me to think. I remember askin' what your white name was and you got angry and spat, "I'm Apache". Never saw the like of that Travis.

"I remember when Black Feather made us brothers, an how I didn't think we would ever see each other again.

I remember you surprised the hell outta' me in Nogales, when out of nowhere you ride in with your renegades!"

He shook his head sorrowfully, as he gazed at the inert body of McCord, "I remember when we was with the army, we was goin' after Mangas Coloradas and somehow we got ourselves caught in that box canyon.

Remember how the warrior's came on us sudden like, an we got ourselves trapped in that canyon, how you fought like hell protecting me an them two women from them. An you had to carry me out.

You saved my life that day partner." His voice soft and low.

"I remember the day you an Carrie got married, how happy you seemed to be, how Carrie would not let you out of her sight." He smiled then said, "And how Black Feather had given you that black devil of horse you ride." he said, as a faint smile crossed his face. Me and the rest of the Marshals got you that gun you carry.

"I remember that fight you an me got into the day you left, you could'ave killed me then, but you didn't. Thought about that a lot over the last year. Heard you finally found the hole in the wall took out the Ault brothers. Heard you just walked in, I wish I coulda' seen the look on Calhouns face." He said with a smile. Pausing, "How many times did you an me go after him, an he'd lose us up there.""I remember ridin' to your ranch that day," he said, his voice full of emotion, as tears welled in his eyes. I panicked when I thought you was dead! An how the doc didn't think you'd pull through," Pausing. "like now," He breathed softly, "you got to fight this Travis! He said his voice choking with emotion.

"Come on Travis," he whispered as tears clouded his vision.

Morgan raced into the town and ran into the saloon. As she saw Logan, tears welled up then she saw McCord laying still on a makeshift bed, his face ashen, his breathing labored and raspy.

"Oh My God," she breathed as tears fell, kneeling down beside him she gently kissed his still lips. Tracing his face with her fingers as tears fell.-Sobbing, panicked, she searched Logan's face anxiously for some sign,...something,..... anything!

"Logan.... Logan...." she whispered fearfully, her voice thick with emotion, without saying anything, he just shook his head. She put her arms around him and they held each other as they sat next to McCord.

"Why don't you two rest." Said Clemins gently, "I'll be here with him, if anything changes I'll send for you." Looking at each other, they shook their heads choosing to say with Travis.

For days, McCord lay, his life hanging by a thread. Clemins just shook his head, each day McCord lived, it made recovery more likely. Finally they were able to move him to a room at Bernice"s. Never alone, either Morgan, Logan or Clemins was with him.

For days, the ranchers, and Chad combed the hills and valleys around Castle and still found no sign of Stanford. Daily Chad would returned with an update for Logan. They found a trail leading up into the rough, broken back country of Indian Peak.

The ranchers had gotten together and had quickly built a jail out of logs. The blacksmith had donated rough iron for the bars. Within a week Kincaid was moved to the new jail.

On a moonless night, a shadowy figure crept along the outskirts of the town. Coming around the back of the jail he peered in and saw Kincaid huddled in a corner.

Silently he crept around the corner, and looked through the window. Inside he saw Garret Shannon sitting at a desk. Then slinking back he waited in the shadows. Hearing a noise, he backed slowly under some stairs as two men passed by. It was Chad McKindley and Logan Teel.

He watched as they entered the jail. Turning he sneaked up the stairs and into the hallway of Bernice's.

Hearing a noise he silently faded into the shadows. He saw Mattie the owner of Bernice's come out of a room with dishes and walk down the stairs.

As footsteps came up the stairs he quietly snuck down the outside stairs. He paused for a moment and glared up the stairs toward McCords room.

"Later marshal." Stanford sneered, his eyes glowing with anger, though clenched teeth. Then headed back toward the jail.

Looking inside, he saw no one. Testing the door, it opened! Quietly he stepped inside, grabbing the keys from a ring on the outside of a door he opened it and slipped inside.

Kincaid was sleeping. He opened the cell door then awakened Kincaid. Motioning for silence, the two men stepped out the door. A moment later both mounted the horses he had left and rode into the darkness.

Logan was sitting with Travis when Garret ran up the stairs into the room

"Logan, Kincaid is gone!" He breathed as he came in.

"How the hell did that happen." Snarled Logan angrily, as he stood up glaring at Garret.

"I left for just a few minutes, when I came back, I noticed the keys missing, and the cell door was open and he was gone." Stated Garret angrily.

"Get a posse together," He ordered, then added, "we'll go after them in the morning."

As he sat back down, he knew as long as they were out there McCord's life was at stake. He knew they would come after him.

It was late when Travis opened his eyes. His body was wracked with pain. As he tried to move he felt a stabbing pain in his chest, and gasped. A moment later he saw Logan's face above him.

"Water," he gasped. Then felt hands lift him as water was placed on his lips.

"Travis," breathed Logan as a slight smile crossed his face, his voice full of emotion. Then added, "welcome back."

Able to only nod his head, Travis closed his eyes and slept.

"Get the Doc." Ordered Logan. As he looked at Chad.

Moments later, Clemins ran in. He felt McCords head, then checked his wounds.

"You know Logan," stated Clemins, "I didn't give him one chance in hell to live." Adding, "I just don't know how he did it."

"Doc, it's the anger inside him that won't let him die!" Said Logan softly, "He has survived this long because of it."

Logan was sitting next to him when his eye's opened again. Grasping his friends hand Logan smiled and said in a whisper,

"*kiz Zen* , my brother." Said Logan in a faint whisper.

"*kiz Zen* my brother." Whispered McCord weakly.

"I.....I ....got him." Said Travis thickly.

"He got away Travis." said Logan softly.

"What.....what....the....hell." He breathed as he stared at the ceiling of the room.

"I....I....thought ….it...was...over." he mumbled thickly, as he closed his eyes.

"Travis, I got men out looking for them." Stated Logan quietly.

"I.....I...just ….wanted...it over." he breathed.

A few days later Clemins came into the room, seeing Logan and Travis he walked up to the bed. "Feeling better Mr McCord." He said as he checked him over he said to Logan "did you tell him?"

"Tell me what." Said McCord weakly giving a questioning look at Logan.

"Son.... you still got a bullet in you." He started gently, "its near your heart. Lodged in a rib."

Then said, "it has to come out, if it moves..... it'll kill you. If we try to move you it could move on it's own," he added quietly. "I think your strong enough now where I can take it out."

Pausing, he added quietly, "But there are no guarantees that the operation won't kill you. Son,".....said Clemins, his voice full of emotion, "nobody but you can make that call."

Leaning back, Travis closed his eyes then said, his voice weak and raspy, "sounds like I ain't got much of a choice," he breathed, then added hesitantly, "then do it Doc."

Clemins left then returned with a green bottle and several pieces of cotton. He told Logan to get hot water as well as clean towels. Then they needed to turn McCord on his stomach.

McCord gasped as he was moved, the doctor took the bottle he brought and said "this is chloroform." then poured a large amount on a piece of cotton. As he put it over McCords nose and mouth he told him to breath it in.

Within a few minutes, McCord was out. First the Doctor cut the bandage away. Then he cleaned the wound with iodocal. Taking his forceps he put them in the bullet hole.

Sweat beaded on his forehead as he worked. Clemins teeth were clenched as he felt for the bullet. Logan heard him breath, "Got it!" then he carefully removed the forceps with the bloody bullet grasped in it. As blood rushed out, Clemins swabbed with the idoprocol.

"The knife please," he said to Logan. As Logan handed it to him, McCord started to awaken

"Take the chloroform and pour it on another piece of cotton and put it over his nose and mouth." He instructed.

As Logan did, McCord's breathing became deeper. The doctor then took the knife, it's edge glowing a dull red, he laid it on the wound. The smell was arid as the knife seared the wound closed.

"Now," stated Clemins as he sat down tiredly, "we wait." Adding, "it's up to God and him."

Chapter Nineteen

The sky was overcast, thick gray clouds hung along the sides of the mountains as two men rode toward the town. The horses walked carefully, their hooves slipping in the half frozen mud of the trail.

As the wind began to blow and snow scattered around them, the men pulled their hats down. It offered little protection from the now freezing wind and pellets of snow that buffeted them.

Through the snowy mist they saw the soft glow of oil lamps from Dowds Junction. Walking into the saloon, they felt the welcome warmth of a large stone fireplace, shouldering their way past ranchers, cowhands and miners that all seeking shelter from the incoming storm.

Finding a table toward the back, one sat down, as the other one went to the bar a moment later he returned with a bottle of whiskey and two glasses.

Pouring each of them a shot of the amber fluid, one of them shoved a glass to the other. They were dressed in woolen shirts, each had a dark beard and their hair hung in long matted strands. In their eyes there was a hunted look. Their faces gaunt and lined, their eyes sunken and hollow. They watched the others with fear and suspicion.

The door opened and an older man with a limp stepped inside. Dusting his hat against his leg then wiping off the snow from his jacket, he limped to the bar,

"Duffy....you ol' hound dog." smiled the barkeeper. Then added, "ain't seen ya' for awhile."

"If'n it ain't Big John!" said Duffy, his voice cracked and loud.

"Got me a job up ta' J-Bar." He said, licking his lips, he added, "gimme' some o' that there whiskey John."

"These ol' bones o' mine or gonna stay warm this winter." he said as John poured him a drink.

Taking it he slammed it down then looking at John he said, "another."

"Sure gonna play hell out there tonight." Said Duffy as he drank the second. Adding, "Pity anyone out there tanight'."

"How's that McCord gent." Remarked John, as he poured Duffy another.

"Bad..." said Duffy shaking his head. "The Doc had to do whats called and.....uh....opreation'

"You mean operation." Laughed John. As he washed and dried the glasses.

"Hear anything bout them scoundrels Stanford and Kincaid." Asked John casually as he wiped the bar.

"Them Marshals," started Duffy as he pushed his glass toward John, "they's been outta' hunting them an ain't seen hide nor hair of them. ......heard the one named Teel say he thinks theys' gone ta' Denver." Added Duffy.

At the mention of the names Stanford and Kincaid the two men looked at each other as they heard about McCord they both smiled. Standing up they walked out into the storm.

"So he's feelin' poorly." Remarked Stanford, then added, sneering, "why don't we go pay him our respects." The other man, Kincaid smiled evilly as they headed to their horses. Then up the trail to Castle.

The night was cold, the snow swirling and was being driven by the now blowing wind. Two men fought the cold and snow as they furtively kept to the shadows of the buildings.

Slowly they crept toward Bernice's. As they came around the back of the livery, they walked quietly toward the back stairs of the building.

Stanford flattened himself against the wall and motioned for Kincaid to do the same on the opposite side. Slowly Stanford raised the window. A moment later, they were inside.

Kincaid went to the door, as Stanford saw McCord laying in the bed, Stanford smiled evilly as he silently approached him. Taking out his knife, he walked to the bed and laid the cold, steel blade against McCords neck as he leaned hard onto McCords chest!

Gasping and choking, McCord fought his way to consciousness, he felt the cold steel on his neck as his eyes blinked open. Hate poured through him as he saw Stanford's evil face above him.

"Heard you was feelin' poorly." Hissed Stanford as he dragged the blade across McCord's neck, then watched in satisfaction as small droplets of blood followed the knifes edge.

"I'm gonna take your pain away." He said as he lifted the knife above McCords head.

Balling his fist under the blanket, with every bit of strength he had, he raised his left arm and blocked the knife as his right fist hit Stanford's cheek, sending him back into the dresser! The knife slashed McCord's arm and went deep into his forearm! McCord gasping in pain rolled and fell off the bed!

At the sound of boots running up the hall, Stanford and Kincaid, went back out the window and disappeared into the night. As Logan ran inside the room. Worriedly he looked at McCord, his face ashen, and twisted in pain. Then he saw the blood flowing from his arm.

"Get Clemins Now!" He screamed as he saw Travis lying on the floor.

He picked his friend up and laid him back on the bed. Looking at his hand he saw it covered in blood. Seconds later Clemens ran in.

"What the hell happened here." Demanded Clemins as he tore the sleeve from the shirt Travis was wearing. The knife had sliced through his forearm, just above the wrist, leaving a three inch gash.

"Hand me my bag," He demanded angrily.

He swabbed the wound, then he pulled out a needle and sutured the wound closed.

During this McCord lay still, unconscious. Logan paced back and forth. Knowing it was Stanford and Kincaid he knew there was no way to go after them tonight.

"He can't be left alone." Said Clemins angrily. Adding, "least ways not if them two owl hoots are out there." Then he said, "he may not survive another attack."

The following morning a posse attempted to try to track them but lost the trail in the deep snow of Indian Peak. As they rode back to town, Logan could not shake the feeling they were being watched. But from where.

Pulling up at Bernice's, he walked up the stairs to his friends room, he met Morgan coming out.

"Docs in there now with him." She said as she glared at Logan. Adding, "Where the hell were you!"

Ignoring her outburst, he shouldered past her into the room and saw Travis sitting up. His face was pale, as he looked at Logan.

"Found no sign of em Travis," he said quietly. Shaking his head, he sat down heavily in a chair next to the bed.

"Logan," said Travis, his voice weak and raspy, "use me as bait." Seeing the Logan's face, Travis added, "it's the only way to get em' to come back here."

"No." He said emphatically, "there is no way that will happen!"

"It's the only way," breathed Travis. Adding, "give me a gun."

"No!" Again Logan stated angrily as he stood up, pacing back and forth he glared down at his friend.

"Logan," gasped Travis as he fought through a twinge of pain, "Morgan is in danger as well as me. They have already tried to get me. Whats to stop them from taking her, they know I will come after them if they take her." then he added quietly, "Logan, they know how important she is to me."

"I want Morgan in town." He added weakly, then said, "they will stop at nothing to get to me." Adding, "If we do it my way.....then we can control when and where they come."

As Morgan came into the room, she looked from Travis to Logan. Sitting down, Travis grasped her hand in his.

"Morgan, with Stanford and Kincaid out there," he paused, his voice of emotion, "I want you here." Stated Travis softly. Seeing tears running down her face, he brought his finger up and wiped a tear from her face. Then added, "they know how important you are to me. Then said, his voice soft and low, "and I need you here beside me."

"Please." he said as he pulled her face down to his and kissed her gently on the lips.

Able only to nod her head, she laid her head on his chest and listened to his beating heart as tears fell from her eyes.

Days passed, and Travis grew stronger. No longer feeling the pain he had had before, he looked at Logan and Morgan.

"Put the word out." he said softly, his eyes narrow with anger, "that I can barely move." Maybe that'll bring them in. "Just make sure your ready for them."

"I'm not sure about this Travis." Said Logan.

Garret knocked on the door, seeing Logan he motioned him out into the hall.

"Brady's men found tracks this morning out behind Morgan's ranch." Adding, "its a good thing you made her come in when you did."

"Morgan," stated Logan worriedly, as he walked into the room, "there were tracks out behind your ranch house this morning, some of Brady's men found em'."

"You will go nowhere without an escort. Not even here in town." He told Morgan flatly, as she started to argue with him he just looked at her, his blue-gray eyes like steel. Seeing the look, she held her tongue.

"Travis your right. The only way this will end is if we get Stanford and Kincaid." He said quietly turning to his friend.

Morgan listened then asked, "what do you mean." Motioning for her to sit down, he told her the plan. At first she fought the idea.

"It's the only way darlin'." Said Travis, his blue eyes as cold as the windswept snowfields and narrow, his voice low and deadly. "Its the only way I or we can protect you from them."

CHAPTER TWENTY

In an abandoned cabin, deep in a canyon, underneath Indian Peak, Kincaid and Stanford sat as the fire in the fireplace crackled and popped. They had found this cabin several months ago. It lay nestled in a small canyon just on the lee side of the mountain.

"That bitch has moved into town." Said Kincaid angrily. "overheard several riders talkin." Then he said, "to hear them talk McCord ain't doin' to good." Then with a grin he said, "they say he's close to dying'."

"Now ain't that a damned shame." Remarked Claybourne. "Maybe we should just pay him another visit. And help to eliminate his terrible sufferin'." He added, his face twisted in hate with an evil grin on his face.

He stood up, picking up a log, he threw it on the fire. He watched as the log caught then he glared at Kincaid.

"That son of a bitch cost me five years of my life." His voice caught, "an the only woman I loved." he slammed his fist into a wall, "I want him Kincaid." pausing, "I want that son of a bitch dead."

"So do I." Said Kincaid, his voice soft and low, adding, "so do I."

The night was cold, a thin veil of snow fell as two men made their way cautiously through the buildings of the town. Motioning for Kincaid, they climbed the outside stairs to the room McCord was in.

Silently they opened the window and both crept in. Seeing McCords form on the bed, Stanford crept silently to the bed, for a moment his face broke into an evil grin as he took his knife and brought it down hard!

Then from behind him he heard the ominous click of a navy colt. Turning on the balls of his feet he stared into the hated face of McCord standing infront of him.

"Looking for me." Snarled McCord.

With nowhere to go, Claybourne screamed, "it's a trap!" then threw himself at McCord! He hit the gun, just as it fired! The bullet aimed at him went into a wall!

At the sound of the gun, Logan ran inside and saw Kincaid crawling out the window, he fired! Kincaid slumped down on to the floor dead.

Stanford grabbed the front of McCords shirt and slammed a left cross to his jaw knocking him to the floor. For a brief moment he stood over glaring at him, breathing heavily and clenching his fists, seeing Kincaid dead, he ran to the window and jumped out.

McCord, his head roaring in pain, his vision blurred, he struggled to his knees, he brought the gun up and holding it with both hands, he fired at the fleeting Claybourne.

"It's over Travis." Said Logan gently.

"Stanford........Stanford." mumbled Travis.

"Travis." said Logan gently, "give me the gun."

"Is.....is ..is............" his voice faded, the gun fell to the floor as he slumped forward..

Clemins ran inside the room and helped drag the limp body of McCord to the bed.

"Are you ok?" asked Clemins.

"Yeah Doc......just real tired is all." Said Travis as he weakly smiled. Then added, "just real tired." Closing his eyes he went to sleep.

Worriedly Logan looked out the window where Claybourne had jumped. Twenty men had gone out looking for him. No one had returned yet. Anxiously he waited for word from Chad or Garret. Several hours passed then he saw the men come up the deserted street.

Walking out of Bernice's to greet them Logan saw Garret shaking his head. "He got away Logan."

"What the hell do you mean," demanded Logan angrily.

"He got away." Garret repeated. "He flat disappeared on us."

Stanford had waited until all the riders left then headed to the cabin at Indian Peak. As he sat at the rough hewn log table in the cabin, he drank a cup of steaming coffee. He was angry, his face dark with anger, his dark eyes narrowed.

"How stupid," he thought as he slammed his fist into the table. They had been lured into a trap and now Kincaid was dead.

"Another time Marshal," he swore, as he looked out at the heavily falling snow, "Soon!"

As McCord opened his eyes, he saw Morgan sitting next to him. "Hi there." He whispered,

"Hi," she whispered, her eyes welling with tears, as she touched his face. Then bent down and gently kissed him.

He brought his arm up and put it around her. Touching her hair, he hugged her. "I'm glad your here." He whispered.

"I am too." She said softly.

They were interrupted as Logan walked into the room with coffee in both hands. Seeing Travis awake, his somber face broke into a smile. Handing a cup to Morgan, he stood next to them.

" 'bout time you woke up." he said with a grin. Then added, "how are you feeling."

"Like I've been stomped by a horse, then rolled on." Remarked Travis with a weak smile as he grasped his friends outstretched hand.

"Morgan," said Logan with a smile, "why don't you go down and tell Mattie to bring some coffee up here and some food too."

A moment later Mattie came up. Seeing the two men talking, she left a hot pot of coffee with biscuits and eggs on the mantel of the fireplace that was crackling and spitting keeping the room warm.

Logan poured Travis a cup of the coffee, as Travis sipped the brown liquid, relishing it's taste,

feeling it's warmth course through him he said, "been awhile."

"Do you remember much from the other night?" Questioned Logan.

"I remember they came," he said softly, "but not much else."

"Kincaids dead........"said Logan hesitantly. "Stanford?" interrupted McCord.

"He made it out the window," said Logan shaking his head.

"Damn!" Breathed McCord as he closed his eyes and leaned back against the pillows.

"Travis," said Logan as he stood up and put another log on the fire, "I've had men out in the snow looking for him. No tracks, no trail." He added quietly.

"He's out there Logan." stated McCord quietly, his eyes narrow, his voice low and quiet, "he's gonna wait now."

Their conversation was interrupted by two men walking in, it was Morrison and Jenkins two of the ranchers Travis had met at the gap.

"Heard you was awake," Said Morrison with a smile.

"Had to come an pay our respects. " Added Jenkins as he grasped McCords hand, then said, "we owe you two for saving our hides."

"Everybody out!" Demanded Clemins with a smile as he walked in. "he needs his rest."Adding, "an that means you Logan."

Later Morgan silently entered his room, as she turned down the oil lamp, he grasped her hand and quietly said, "don't go."

"I won't," she whispered as she touched his face, and stared deep into the eyes that once were like ice, now there was a warmth she had never seen. He pulled her down to him and kissed her passionately on the mouth. As their bodies melted together, he felt feelings he had not felt since Carrie.

Later Mattie walked in and found them embraced in each others arms sleeping with a sly smile she quietly left.

Sunlight shining through the frosted window was the first thing McCord saw as his eyes opened.

Hesitantly he sat up, lightheaded at first he sat on the bed for a moment, as his head cleared, he stood up. He put on a shirt one of the ranchers had brought him, rolling up his sleeves, then put on his jeans and pulled his boots on. Buckling on his holster he walked down the stairs.

He saw Logan, Chad and Garret, but did not see Morgan. Logan's face broke with a wide grin as he saw his friend.

He made his way slowly to his friends. Reaching the table, he eased his body into a chair.

" Why if it ain't Mr. McCord." Said Mattie as she came to the table with a pot of coffee. Putting a cup infront of him she poured him a cup. Adding, "it's wonderful to finally see you up and around."

He gave her a broad smile as he took a drink of the coffee. "Thanks

Mattie," he added, "your looking beautiful today." She blushed at his words and hurried back to the stove.

"Where's Morgan?" He asked.

"Back to the J-Bar." said Logan, adding, "Brady's Vaqueros are with her. Nodding his head, Travis looked out of the frosted window to the frozen landscape. A snow storm had dumped two feet of the white stuff and had shut everything down,

Drops of water dripped down from the icicles that had formed over the windows. The street outside was a mixture of half frozen mud, snow and water. Snow lay in drifts around the doors to the buildings.

"Say," said Logan, "Morrison dropped these off for us." Showing his friend several coats made from elk hide and deer.

As he finished eating, he leaned back in the chair, Logan offered him a cigarette. Gratefully, he accepted it. As the ranchers all came in, they stopped at the table shaking McCords hand and thanking him for what he had done.

Across the street was the candy cane sign of a barber. Walking in, he sat down as a burly man came up to him.

"Need a shave." Travis said, "an a haircut."

Seconds later, a warm towel was wrapped around his face. Enjoying the warmth he closed his eyes. The man then began to sharpen the razor with the strap, he began to take off the weeks worth of beard McCord had grown.

Then the barber began to trim back his hair. Looking at his reflection in the mirror. He looked completely different. He payed the man and walked outside.

He felt the bite of the cold air on his face, he could see his breath as he walked down to the livery. Walking inside he heard the stallion snort then kick the side of the stall. As he opened the door and walked inside, he whispered in Apache, "*Ya a ch Sh ils a ash*", "hello my friend."

Opening the door to the stall he walked the stallion to the corral. Then laughed as the stallion took a tentative step into the snow.

Moments later the stallion half-reared then whirled on his hind feet and bucked, throwing the snow all over and then tossing it's head, it turned toward McCord and raced toward him. At the last second, McCord side-stepped then slapped the stallion on it's hindquarters as it went past.

Smiling, he remembered the day Black Feather had given him the horse. It was his wedding day as the tribe came in for the celebration, Black Feather took him aside.

As they walked to the corral, Black Feather motioned for him to stand still, then with an Apache cry three men rode up with a black colt. Taking the lead for the colt, Black Feather gave the lead to him.

"*Ci ye* (my son), I give you this *di thi th t th ii*. (black horse) as a gift. He will grow and be your brother in spirit and a warrior at your side. Treat him wisely and he will be like the black raven. He will protect you and will keep you from harm."

As he looked at the mountain, known as Indian Peak, he remembered Black Feathers words,"To beat your enemy, you must know him, you must become him, you must become *"the go de"* the black spirit that enters his mind*. You must know how he thinks, and what he will do.

Logan walked up behind him. As they stood watching the horse, Travis asked, "Any sign?"

"No," replied Logan worriedly.

"You know Logan, he's up there," stated McCord quietly, "an he's waiting for me." Turning to his friend, he added with a slight smile, "I'm getting' a bad case of cabin fever."

As Logan started to laugh, he added, "so am I."

"See this." he said as he handed a piece of paper to him. Travis read it and his eyes narrowed as he looked at Logan.

"So Governor Baker wants you in Denver." He said. "Any idea why?"

"Something about Chad and Garret most likely," Said Logan, then added, "It's not the right time to go. It ain't finished yet." He added as he gave McCord a hard look.

"When you planning to go," He asked as he touched the horses forelock.

"Thought the two of us would go, say maybe next week if your feeling up to it." Replied Logan . "I figured Chad and Garret can stay here and keep things under control until we get back." He added.

Logan he's up there waiting." Said McCord quietly, "you go, just in case he makes a move, one of us should be here."

As Logan nodded his head in agreement, Travis, his eyes narrow, cold as steel, scanned the mountain.

"I know your up there." He thought angrily, his blue eyes glowing with hate.

Stanford had been watching Morgan for three days now. Each time he thought he could take her, she always had the men from Brady's ranch with her. He had to come up with a plan where she would be alone or at least just with the new man Duffy.

He had been hiding up here above her ranch for the last week. He knew each morning she fed and watered the horses, he knew she would then feed the chickens. She had the cattle brought down from the mountain and put into a large corral near the barn.

It was necessary to give them protection from the weather and the various predators like the mountain lion, lynx, bob cat, wolves and coyotes that were preying on the cattle this time of year.

Again though, she always had those vaquero's with her. Garret, her top hand had moved to town and was McKinley's deputy. He did not have to worry about him. He did have to worry about the vaquero's.

They were crack shots and they were expert trackers. Twice he had almost been found by them. Even the man Duffy seemed to know when not to leave.

He had overheard several of the riders mention that Teel was leaving for Denver sometime in the next few days. He knew he could deal with McCord himself but not with the two of them.

The day dawned clear and cold, from where he was he heard the sound of horses slowly coming up the draw toward him. Using his field glasses he saw two riders flanking Morgan and Duffy.

He brought the rifle to his shoulder and fired. One man went down, as Duffy slapped the reins and the horses began to gallop. His second shot hit the other vaquero knocking him off his horse into the snow.

Mounting his horse, he rode it down the trail and intercepted Duffy. Duffy pulled the horses up and he saw fear in the face of Morgan as he glared at her.

"Get the hell down outta' that wagon." He growled. Seeing Duffy move, he fired, a moment later Duffy lay dead.

Morgan took off running as Stanford kneed his horse and rode after her. Fearfully, she glanced over her shoulder as she ran to the trees. She fell in the deep snow and before she could move, he was there.

As he grabbed her, she fought back, kicking and screaming. She bit his hand and he slammed her jaw with his fist and she fell unconscious into the snow. Picking her up, he placed her unconscious body in front of him and road back to the wagon.With an evil grin, he wrote a note, then stuffed it between Duffy's jacket and shirt.

He guided the horses back onto the road then shot his gun into the air. A moment later, the horses took off at a dead run, the wagon bouncing along the trail. With a grin, he turned his horse toward the trail leading into Indian Peak.

"I'll be back sometime in the next five days." Logan said to McCord as he boarded the train. McCord nodded his head and grasped his friends hand,

"See you went you get back." Said McCord as he stepped away from the train.

Black smoke billowed out of the smoke stack of the engine, as the wheels slipped then began to turn, slowly, the train began to move and started moving up the track into the high mountains toward Leadville, it's first stop on it's way to Denver.

It was now mid February, he still had moments of pain but not as bad. Although the sun was shining in the clear, cloudless day it was still cold. He could see his breath as he walked, the snow had turned to slush, the road was a combination of ice, slush and snow.

The mountains were covered in a fresh blanket of snow and seem to glow in the sunlight. Standford had not been seen since the last attack. Travis found himself thinking more and more of Morgan and Carrie.

Not knowing what to do, he found himself heading down to the livery. The stallion greeted him with a nicker.

Grabbing a brush, he started to brush the stallion, then thinking better of it, he opened the door of the stall and guided the stallion to the snow covered corral. He stood for a moment then grasping Raven's mane he pulled himself on to his back.

"*Hoppo! Sh ils a ash*" "lets go my friend." He whispered in Apache as he slammed his heels in to the stallion, the stallion whirled then headed to the fence and jumped!

Landing smoothly on the other side, the stallion ran hard as the man with only his voice and knees guided the stallion toward a snowfield just out of town.

As the horse slowed down, he heard the thunder of hooves and the jangle of traces then a wagon flew into view. The driver was laying sideways in the boot. The horses, totally out of control.

He kicked the stallion and raced toward the oncoming wagon. As the stallion half-reared the horses slid to a stop. He knew it was Duffy and he had been shot. A note was stuffed between his jacket and his shirt, it read, "shes mine now you want her come find her!

CHAPTER TWENTY-ONE

Crumpling the note, he threw it angrily into a snowbank. His ice cold eyes looked toward the mountain known as Indian Peak, his jaw set, his face dark with anger. He slammed his fist into the wood of the buckboard.

Climbing in, he slapped the reins and the horses began to move as the stallion trotted next to them.

The horses raced toward Castle, pulling them to a sliding stop outside the jail, he leaped off and ran into the building.

"He's got Morgan," he snarled to McKinley, he grabbed a Henry rifle and several boxes of ammunition. "Tell Logan when he gets back that I am going after that Son of a Bitch," he snarled.

"Travis no." started McKinley as he stood infront of McCord. "we'll put a posse together."

"outta' my way Chad." Stated McCord his voice soft and deadly, He pulled his gun on McKinley, "When Logan gets back, tell I'm heading into Indian Peak."

"Now move aside Chad," stated McCord, his eyes narrow and cold.

"Travis, your in no shape to be going after him." Argued McKindley angrily.

"Chad, don't try to stop me." Travis said softly. "If you try, I will not kill you but I will hurt you." Turning his back he left.

He ran into the mercantile, grabbing several blankets, a pot, canned goods and gloves he stormed out. Within an hour, he rode Raven out of town toward Indian Peak.

McKinley ran to the telegraph office. Logan was on his way to Denver but the train had had to make an emergency stop in Leadville due to the snowstorm. The snow had covered the main rail head and they were waiting for the snow train to dig them out.

"Wire this message to Logan Teel in Leadville," said McKindley breathlessly.

"*Logan* stop *Morgan taken* stop *Travis gone* stop"

Reading the telegram the man just looked at him and nodded his head.

McKinley ran up the street to the saloon. Seeing Garret, he told him what had happened. Together they organized a posse and waited for a reply.

Logan was sitting in the train station as the stationmaster came running toward him. "Your name Teel......asked the stationmaster, as he nodded his head, he said. "this is for you...just came in."

Reading the wire, he gave the stationmaster a hard look. "Whens the next train to Castle."

"Now." He said, then added, "knew you'd be heading back. I'm holding it for you."

Running as the train started up the track, Logan raced to the last car as two men helped him on board.

As McCord rode, the going was treacherous. Low ominous clouds were building on the horizon. The temperature was dropping fast. He covered his face with his neckerchief as the wind and snow began to fall. He had leather gloves lined with wool from mountain sheep, his coat was elk hide also lined with the wool.

Even this was not capable of stopping the cold. For two days he searched the lower canyons and valleys. On the first day out, the stallion tossed it's head and pawed the snow. Taking his gun, he searched the camp and found the tracks of a large mountain lion.

The cold was ferocious. His hands were numb, his nose and eyes felt frozen. Ice formed around his mouth, that night, shivering, he built a small fire, then placed three good size rocks in the fire, he waited then pulled them out, he coaxed the stallion to lay down then piled the rocks beneath a blanket then he laid down next to the blanket and put another blanket over both him and the horse, the body heat from the horse and the rocks kept him alive.

Snow was swirling around him as he stood up shivering, brushing it off, he walked to the almost dead fire, taking some dried branches and leaves he coaxed the fire back to life. Using several small rocks he heated them in the fire then pulled them out and wrapped them in a blanket and held them under his coat.

Making coffee, he poured a cup, with steam rising, his teeth chattering and his hands shaking from the cold, he warmed his hands around the cup then drank it and felt it's warmth go through him. He melted snow for the stallion to drink. As he was gathering the snow again he saw the tracks of the mountain lion and realized big cat was stalking them.

Mounting the stallion, they headed higher into the back country, as the snow became deeper, McCord had to dismount and had to break trail in the snow making it easier on the horse. Without warning, the stallion reared pulling McCord off balance and into a snowbank!

Turning around he saw the mountain lion crouched infront of Raven, it's black tipped tail lashing back and forth, he heard the cat's low throated growl, suddenly it sprang! Raven reared, it's left front hoof catching the cat near it's shoulder!

The cat fell near the snowbank where McCord was crouched, as it lay stunned for a moment, McCord sprang with his knife! Landing on the back of the cat, he brought the knife down hard into the animals neck killing it instantly.

Shaking, McCord walked slowly to the frightened stallion. He murmured to it and his voice seemed to calm it down. The cats claws had left scratches on the stallions shoulder but they were not bad.

Patting it's neck, he coaxed the nervous animal around the body of the cat and they started back up the trail.

Cresting ridge after ridge he slowly worked his way higher into the back country. For days he searched for some sign of Stanford. He remembered during the summer he had found a deserted cabin on the lee side of the mountain. This is where he was headed. It was the only place he knew of on this mountain.

The sky was overcast, as clouds built on the horizon, he knew the weather was changing and could feel snow in the air.

As he crested a ridge, below him was a stand of pine, the trees would offer some shelter from the wind and snow that was coming, he carefully walked the stallion down the winding trail into the trees.

Using his lasso, he roped three trees together then piled pine boughs and leaves inside it. He notched one of the trees and waited, a moment later black tar leaked around the hole, scraping it off, he spread it on several of the dry branches.

Hitting his knife against a piece of granite, the sparks ignited the tar and a few moments later, fire came to life. He quickly gathered twigs and dead branches and stacked them inside. Outside the wind was beginning to blow hard, as snow pellets began to fall.

That night he sat in the shelter as the wind and snow raged outside. The sound of the trees cracking from the cold sounded like gunshots. Outside he heard the crack as tree limbs broke and fell. As he watched the fire burn he knew he could not be that far from the valley. For most of the night he lay awake placing wood on the fire to stay warm.

As morning came the snow had let up but had not quit, looking at the clouds he knew it was going to start again as he climbed a ridge just above his camp. To his surprise, he spotted the cabin less than two miles away.

Using his field glasses, he saw smoke rising from the chimney. The cabin was built toward the back of a wall of sandstone and the forest had been cleared leaving no cover, it meant he had to wait till the storm hit.

As he trained the glasses on the cabin he watched as a heavy set man came out, even from this distance he knew it was Stanford. He watched as Stanford chopped wood, then went back inside.

The wind began to blow and snow beginning as flurries turned quickly into pellets then without warning, the snow began falling hard.

Morgan sat fearfully in a corner, her hands and feet tied, as Standford walked inside with an armful of wood, as he glared hatefully at her. He had already hit her once. They had been there for nearly three weeks and she had just about given up.

She had convinced Duffy to take her to Castle to be with Travis. Flanked by two of Brady's vaquero's she had felt safe enough. Halfway down the trail. Gunfire exploded, Duffy slapped the horses as she held on and watched as both vaquero's where killed.

Duffy put up a fight, then was shot as Stanford rode out of the trees toward her. She had tried to run but with the snow, he caught up with her. He grabbed her hard by the collar of her coat, she had tried to fight back and that's when he hit her hard in the face and knocked her out. The next thing she knew she was here at the cabin tied up.

Her face was bruised, her lips cut and swollen, one of her eyes was swollen nearly shut. There were scratches on her arms and her blouse was torn at the sleeve. Blood was caked over her one eye, He looked down at her with satisfaction.

"You gonna behave yourself if I cut your hands loose." He sneered.

As she gave a curt nod of her head, he cut her hands loose. Her wrists were bleeding from the ropes. Rubbing her hands together, she gazed fearfully at him. He threw a plate of food infront of her, then gave her bread. Starving, she hungrily ate as she fearfully watched him.

From outside the wind had begun to blow and howl through the branches of a old cottonwood, snow was beginning to fall hard. Embedded in the howling wind came a distant forlorn howl of a lone wolf. He grabbed Morgan and tied her hands again leaving just enough slack that she could eat.

"Damned critters been hangin here in this valley for two long," swore Stanford angrily, he grabbed his rifle, looking at Morgan he snarled, now don't you be getting any ideas." then walked outside.

From the shelter of the far side of the wall, Travis saw Stanford leave, through the near blinding snow, he quietly stepped onto the wood porch and made his way to the door of the cabin.

Looking through the oil cloth that covered the window, he vaguely could see the outline of a figure at the table. The door opened silently as he used the barrel of the rife to push it open. Quickly he stepped inside, he stopped for a moment and looked to see where Stanford was. Not seeing him he closed the door quietly.

"shhhh........." he whispered , running to her, he quickly cut the ropes. The anger welled up in him as he saw the bruises and the rope burns around her wrists. Angry, his eyes narrow and cold, he held her for a moment, his eyes cold and narrow, he caressed her hair as she sobbed quietly into his chest.

"It's ok Morgan, I'm here now." He whispered gently, as he held her close, her body trembling as she cried. His eyes like steel, he moved her back as he heard the sound of boots on the porch.

Stanford checked the animals then looked around and found nothing. The snow was blowing sideways in the now howling wind as he walked back inside the cabin. As he entered it. The rifle was knocked from his hand and slid across the floor.

Then a fist knocked him to his knees, his vision blurred then focused on the hated face of McCord, as he was hit again.

Gritting his teeth, he sprang to his feet. Tasting blood, his eyes full of hate, his face black with fury, he lunged at McCord. They both fell out the door and into the snow.

He grabbed a piece of wood and swung it hard. McCord dodged and rolled to his left and springing to his feet.

The two men circled each other; each driven by rage, McCord charged him, he grabbed him by the coat and with a right cross he slammed Standford in the chest sending him falling into the rocks.

Grabbing him by the shirt McCord pulled him up and slammed his fist hard into the mans stomach, followed by a left uppercut to the chin! Stanford folded to the ground!

Seeing red, McCord picked him up again and snarled "You son of a Bitch! You killed her! With all the hate and anger inside him he picked him up and threw him into a wall of granite.

As Stanford sank to his knees, his hand felt a rock. As McCord came at him again, he slammed the rock into McCords side. Falling, McCord lay nearly paralyzed by the pain. He felt rather than saw Stanford come after him again with the rock, this time he rolled to his left as Stanford fell hard into the into the snow.

McCord staggered to his feet and grabbed him from behind, kneeing him in the back as he wrapped his arm around Stanford's neck. Stanford, choking, slammed his elbow into McCords side and broke free!

McCords eyes were flaming with anger as they circled each other then Stanford lunged for McCord, driving him into the rocks. This time

McCord, with all his hate and anger behind him, slammed the big man with his fist and Stanford went down.

Breathing heavily, McCord tasting blood from a cut inside his mouth, walked up to Stanford and picked him up by his coat collar. He grabbed Stanford's neck in his hands, choking, Stanford brought his arms inside and broke the hold.

He tried to crawl away but McCord grabbed him again. With his fist, he drove it hard into Stanford's jaw and Stanford fell unconscious into the snow.

McCord stood over him, breathing hard, his hands bleeding, he pulled his gun, glaring at Stanford he cocked the hammer and aimed it at him..

"Travis no!" Said Logan from behind him.

"He killed Carrie!" Snarled McCord hotly, his eyes never leaving Stanford. "Logan don't interfere!"

Again he aimed the gun, behind him he heard the click of a colt. "Travis, drop the gun." Ordered Logan quietly. "Now!"

"So help me God Logan don't....He.....killed her!" Travis panted furiously, his eye's glowing with hatred, his teeth clenched, his voice catching as he spoke.

As he turned his head to look at Logan, Stanford's face broke with an evil grin.

"Goodbye Marshal!" He snarled as he fired the derringer!

The single bullet aimed at his heart burned into McCords arm instead, the force of the bullet spun McCord around, he fired the colt just before he fell into the snow! Stanford face registered surprise as he felt the white hot bullet burn deep into him. The last thing he saw was McCord falling, as he fell dead, face first into the snow.

"Damn you Travis." Stated Logan worriedly as he ran to McCord,

His eyes glazed with pain, McCord looked up at Logan, weakly, he whispered "Hi-dis ho*o kiz zen* it is finished, my brother."

As Logan nodded his head, he echoed softly, " Yeah, hi-dis ho*o* it is finished."

McCords eyes closed as his body went limp. "Get him into the cabin now!" Ordered Doc Clemins as he ran up to Logan. Clemins had decided to ride with the posse just in case.

As he was carried into the cabin and laid on a bed, Clemins cut the sleeve of the jacket then the sleeve of his shirt. The bullet had hit the bone, then ricocheted up into the muscle.

Clemins worked for over an hour repairing the damage as McCord lay unconscious in the bed. He looked at both Morgan and Logan.

"He'll be alright, he's exhausted and he's lost a lot of blood." He said as he put McCords arm in a sling, then he walked over to Logan and placed his hand on his shoulder and sat down infront of the fireplace.

The sun shining into the room was the first thing McCord was aware of as his eyes opened. Logan was sitting next to him, as he moved his head, he closed his eyes against the pain.

"*Ashoge kiz zen*- thank you." He whispered weakly. Then added with a half smile, "You look like hell."

"*A he ya eh kiz zen.*"you are welcome," Replied Logan softly as he grasped his friends hand in his. Then added with a smile, "You don't look so good either partner."

As Clemins came in, his worried look turned to a smile as he saw McCord awake for the first time. Checking his wound, he shook his head then left. As Morgan walked in. Tears fell as she bent over and kissed him lightly on his lips. She had several bandages on her face as Clemins had checked her wounds.

Reaching up, he pulled her face down to his and kissed her passionately. A moment later, she looked at Logan, and blushed as she stood up. The snow had finally stopped, mounting the horses they headed back to Dowds Junction.

A week later Travis was in the corral with Raven when Morgan rode up. Turning he smiled at her and walked over to the fence as Raven trotted up and playfully grabbed his sleeve.

Logan had gone to Denver and was due back in three days. The day before Travis had received a wire from the Marshals office in Phoenix requesting their status. He had not sent a reply, but he knew he had to and soon.

Grabbing a handful of mane, McCord swung up on to the back of the stallion, he rode the stallion to the fence where Morgan was sitting, then with a smile pulled her on to the stallion with him.

"Don't know 'bout you, but I got a bad case of cabin fever." He said, as he turned the stallions head toward the gate.

Seconds later they rode toward a stand of trees. He slowed the horse down then slid off it's back, and helped Morgan down. Walking hand in hand, Travis looked at Indian Peak.

Snow had fallen the night before, the peak gleamed and sparkled in the sun beneath a crystal blue sky. It had started to warm up in the high country as spring was coming. Buds were on the trees and the tops of small wild-flowers were poking up through the snow.

He pulled her close to him as his lips gently caressed her forehead. . Looking down at her his eyes glistened with tears.

"Morgan," he started his voice full of emotion, " I have spent the better part of two years chasin' Stanford and Kincaid. Now thats it over, I have thought about you everyday, you know how very important you are to me." Leading her to a deadfall he picked her up and sat her on the tree.

"But I'm not sure." He said clearing his throat, "For two years every waking moment was spent looking for those two." As she started to speak he shook his head and said, "No, let me finish darlin'."

"I don't know if I'm ready yet to be with you or anyone." He said as he looked at the mountain in front of them. "I need time to sort out what has happened........ an it's not you." Tears fell from his face as he took a deep breath. "I....I...never thought I would find anyone like you."

"But," he added softly, "I.....I...promised Carrie..........."

"I need time Morgan." He said hesitantly. Then he added "It's my job also, Carrie died because of what I do.....I almost lost you twice."

"Darlin'," said McCord as he took her into his arms, "Logan and I are leaving day after tomorrow, but....but... please understand this is something I have to do and," his voice in a whisper, "I will come back here."

"How could you!" She snapped as she pulled away, wiping angry tears from her eyes. "I really thought"...she added sobbing, "that, we would be together after all of this. How could you just walk away from me, you said I was "Important" to you and now you expect me to just watch you walk away? Well I can't! Just leave me the hell alone." She added, her voice trembling as tears fell.

"I'm sorry Morgan." Said Travis, as he went after her.

He ran after her and turned her to him. Sobbing she pounded his chest with balled fists and spun away from him and ran to the stallion. As he came up behind her he turned her to him.

"Morgan, I'm sorry if I hurt you. You are important to me but, I have to go back." He said, his voice gentle and soft. Adding, "I don't belong here but you do."

"When are you leaving?" She asked, in a trembling voice as tears fell.

"We're leaving in two days." He said quietly.

As they walked to the horse McCord lifted her onto it's back then mounted the stallion. They rode in silence back to town. She jumped off the back of the horse and ran toward hers.

"Morgan," said Travis as he walked after her, she stopped for a moment shook her head then mounted her horse and left headed for the J-Bar.

"You wanna' talk about it?" Asked Logan, walking up to his friend.

"No." Was McCord's terse reply.

From around the bend clouds of black smoke and the lonely sound of the whistle announced the trains arrival.

A moment later, the train rumbled to a stop. The two men loaded the horses in the last boxcar. Pulling up the ramp they boarded the train. Travis looked again for Morgan, she was nowhere in sight, shaking his head he turned and boarded the train..

Morgan watched tearfully from a ridge above the town, but she knew there was nothing left to do. As the train pulled away from the station, tears fell as she turned her horse around and rode back to her ranch.

For three days, the train moved slowly out of the mountains and into the desert. The sun was just coming up as suddenly the train began to slow and then stop. The conductor walked up to the seats of the two men they had stopped for.

"Your stop Marshal." Said the conductor as he shook the shoulder of one of them. He nodded his head tiredly then shook the other. The other man was pale as both stood up.

They walked to the last boxcar. Opening the door, they brought down a loading ramp, then unloaded the horses. It had been a long ride and the animals were skittish. The air was hot and dry, in the distance silhouetted against the rising red sun, stood the Suguaro cactus. Kicking their horses, they rode deep into the red sandstone cliffs of the white mountains toward the Big Sandy river and into the Joshua tree forest.

It was spring in the desert, the rains had come and the cactus were blooming, small white flowers decorated the huge cactus. Riding up to one, Travis picked one small flower then rode alone toward a bend in the river.

As Travis came over the ridge, for a moment he paused as tears clouded his vision when he looked down at what had been his and Carries home. The wildflowers she had planted were growing and blooming, reds, pinks, blues and yellow flowers, they seemed out of place in this arid country, it was as if Carrie was welcoming him home.

Nudging the horse, the stallion walked slowly through the blooming wildflowers that seemed to be everywhere, toward a small grave next to the house.

Dismounting Travis took off his hat nervously turning it in his hands, he stood in silence as tears fell from his face.

"I left you my darlin' with my heart full of pain." His voice a whisper, adding, " I made you a promise that day, I ....I promised you. I would get them....and I did," he said, his voice trembling, "and I made them pay Carrie with their lives."

"*Shi'aad hi-disho* my wife it is finished." Then added softly, "I miss you so much my love."

Overcome with grief, he fell to his knees, tears streaked his face as he tentatively reached forward and placed his hand gently on the grave. In Apache he whispered softly, " *shil nz hoo"* I love you."

His voice caught as he whispered through his tears, "I....I... picked..... this.... for ....you. I thought you would like it."

He then placed the single white flower on her grave. He sat for a long moment then he took off the agate and laid it on the grave next to the flower. Standing up, he stood a moment longer then turned, mounted Raven and rode up the ridge.

Pausing a moment, he looked back at the place that had once had been his home, his face streaked with tears, he whispered softly, *"Ego ga han shi'aad shil nz hoo"* until we meet again." Then he kneed the stallion and rode to Logan.

"You ok?" Asked Logan quietly, as he saw his tear stained face.

"Yeah." Replied McCord quietly as he nodded his head.

Turning the horses south they rode toward Phoenix, the headquarters of the Arizona Marshals.

A man, Miguel Sanchez, walked up the pathway to a grave carrying a bouquet of pink fairy duster, red globe mallow, gold poppy and many others.

For two years he had been taking care of senoras grave. In the distance he saw something different, he began to run to it, then he saw the single white flower.

Turning around he ran back down the path screaming. "Maria …...Maria," When she finally came to the door of their small home, he breathlessly ran up to her pointing excitedly at the figures of two men fading into sunrise and said. "He has returned...Maria, El Cetan Nigrin, Maria it is him, the senor has returned to us.

The End